Wizard

by
Sophie Wainwright

THE NOVICE'S QUEST

Published by Aultbea Publishing, Inverness

Copyright details

Wizard
Part 1: The Novice's Quest
by
Sophie Wainwright

First published in Great Britain by
Aultbea Publishing Company in 2005,
106 Church Street, Inverness IV1 1EP

Second Edition

ISBN 0-9549340-7-5

Cover design by Al Knight

Printed by Highland Printers Limited
Henderson Road, Inverness IV1 1SP

Dedicated To:

Jenny my big sister.

You were the first one to read it, and the first one to believe in it.

Thank you.

Thanks To:

I'd like to thank my family, friends and teachers for their support and encouragement. They were a tremendous help and I would have lost the patience to persevere a long time ago if it hadn't been for them. I'd also like to say a huge thank you to all of those people at Silklantern who helped me develop as a writer.

WIZARD
The Novice's Quest
SOPHIE WAINWRIGHT
Prologue

The wind howled like a pack of wolves on the hunt and the ocean rolled fiercely, tossing a small, battered boat around in its rage. The vessel held two figures and a bundle on its deck, a man, a woman and a month old baby. The man was wrestling with a taut rope and a sail made from a hard cloth that had been waterproofed by a mixture of oil and herbs. His fingers were red raw and blistered, his face, covered by masses of dark brown hair, was haggard and gaunt, his clothes were soaked and his feet slipped on the wet deck, making him fall. Staggering back up, he grabbed the rope, which now flailed around in the ferocious wind, flaunting its newfound freedom to the world, and started his battle all over again.

The woman hugged the infant close to her body, hushing his loud cries. Then, securing him into a wooden crate lined with straw, she yanked a handful of leather thongs from her belt and strapped them across the crate, making sure they wouldn't break and let the child be tossed out and on to the deck. Placing a soft kiss on his already wet brow, she set the crate on her seat. And finally she rushed over to her struggling husband and grabbed the rope with both hands; they exchanged a brief, brave smile and then concentrated wholly on the task at hand. Together they battled the storm which threatened to overturn the boat that had been their home for the last few months, defying the elements and the water gods with their show of strength. Suddenly the sea gave an extra violent start and the woman rolled forward, head over heels, hurtling into the boats side. Her fingers clasped at the wooden rail and she prayed to Vigorr, Goddess of Strength, to let her hold on and not be plunged into the icy, black surface that lay a few feet below. Her husband dropped the rope and jumped to her side, grabbing an arm, roughly pulling her back towards the mast and safety. She gasped and held onto his arm. A shrill cry to her left made her turn. With wide eyes she saw the crate she had placed her son in soar forwards with a violent jerk and skip over the white crested waves like a stone. Her husband grabbed her middle and held on tightly as she scrabbled to jump into the waves after the crate; she screamed her rage and cried her sorrow out to the winds and hit him and hated him for holding her back. He took it all in a grim silence as it started to rain and the fresh drops mingled with his salty tears to slide down his face. They prayed together, prayed out loud till their voices went hoarse and prayed in their minds for days, prayed to all Gods, all Goddesses, anyone who could help, anyone that would take pity…anyone…

*

Dawn came; she was Goddess of the morning and came in style, with a burst of light and life, pushing the night's shadows back into their hidden holes under the earth's crust. Her main job done for the day, she floated around in the sun's rays, drifting from place to place with a happy tune on her lips and smiling eyes. Dawn's skin was golden-brown and her eyes were white with silver pupils. Her hair glistened like freshly grown straw bathed in sunlight and waved about her in long strands that reached her feet; her long nails were delicately rounded and seemed to glow softly like little lamps. She flew gently down towards the sea and skimmed her feet into the smooth waves.

As she played with the water and watched the ripples on the shining surface, her mind caught the edge of a prayer. Looking up with interest, Dawn floated forward a few feet and then she shot upwards into the sky. Soaring forwards once more, her sharp eyes saw the source of the prayer, a small boat with two small figures kneeling on the deck. Their eyes appeared listless and looked out to the west over the sea and towards the horizon. The Goddess moved nearer to them and heard the prayers that they said silently inside their heads.

A baby? A little boy, hmm. Dawn placed a finger on her bottom lip. She didn't having anything better to do that day. And though she could not return the child to its parents without breaking a dozen of rules set down by the King of the Gods and the Queen of the Goddesses, she could see him to safety. With another gaze into the two mortals worried minds she flew off towards the west, to find a small crate that held a precious bundle of life inside.

*

Dawn had been searching for hours, and she was considering giving up when she saw something bobbing in the water. With a smile of delight at finally finding the child she went down to him and floated atop the water as she looked inside the crate. He had hazel eyes and soft eiderdown tufts of brown hair. As Dawn peered at his face he gurgled and smiled, waving a chubby arm in the air. The Goddess smiled and reached out with a finger, smoothing his head and kissing his nose; as she leaned back her eyes caught movement in his. A gold rim had appeared around his pupils and the hazel in them appeared lighter. Dawn caught the bottom of a delicate lip in a gasp as she saw a gold kiss-mark on the child's nose sink into his skin and add to the intensity of the gold around his pupils. She quickly drew her hands away from him and onto the crate. The boy had stolen some of her magic, but how-? Dawn stopped short and closed her eyes; she searched amongst the stars and into the child's future, and she knew he would be a wizard...She kept her skin away from him. Mortals with the ability to wield magic absorbed it from Gods and Goddesses such as herself. That small stroke on the head had just given him immense power; and her kiss had hidden it from him, at least till he could control it properly. She swept back a crisp golden strand of hair that had fallen forward over her face and started to push the crate forward, towards the Western Isles that were a few miles away. They held the mage guild of Mog and this boy would need all the training he could get as soon as he could get it. Not that the mages would know of his power, if it wished to stay hidden then no mortal would be able to sense it. However they *could* bring him up with more control then anyone else, and who else did the child have now his parents were no longer with him? So she started to push the child towards the small patch of islands in the west, wondering what would happen with the power of the Gods lying dormant in his mind.

CHAPTER ONE
A Wandering Wizard

Jed was a wizard. He had the unofficial (yet strictly professional) long, flowing beard that wizards usually have. He had ankle-length robes and a pointy hat that tended to flop over. He also had a staff; it was as tall as himself and had many intricate carvings on it, most of which he couldn't make out, and a round white gem set in the top. It was a magical staff. Jed was thirty and as such was considered young and excitable by all wizards over the age of one hundred and eighty-three. He had an untidy mop of thick mousy brown hair that hung to his waist, a long, traditional beard that tripped him up every now and then and murky hazel eyes with gold rings around the pupils and inch-thick glasses with green crooked rims. All in all, Jed looked like the man the Gods had created for people to pick on.

However, there was one advantage to being Jed; he was a power-ful wizard. If he thought about it long enough he could create his own type of wizardry. If he thought about it some more Jed would proba-bly call it 'Jedism'. But Jed didn't think about it.

Instead he was currently traipsing around the planet trying to find a quest. He didn't want to go on a quest but his guild leader, fed up with turning around and finding Jed mimicking his every move (it was considered good practice to follow others and learn their crafts in wizardry) had sent him to find one. So there Jed was, nearing the Inn of the Drunken Hedgehog, in the town of Gin'ne on the planet Mog. (Ancient scholars believed that when the God who made the planet came to naming it, they had favoured cats. In a far off isolated island in Mog, people worshipped cats to gain favour with the God. However he was currently in favour of dogs and the worshippers kept dying in the most unusual ways.) As Jed waltzed along the road his staff whizzed around him; it made an annoying buzzing noise and zipped about like an anxious dog wanting to explore everything in record time. Eventually Jed sighed impatiently. He stuck a hand out, the staff jerked into it with a thud and his long, spindly fingers moved to the white gem set in its head. Yanking upwards on the stone, he felt the gem rise into the air and all at once the amazing, intricate carvings started to move, slowly at first but getting faster and faster till all of a sudden they slithered under the gem like a snake and down into the staff. Pushing down and replacing the mystical stone, Jed smiled to himself as its texture changed from a rare gem to that of old wood. Now, having locked the magic of the confounded instrument inside itself he might have a bit of piece and quiet. Perhaps people would take him for an honest traveller instead of a high and mighty wizard and leave him alone.

*

Stepping into The Drunken Hedgehog, Jed surveyed the dark corners warily. The grimy floor held footprints and leaves that had been blown in by a gust from the street. When most wizards step into a building the door flies open and a burst of air flaps their cape forwards, swirling it around them majestically. Jed had no such luck. Instead the door had creaked open stiffly, nearly rebounded into his face and everyone stopped talking to stare at him. It reminded him of a scene from one of the books he had favoured in his childhood years, where a stranger walks into the tavern and everything stops whilst he orders a drink and appears at ease. Then the fight always breaks out. However, as suddenly as everything had stopped, everything started again.

One man leapt out of his chair and waved a mug in Jed's general direction.

"Get 'im! E's a wizarrddd!" came the drunken cry and every man at the table stood up and ran to confront their magical and very surprised foe.

Jed made a mental note to hide his pointed hat as well as his staff in the future.

"Arrgh! Ge' lost! No magic foolery in this town!"

"Yeah! Pack yer bag a' tricks and leave now!"

The shouts carried on for some time as the men stood and waved their hands about, there were three altogether and each man had a face that looked as if someone had trodden on it at birth. The first man was short and hairy and very dirty, built like a baboon, with ratty garments marked by stains on them. His hands held an old copper knife and a brass knuckle-duster, but he seemed content for someone else to make the first move. The second man was tall and thin, like a stick, with large fingers that groped the air and pointed accusingly in Jed's direction. He wore a snarl and was the one who held a mug in his soiled hand, with grubby clothes that had once been fine and threaded with gold. Now the cloth was faded and the man himself had bloodshot eyes and wrinkles of worry on his forehead. The last man was quieter than the other two and his eyes darted everywhere, like a rat's. His nose resembled a snout and he held a spiky silver disk between two fingers.

Jed saw the first move coming; the little man shot out his hand and the sharp, metal disk flew towards Jed's face.

Raising his disguised staff and grasping it with both hands, Jed smashed it down hard on the tavern floor. The dirt and muck slid away from the mystical rod in a pool and a white light was thrown up around Jed's form, where it seemed to dance and glitter ever so slightly. The disk bounced harmlessly off the shield and whirled into a dark corner; there was a choking noise and the sound of a body falling to the floor.

The three men had watched the disk and now stood with their mouths open and eyes wide. They probably thought a wizard was more like a magician or a trickster. Jed frowned at the notion. Some towns had been without mortal magic for far too long. He lifted the staff from the floor and held it over his head, with his other hand thrust out in front of him, the words of magic flowed from his mouth in a wave.

"Away and out! Be gone and leave,
Never to return lest it be for great need!"

The men turned and ran. Well, they tried to run, but found themselves dangling in the air. Jed moved from the doorway and they floated out a good hundred yards before dropping to the ground, scrabbling to their feet they turned tail and ran.

But the fight had not ended yet.

Blood pooled from the shadowy corner where the dead man lay and another shadow moved forward, silently and cautiously. Without jibing or shouting he made his way to Jed; and Jed knew that the silent ones were the ones to look out for.

The man didn't remain silent for long.

"If you hadn't conjured up that magic trick my friend would still be alive, wizard!" His eyes never left Jed's and fury burned in them. Jed opened his mouth to protest that he was only protecting himself when chairs scraped around the room. Everyone was silent and they all stood looking at him. His mouth dropped and he moved back towards the door. He couldn't get them all in time, could he? He didn't have to. The door behind him flew open with a crash and a tall, lithe figure filled its frame, the cowl of her hooded cloak shrouding most of her face in darkness, revealing only a bare glimpse of curving lips that smiled softly. Her voice was quiet but, for some reason everyone was sitting down now and trying very hard to make themselves as inconspicuous as possible.

"Good day, gentlemen, I was on my way here to have a friendly drink with you all when I saw some acquaintances being thrown from the building...by air," She chuckled. "I hope you have all been good to any magic wielder that happens to be passing through. After all, I would hate it, if harm came to anyone in this town," the mysterious figure told them. Her hands suddenly held a gleaming sword tightly, she flicked it in the air with ease, catching it gently by the blade and balancing it on a finger, almost playing. Jed's eyes narrowed and flicked back over the woman. A flash shone in the dark and he concentrated harder. Her eyes shone out from the gloom that was the hood's shadow on her face; they were like slits of green, luminous cat-eyes staring in the night. The men in the tavern shook their heads and mumbled into their hands, looking at the floor and away from Jed. The woman stood straighter and her head turned to Jed. "You will come with me now," she told him. She went out onto the street; Jed followed quickly, trying to keep up with her long strides. "I say!" he called as he caught up with her, not quite knowing what to say, "Err...thank you miss?" No name came from the depths of the hood and he floundered on.

"Well, anyway...thank you. Might I ask why those men in there were, well, were going to attack me for walking into a tavern?" he said, still trying to peer into the hood and get a glimpse of his saviour. This however proved difficult. She was much taller than he was and walked faster, making a beeline to a large building further down the lane. The answer that came was short and simple, but softer than the hard voice she had used earlier. "Because you wield magic, and they do not. Jealousy is common in mortal men. It has also been a while since a wizard ventured out from their homeland in the west...over ninety years if I am not mistaken."

Jed nodded. It was true; the last Archmage had not let any leave the guild for some time. The reason he had given was that two terrible powers would join and sweep the land, destroying what they could not claim; he had read the stars and they had plagued his dreams. But the old man had died and after many councils had been held the new leader of the mage guild had let them out, but warned them to return in times of danger. Wizards would be needed to reshape the land if indeed a hidden danger destroyed most of it. Jed's thoughts came back to the present; he suddenly realised that he had been told to follow this woman and so far he had no idea why.

And so, being curious he asked, but again he received no answer. Instead she pointed to the building in front of them and they walked in.

Jed found himself in a world of white, void of all other colour; the carpet on the floor was spotless, the walls shone the colour white, the seats of the chairs were white and so was a door at the end of the room. Even the secretary was white; with permed short hair and white glasses that stood on the end of her nose, she also looked very strict. Tapestries and paintings hung from the walls in all shapes and sizes, all in different shades of white and cream.

"You will have to wait, I'm afraid," the secretary said.

Jed looked around the obviously empty waiting area.

"Why?"

The secretary sniffed and pointed to the woman who had led him here as she opened the white door and entered, shutting it firmly behind her.

"Ah, I was told to come with her…"

"She will report to thee Mayor and you will be h'informed when you h'are required," she said, nose in air and perfectly plucked eyebrows raised. Jed sighed and twisted his face into a scowl. On someone else's face it would have been intimidating, on Jed's it looked as though he was sulking like a small child.

Sitting in a comfortable looking, yet extremely uncomfortable chair, he waited. Shifting around to find a comfy position he wriggled and sighed, kept crossing and uncrossing his legs, changed his staff from hand to hand; his hat came off and went back on again, then off and then on then off. His long flowing beard was flicked about and curled with skinny fingers, then swept over one shoulder and juggled to the next. The hat went back on and his staff was leant against a chair. He could turn sitting on any seat into a gruelling experience. It was one of his rare talents.

After ten minutes of this the secretary stood and, moving over to the white door, tapped politely with one hand. The door stayed shut. She tapped louder and still no answer came, Jed re-flicked his beard and gave the poor woman a faint, airy smile. She smiled back and thumped the door as hard as she could. It opened and a short balding head appeared, followed by a rather round body.

"Yes Mistress Penyaol?"

"Oh Mayor, this wizard was informed by Mistress Lanoelin to wait here."

"A wizard eh? Haven't had one of you lads down here for some time. Might I know your name?"

And once the mayor was told he then beckoned for 'such a fine wizard like yourself, sir' to come into his room. Jed stood and put out his hand in a grand gesture. The staff leaning on the chairs seemed to turn slowly, as though considering Jeds choice of actions. It stayed where it was. Sighing, Jed picked it up, reminding himself that it had a mind of its own. He stepped into the small, brightly decorated room and sat on a large wooden chair, trying not to wriggle. Looking around, Jed saw the woman who had led him here seated in a corner, her cloak hung on the wall at side and he was able to see her face. She had hair that was black as pitch and fell to her waist in lightly curling locks with hints of blue where it caught the light from the sun's rays as they poured in through an open window. She was the tallest woman Jed had ever seen but her height wasn't what caught his attention. Her eyes glowed like green fire and were the perfect shape of almonds; her skin could only be considered a warm shade of pale. Her ears were pointed and reached an inch above her head, with four sets of delicate garnet and opal gems studded in each.

He turned his concentration from her obvious beauty to her garb. Her ankle-boots were of fine, worn leather; she also wore a pair of blue-grey, skin-tight breeches and a loose shirt made from layers of silk and cotton that had been patterned to look like maple leaves overlapping and sewn together.

On the lady's back was a beautifully crafted and carved longbow of yew and the bright silver short-sword that she had unsheathed only minutes ago. On her hip was a quiver full of razor edged arrows. Hanging from a belt knit of leather and cloth were four daggers of varying shapes and sizes, a heavy looking purse, a set of pipes and a wooden flute.

She was one of the Azale.

*

Millennia ago, when the worlds in the universes were newly made and the God of Mog still favoured cats there existed the Azale, the Eternal. Azale are the most powerful beings ever created. There are many different clans, each unique and different to the last but every

9

Azale has many things in common. They are immortals, living forever unless fatally injured and only showing signs of age when they reach five centuries old, but because of this they can only ever bear three children. One of the Eternal is harder to kill than two armed warriors, even though their bodies are very slight and willowy, they can take incredible hurt and still battle on. It is rare that a human can use a bow as well as an Azale and it is virtually impossible for any society, be it human or dwarf, faerie or beast, to see further than an Azale. The Eternal make no sound as they move and give no warning as to their presence. Azale of the high blood can heal wounds that the strongest wizard, seer, priest or priestess cannot. The Eternal can grow anything just about anywhere and they are intelligent, very intelligent.

But no matter what they can do, there is a weakness in us all. The Azale's weakness is us humans. We amuse them, we befriend them and we let them into our land when other life scorned them for their talents. Any of the Eternal would lay down their life for a human; they have to. No matter if that human was a friend or someone they just found on the ground, on the brink of death and with the light of their life flickering too low. It is part of the pact made by all clans with all humans.

You see, once there were very few of the Azale left on Mog. Dangerously few, they travelled the land like gypsies, always forced to move on in the end. Usually by magical monsters, and at times dwarves. They moved on and away and eventually came upon humans. They were so alike and yet so different. But the humans saw themselves reflected in the Azales' faces and, instead of picking up rocks; they picked up food and water and gave it to them. They led the Eternal to the forests and helped alongside them as their first real homes were built. They fought off those who would seek to destroy the Azale when weak and in return for all they gave, they received the pact.

> *'Human lying by the road,*
> *Whipped and hurt by life's heavy load,*
> *An Eternal comes by and if he sees,*
> *He will lay down his life for thee.*
> *One and one and one is three,*
> *If he lays down his life for thee,*
> *If thee accept, beware the change after,*

Come and join us in our laughter.
Now we join our hands and sing,
Will you join the song's sweet ring?'

But these days the Azale thrive, the largest of any community and still growing. They grew too many for the woods to hold and some sought out homes elsewhere. In the valleys, in towns littered across the countryside, in high mountains cut off from the rest of society and hidden deep in their own country, hidden from mortal men's roving eyes in the world of dreams.

There were always the Azale.

*

Jed gave a seated bow to the female Azale in the opposite chair; she in turn nodded and looked back to the Mayor, her eyes flickering and reminding Jed of fire.

"Ah Mr Jed. This is Karma Lanoelin, an Eternal from the Woodland clans. Karma this is Jed, and from what you've told me, you already know he's a wizard".

"Yes. He has not learnt to hide his talents," Her voice was smooth and the words seemed to roll off her tongue like music, quite unlike the tone she had used in the tavern. No human could speak as gracefully as an Azale.

"Your voice?" Jed asked, unsure.

"Oh that, it changes from time to time to suit my mood and purpose. Not everyone trusts my type and not everyone likes our echoing voices," She sniffed and sat upright, hand on chin, "Why do you come to this little town after so many years of neglect from you and your kind?"

"Um, well, I...I'm on a quest"

"And what quest would you be on, Jed?"

"Well, right now I'm on a quest to find a quest".

"Oh".

There was silence; the Mayor had started to shuffle various bits of paper around on his desk at the word 'quest'.

"And what do you do, Karma?" said Jed.

"I sing, heal, kill and do quests for money, Jed," she answered in a silky accent.

Jed's mouth formed an 'O' shape and he wondered why she had

11

brought him to the Mayor and what for. He glanced back to the mayor, who was still muttering and still going through the papers. Had he done something wrong? He'd never been outside his guild before; perhaps the rules were different?

"How old are you, Jed?" The question came from nowhere and almost caught him off guard.

"I'm thirty, Karma. What might your age be?"

"I am two-hundred and twenty-four years old, Jed".

Her eyes twinkled with amusement and her lips curved into a soft smile. As if she found him entertaining.

"Ah-ha!"

Both Jed and Eternal turned their attention to the Mayor, who was holding aloft a piece of tattered script.

"Here it is, Karma, you came to me only a few days ago seeking a quest, but then I did not have one for you to take on alone. You now bring Jed to me and he also needs a quest," His voice sounded as though he were suppressing excitement.

Nods were exchanged; this was indeed true.

Jed pricked his ears. He would be going on a quest with someone he hardly knew? How had that happened?

"Well, this is the nearest town to both of your homelands and I guess I should be glad of that fact. An Eternal runner burst in here one day and thrust this on my desk, telling me to appoint the task to someone capable of great things. Now, it's not for me to judge, but wizards are well known for their power, wisdom and common sense and Azale, well, Azale are Azale! So maybe this will suit you?"

He handed it to Karma, who read it. Her eyebrows twitched upwards in surprise, and then she handed it to Jed. His eyes flickered over the hurried scrawl before him, his jaw dropped slightly and he muttered "oh no" under his breath.

He read:

A man rises in power amongst the High Azale in the Northern Reaches. He was nearly dead when he reached us but the pact was given and his life restored…in a fashion. However his soul is corrupt; he has already run us out of our home and he seeks to gain our power and steal our magic. His name is Ragea Atia and he has support, we cannot get near him but someone must kill him soon or our way of life may end. We ask for your help.

Anann Versa
Runner from the High Eternals in the Northern Reaches

Handing the paper back to the Mayor, Jed thought about his options. He could go on this rather daunting quest and hope to succeed, he could turn back now and be thrown out of the guild and be stripped of his staff and powers for disobeying the Archmage...or he could hide. His mind was swerving to the last option when Karma stood.

"Well, I for one will go on this quest. It cannot be helped. Sadly, all Eternals' magic is with the High Azale, huh, you'd think they were Gods the way they stay in their old castles acting mighty and grand. A good Eternal should always have an ear on the ground, not in the stars and mixed up with new magic.

Will you join me, Master Jed?" Her voice held a hint of disgust for the high Eternals, and seemed offhand when she asked for him to join her-but she smiled brightly at him too; she did have a lovely smile.

Jed realised he was supposed to answer and pulled away from his private thoughts of cowardice.

"Yes I think I will. Good day, mayor"

He was vaguely aware of a small voice in his head saying, *"Hello? Did you listen to me before? I thought we were choosing option three!"* He squashed the voice and trailed behind his newfound companion out on to the streets.

CHAPTER TWO
New Friends

Outside Karma immediately took charge; this seemed to come naturally to most women, Jed thought, and he was happy to follow anyone with authority.

"Right, Jed, let's start walking. We have a good day's journey still ahead of us and we can talk whilst we walk; it's better for you," she said.

"Yes, Karma" Jed mumbled obligingly.

"And if you're worried about supplies and horses and such, don't. I have some friends waiting for me on the forest path and they have all we will need".

"Yes, Karma"

She slid a sideways look at him, "Are all wizards like you, Jed?"

"Oh no, Karma"

She nodded and set off at a brisk walk, Jed had to trot to keep up with her lengthy strides, hampered by the added nuisance of his long dragging robes. He wondered what they'd say back at the guild if he wore anything other than the heavy, itchy robe that was traditional wizard wear. He sighed and kept on trotting.

*

They had entered the forest. The surrounding view was trees and more trees, with a muddy makeshift road running through them. Most of the trees were two hundred feet tall with trunks so wide that it would take at least several people to give one a hug, Jed thought. Their canopies stretched wildly around and tangled together in places, as though clasped in a permanent handshake. Though it was autumn, where there should have been browns, reds, yellows and golds melting into each other and painting a marvellous picture of light and magnificence. Jed found it muddy, dark, spooky and tediously fly-ridden.

As they walked, Karma discussed minor issues with him, for example the reasons why some Azale clans disliked others. The plain fact was that everyone was different and anyone who had a different opinion to the majority of people was classed as a rebel and wrong. Their discussion reminded Jed of wizard school; just because one boy had a magical staff that was smaller than yours did not mean that they aren't as strong as you when having a duel.

He was wondering whether Azale ever went to school when a small grey bundle dashed out from behind an innocent-looking tree and slammed itself into the Azale's midriff. Instead of drawing sword and launching into battle she chuckled and patted it on the head. Catching Jed's look of confusion, she reached out and pulled the grey cloak from it.

Underneath the large and tattered cloak was a small boy; he had royal blue eyes that sparkled with laughter and bright ginger hair sticking out at odd angles. His grin was of a cat who had got the cream without anyone finding out. Before Jed could get over the shock of the lad, another blur moved into view. This one was clad in elegantly cut black and dark blue and had a dagger to Jed's throat before he could so much as move an eyeball in its socket.

The man was as tall as Karma, quite slim, with a dark look about him, the way he moved, the way he stared. He would have been handsome if he didn't have a collection of scars around his neck, throat and face. He had short-cropped, spiky black hair; his eyes were midnight blue, almost black, and took everything in, flickering over Jed with speed and without emotion. His breeches were loose and black, his boots were knee-length and also black, his shirt and coat were the dark blue of his eyes and he wore a wide-brimmed black leather hat, his cloak was short but of very fine craftsmanship. On his belt were four small bags and three open pouches; also five small throwing disks, all with vicious points round the edge. He moved like a cat and strangely, it seemed as if he wasn't even holding the razor-edged dagger.

"Good day Karma, who's your friend?" The words flowed like Karma's but not with that warm edge; this voice held nothing in them but slight amusement and an arrogant tone.

Karma smiled as Jed gurgled and put up both hands. His staff stood still in the air. The man watched him like a cat watches a mouse, no, like a tiger sizes up his prey.

Then the Azale turned to the small bundle still hugging her midriff. Patting it on the head, she gave it a grin and said, "Hello Lance". Then her attention turned strictly to the man and Jed, she sounded like a mother berating two small children for fighting.

"Leave off, Telric. That's Jed. He's a wizard and he's going to help," she announced. "I got the slip, by the way," she patted a pocket. The bulge that had been the script was not there. Lance had such an air of innocence about him, that it could only be considered guilty. He waved the script in front of her with a grin that spread across his face from ear to ear.

"Lance, give me that back! You little thief!"

The lad grinned, flourished an eccentric bow and wiggled his eyebrows. Jed started to smile at his antics and the knife at his throat pushed just a little harder.

What had he done to get thrown in with this crowd?

"Ta Karma, yer not a bad warrior Eternal yerself!" the child's accent took Jed by surprise, compared to Karma and Telric's smooth-tongued words he was utterly uncouth and bold.

Telric dropped his arm and the dagger disappeared about his person, his other arm shot out and gave Lance a clout on the head. Then the dangerous fellow turned back to cast a critical eye over Jed. His eyes went to the staff and Jed put a hand round it, almost embarrassed that the thing refused to move from its position and submit to gravity.

"Erm, good day?" he ventured, on the off chance that a show of friendship might work to calm the man down.

"Hello, Jed. Now here's how it goes." The black-clad arm now snaked round his shoulder and pulled him into a walk, it clinked as it moved and Jed felt the heavy touch of metal through thick material. He was afraid of that one arm.

"My name is Telric Zeal and I am head of the Assassins Guild in Torath'Danar", *(That explains the lack of manners, thought Jed)* "Karma is a good friend and Lance is...Lance is someone I helped. I don't make friends easily, wizard and I don't trust anyone but Lance and Karma and even then they had to earn that trust twice over. Leave me alone and I'll leave you alone. You help, you get paid you leave. Those are the rules. Do you understand them?"

Dark eyes furrowed into Jed's as Telric swivelled him about, and gave away nothing, no clue as to the next move, no sign of what might be happening in his head.

Karma pushed them apart and poked a finger at the assassin's chest; Lance the thief glared at her and moved in the way of the offending finger. (Jed had been shocked by the boy's accent before, and now the language that Lance shot at Karma appalled him).

"Now listen, both of you, we need that slip from the Eternal runner to prove to the high Azale we are there to help. Jed is useful and all he wants is to get this over with, I'm sure, so leave him be. I have half a mind for you to feel the back of my hand, Lance, and I am positive that Telric agrees. Just because he swears doesn't make it acceptable for you to. Now, I'm going to start walking. Anyone who wants to follow is welcome." She stalked off, the essence of anger and the very epitome of leadership, Jed followed quickly and soon Lance and Telric caught up.

Smiling, Karma turned and flicked a finger at Telrics nose, anger forgotten.

"Ha, I knew you'd follow"

The assassin looked at her and then grinned, the grin of someone sharing a private joke. Jed sighed wearily. He watched the young boy as he darted ahead of the adults, stopped and waited, darted back and then darted off after a moment of casual walking. He seemed to have boundless energy. Jed turned his attention to Karma and Telric who were now talking and laying plans.

"Well, you know I like you, Karma, but the High Azale have a vicious and tricky way of dealing with outsiders. Plus they invented the pact and that's not a nice thing for anyone to go through," Telric sounded angry, as though he had been through this conversation before and didn't like repeating it.

"It's the only way we can save a human!" Karma said, "Anyway the woodland Azale always asks if the human wants to be saved first and we tell them what will happen if we save them. And you're changing the subject. This man who's gained the power amongst the Azale, how do you think he got it. Friends on the inside of the fortress, perhaps? And then there's the question of whether he can get to the magic to steal it. He'd have to go through the Keepers and they hold their post higher than life; they may try to trick him with the magic as well" Karma's voice sank to a mumble and she frowned, "You know, if it wasn't for the fact that all Azale magic is controlled through that one small globe they keep I wouldn't even bother to go and pull them from this mess!"

"Why do you always ask me the hard questions?" Telric's voice was laced with agitation now.

"Because you have so many spies everywhere, I've no doubt you've snuck some in amongst the high and mighty magic wielders of this world."

Karma seemed to have hit a sore spot and Telric shut his mouth with a sharp click. Glaring at her, he let himself drop behind. By the time they had ceased with their conversation Jed was decidedly confused. He had to speak up.

"Might I inquire as to what you are talking about? What exactly is 'The Pact' if it's a nasty trick? I thought it was meant to be a gift to humans for saving the Azale from almost certain doom or something…at least that's what I read in wizard school."

Karma frowned at him.

"You really want to know? It's not very nice" she asked.

"Yes I do, I have a right to if I'm going off on this quest. I'd have settled for saving a kitten from a pack of vicious wolves but you persuaded me to come."

"How?"

"You smiled and I think that smiles are a weak spot for me…"

"Don't worry everyone seems to have a weak spot for my smiles." A grin flashed across her face and she fluttered her eyelashes, laughing at his confused look. But the laughter soon died away and was replaced by a frown, "So you want to know. Well its going to take some telling so make sure you don't fall asleep half way through."

And so the telling of the Eternals' pact, how it was made and what it does was told.

"When an Eternal lays down his or her life for a human their soul slips on to the human soul and heals his or her fatal wounds in a certain way. We Azale don't understand how; it was part of the magic we lost from eons ago and all the elders who helped with that magic are long gone. At first the human is overjoyed but after a while their tastes start to change; their ears grow longer and sharper, weight seems to drop off them and height is gained. Eventually they themselves become an Eternal and flee to other lands where they were not known before, but in most cases another Eternal finds them first and the 'Newly formed Eternal' is drawn to their fireside and the music. You see most of our power is natural and music has a nature of its own hidden inside it. Music is our strongest link to the human." She stopped and waited for Jed's reaction. He only nodded and gestured for her to carry on with the tale, eagerness on his face.

"Songs are played around a large fire and the new Eternal is led into a dance, they have not learnt to control their power of magic yet and therefore any sort of magic from us is like a demonstration. They join the dance to feel their own power without even knowing it. Every other Azale there concentrates, the new Eternal dances and sings and listens to the music and another change takes place. The soul of the Azale who died for the human is brought nearer the surface and eventually can gain control of the one they saved; it's as though they are taking over that person's body. At times they don't gain control and it's like having another person in the changeling's head talking and suggesting, teasing and bullying; those types of Azale go mad. Their skin becomes dark and their eyes look like a snake's. They then flee to a place that pulls them, that place is where the dark Azale are. It is there that two Eternals in one body plan and rage about vengeance, as they believe the other Azale did not try hard enough to let them gain control and sent them mad instead.

All in all, very complex; most Azale do not bring the other soul near the surface and eventually that soul slips away and goes to death, leaving the human-turned-Eternal to sort its own life out. Sadly, some do not and waste away, mourning for what they have lost...but that is the only way to save the human species' life, to change them into our own species. The wood Eternal that originally invented it were the keepers of our magic; they looked down on others who weren't as powerful in the magical world as they were and eventually took off. They took the name the 'High Azale' as though they're better than us common war-mongering, woodland types. It's disgusting really. I'm sorry, Jed". For once Karma's bright eyes didn't reflect the light of living, but appeared dulled as a sad flower, wilting from lack of sun.

Jed's eyes, on the other hand, were still shining as he absorbed this fount of information hungrily before the realisation of what he had been told hit him. His eyes took on a brassy glow and his face fell, sadness left its imprint in the way his forehead wrinkled and how the slight dimple on his left cheek disappeared as the smile, which had been on his face a few moments before, sunk into a blank line. How could such wonderful seeming creatures be the cause of such evil and suffering? Karma was right, it was disgusting and no excuse could be given for taking over another's body and pushing the owner out.

Before he could tell her this, a shout came from a little way down the road and Lance told them to hurry up as the camp was already in sight and he was sure that the horses were getting impatient. Telric grimaced when he passed Jed as though being reminded of something he wished would stay hidden. He broke into a run after the boy and once more Jed turned to Karma with a confused look. Now the Eternals sad eyes followed her friend and her face seemed to droop even more.

"What's wrong with him?" Jed asked

"Telric's parents were killed in front of him when he was just eleven," she sighed "He ran from his home that night. He had smiled once, his eyes showed things, but they don't any more. He's empty for lack of a better word. He dislikes the high Azale for one reason: the man who ordered his parents' death was no man; he was an Eternal, of the high order. He once ran an assassin guild for all creatures, humans and magical life forms alike. Telric's parents were some of his best. They wanted to leave and get married, but he still wanted their skills and refused to let them leave. They both snuck away and hid deep in the countryside. This high Azale didn't like that and, well; he hunted them down and killed them. It took him a long time, mind you. They were not his best killers for nothing. They had contacts, they were intelligent, they lived their life in disguise".

They both fell silent as the road started to curve to the right, the humid air made Jed's hands clammy and he felt a trickle of sweat roll down his back. He and Karma walked slowly, waiting for someone to break the calm and to answer the unspoken questions that still lingered between them.

"Telric first killed when he was thirteen. A woman was raising her hand to hit a small child. Since then he has learnt to block out nearly all emotion. You've seen his eyes? Well, they show nothing until he plunges a dagger into some unknown torso, then they burn with light and shine out. He has nothing but his Guild left to him and even then he only has two friends he can truly trust. He is very alone and never confused, which only makes it worse, but always working and his mind always manipulating others to his ways. Some would call him a monster if they knew; I call it a mercy that they don't. He found Lance two years ago in the gutter, without parents and despair clutching him. He saw himself as a child and took him under his wing. I fear that the boy may turn into another Telric and the man hopes for it."

"Then why are you his friend?" Jed framed his question with caution.

"Everyone has a story; it's not their fault if the story doesn't end with happily ever after."

A thought clicked in Jed's head.

"What's your story, Karma?" he asked quietly, his immense thirst for knowledge of other folk and their magic not yet quenched.

A silence entered the clearing and he watched the Azale carefully. Her face became carefully blank as she replied.

"It's complicated" was all she would say, Jed sensed that he should not press the matter and wisely kept quiet.

When they finally reached the bend in the road Telric and Lance were waiting for them on the edge of the forest. Once seen, they submerged into the foliage like living shadows and Jed was led through the trees and bushes to a small clearing. A fire burned in the middle and on it was a black pot that steamed and had a delicious smell wafting from it. Four mountain horses were tethered to a tree, Lance instantly went over to them and patted the great beast's necks and Jed had no doubt that they had planned for another companion on this trip. Four rugs lay on the floor and only three looked slept in. It was cosy and just the way he had imagined a camp out under the stars.

As he moved to sit on the unused rug, he passed the assassin and took the chance to peer into his eyes. Nothing peered back out and Telric sneered, moving over to lean on a tree, his arms folded over his chest and his hat pulled low. Jed hadn't noticed Lance next to him till the boy placed himself in clear view, a cheeky and insolent grin on his face and a swagger in his step to rival any lion.

"'Ere, Jed, can you do some magic?" He cocked his head to the side and his large eyes twinkled.

Jed looked down at the boy, who had his hands behind his back, and patted a pocket.

"I will as soon as you pass me my handkerchief," he answered pertly.

"Awwww! It's silk that is, I could get a real good price fer it where us lot are 'eaded!" The voice changed its tune and became whining and obliging all at once.

"All the same give it back and I might teach you something useful" Lance sniffed, squinting his eyes in a look of suspicion.

"Like wot?"

"Like how to use magic to open a lock"

"Wow! You can teach me that?"

"Yes, but only because you've a spark of atmospherical interference in you."

"Meaning?" The boy raised an eyebrow and scrunched his nose in confusion.

"Meaning, you can learn such a small spell but no more. You don't have the power. Now hand it over"

Surprisingly Lance did so without further comment and sat watching Jed on the forest floor. It was rather fun having an apprentice. Jed looked to Telric and his thoughts changed as the man settled himself on one of the rugs and proceeded to watch him whilst rolling a gold coin across the bridge of his fingers. No not an apprentice, a one-time pupil. Lance already had a master.

By the end of the session Lance had learnt to unlock a safety charm on a leather pouch (which Jed always kept his money in) through magic; he had also promised not to steal from Jed again unless he wanted to be a toadstool for the rest of the trip.

Full night came and the four suns that rose above Mog to create one big sun separated and went their own ways, north, east, south and west, leaving behind the moon shining its silvery light like a candle on a windowsill.

CHAPTER THREE
Danger In The Dark

Sitting on his long, fur-lined cloak, Jed was sulking. The time was around five in the morning and rain fell from the sky in glistening threads. No noise was to be heard and Jed was sulking because he had never had to miss so much sleep in one night before. His staff lay at his side, still disguised from the eye and the white gem still pretending to be nothing more than rotten wood. He picked it up and bounced it on the palm of his hands, thinking about life outside the guild. Deep in thought over these new experiences, he only heard the clank of metal when the bandits were almost upon him.

There were eight altogether. Each carried a huge war axe that glinted golden in the moon's rays and reflected a dozen different jewels moulded into the blade and pommel. Each had a helmet of boiled and toughened leather; all their body armour was different and looked to be of a makeshift style- though each piece could probably withstand a small whirlwind. Every single bandit had a beard down to his chest and most were braided and painted in vivid colours. They stood as tall as a seven-year-old child and were as wide as two men rolled in one and they were all dwarves. Opening his mouth to shout a warning, Jed found that his body had frozen from fear. The dwarves moved faster and the leader let out a roar of mad laughter mixed with rage, his eyes fixed on the Eternals sleeping form. Seeing their intent drove Jed to anger and he raised the staff above his head with both hands, gripping it in a white fury. How dare they try and attack his friends? But before the wise words of magic could be spoken a dwarf produced a lump of wood from his large belt and, throwing it accurately, hit Jed on his skull, rendering him unconscious.

*

The heat and movement of his body being jerked from side to side woke Jed. Opening his eyes blurily, he coughed and blinked twice, trying to shake his head and wake his senses. The first thing he noticed were his hands above his head; they were chained together and stoutly attached to the moving metal cart that held him and jerked from side to side over the rough terrain of the woodland track. The sun beat down on his brow and heated the metal to scorch his skin and make him sweat. Then he noticed his companions. Karma's head and feet were all that could be seen under the pile of chains around her and she had a band of the strange, glowing metal around her hands and neck. Her eyes seemed held in shock and her mouth kept shaking and trying to open; when whispers escaped from it the only words she could form were:

"I can't feel the magic, I'm cut off"

They were said in utter disbelief and terror of such a thought; the Azale's magic was their art. It was what made them who they were, what kept them immortal and without the link of it time caught up and the Eternal were lost.

Lance had a wrist attached to the wall by a manacle. His face was like a black cloud of anger that threatened to burst any moment; however his other hand clutched to Telric's cloak and held onto it so hard that it was white with strain. It was the assassin's attitude that shocked Jed; he would have thought that Telric would be the one to blow a fuse if captured. However he looked relatively at ease, one hand also manacled, the other tapping a tune on a boot. He hummed and smiled slightly, every now and then a chuckle escaped and with it the word, "Fools". Jed noticed that there were only four dwarves on the cart…

Pulling himself into a sitting position, Jed looked at their immediate surroundings. They were all in a metal cage strapped on top of a cart, which was being pulled along by four huge shire horses. Their horses were nowhere in sight and the remaining dwarves were either sitting on top of the cart or on a small platform attached to one side. Each had a flagon of what could only be beer in his hand and most were laughing and joking loudly. One was using Jed's staff to prod the horses on faster and another was sitting next to a mound of small and dark-looking mechanisms. Most seemed very sharp even from a distance. Jed once more glanced at Telric and found the man looking at him and then to the mound. Telric smiled and took off his wide hat, carefully showing the inside to Jed. Attached to the sides with leather straps were a number of long and short picks and one jagged slice of metal that had a streak of green down it, the thing was poisoned. Replacing the hat, he put a finger to his lips and pointed to the sun, and then he made a down motion. He wouldn't free them till night came. Karma had seen the hat and watched it hungrily. Coming to her senses, she fixed her eyes to the ground; staring so much would be noticeable even to drunks. And so they waited.

Night seemed to take a long time in coming but when it did the land cooled and silence settled over them all; the only sounds to be heard were the dwarf's loud snores. They had left one dwarf on guard (and for shame the brute was using Jed's staff to prop himself up on) but after a few minutes he had glanced at his companions and slid down to the floor, and a new snore joined in the already loud chorus. Telric had watched the last dwarf calmly and now took off his hat. At first his fingers twitched over different shapes and sizes of picks but he soon selected two and passed one to Lance. Man and boy set to work and within minutes had both hands free, Telric moved to Karma, hat in hand, and pointed Lance to Jed. Jed watched the boy pout at not being able to rescue the woman but quickly start on Jed's manacles. Jed wriggled and the chains clinked quietly.

"Shh, you'll wake them and we won't have a chance then!" hissed Telric.

Jed sat poker-straight, hardly daring to breathe. After a while his hands were also free and whilst he stretched and rubbed his wrists and back, Lance helped Telric. Karma's chains took longer and the colour-changing metal that covered her hands and neck could not be picked. Finally, everyone was standing.

"We're going to have to steal the cart and horses if we want to get away from these vagabonds. They may have short legs but they can keep running for days without a stop. I'll drive, make yourself useful and push that dwarf off the side, then we can go," the assassin whispered, pointing to the guard, who had slept through all of this. He was the only one on the cart.

Jed nodded and silently went to the cage door. Lance popped up next to him, smiling and holding his hands together. Rubbing them hard, he opened them and pointed his two index fingers to the keyhole.

"Twist and turn the metal bands,
Unlock with magic in my hands"

The lock popped open and the child giggled lightly with joy. Jed went through and the others followed, careful to re-shut the door and move to their positions. Telric leapt neatly off the side, landing on the balls of his feet and making slightly less noise than a prowling panther, waking each horse in turn, gently and soothingly so they wouldn't give the four away. Lance held onto the outside of the cage and Karma wound her legs into the bars, not able to use her hands. When the assassin got into the driving seat he picked up the reins and turned to Jed (who was ready to push the unsuspecting dwarf off) and nodded.

Jed pushed, he had only a moment to grab onto a bar of the cage and to snatch his staff out of the sleeping dwarf's grubby hands before Telric whipped the reins; the horses reared and whinnied loudly. The dwarf woke as he met the ground, and shot up instantly, a shout coming from his throat. This roused the others awake who reached to grab their weapons and give chase. But Telric was already forcing the horses to give it their all; they raced forwards, huge chunks of mud and grass flying up when their shod feet hit the ground, getting faster and faster till they would not stop, fear at the madman attached to the reins driving them on as surely as wolves snapping at their fetlocks.

Jed suspected he would remember that ride very well. He now knew what it was like to be green.

*

Soon they were far from the dwarves and they did not pause for a good few hours. By then there was no catching up. But soon the horses slowed from sheer exhaustion and their steps became shaky and unsure, their heads drooped down and finally they stopped, unable to go further. Telric got off the cart easily and went to each beast in turn and loosened their harness, taking each horse out of its traces. In their current state of exhaustion the huge horses hardly noticed being hobbled and tied to a tree. Karma unwound her legs slowly and almost fell to the floor, her muscles cramped and tired from holding her steady for such a rough ride; instead of getting off the cart she moaned and stayed where she had fallen.

"I am going to sleep, no one is to wake me up or I swear to make this trip miserable for them!" she said with an ominous tone.

Yet, after looking at her closely, Jed noticed that her eyes still shone with desperation, never leaving the softly glowing metal wrapped around her hands...

Lance chortled at her and slid off his own seat to the forest floor. He looked around a bit and eventually climbed the tree to which the horses were tethered. Hugging a branch, he slept and soon small snores came from his open mouth. Jed released his hand from the bar he had hung onto; he rubbed it self-consciously, willing it to remember what blood circulation felt like. Groaning, he flexed his back muscles and carefully climbed down to the ground. He spotted a suitable grassy area under the cart and was just about to crawl under and sleep when a pair of black boots came into view. His eyes moved upwards and Telric hauled him up by the back of his robe, holding him effortlessly in the air. Jed's staff whizzed about angrily, as though watching Telric. The thought came to Jed's mind; *"If Telric does anything I think he'll find himself with a large lump on the back of his head."* He blinked, as the staff seemed to nod to him and positioned itself in a swinging motion. Had it heard? Had that thought even been his? Before he could think more on the matter, he was distracted.

"What did I tell you about trouble? If you had been a bit more careful last night we would all have had a better chance! Let me tell you what being on watch is all about," Telric hissed into Jed's face, then dropped him to the floor.

"It's about spotting trouble and warning your companions before trouble gets to you! What were you doing? Sitting there, looking at the rain and wondering whether or not it was dangerous at that particular moment? Whilst armed bandits sneak up and almost kill us all!"

The black-clad fellow fell silent then, but sighed heavily; as he walked away towards a dark tree Jed could just make out his last words.

"There's always trouble on this sort of quest, and it nearly always gets people killed. I don't want to die, and I don't want Lance or Karma to die. I push that trouble out of the way before it pushes me. I'm starting to wonder whether you're the trouble. I hope your not"

Jed sat for a moment, thinking on those words, then he set his face. It wasn't that he caused trouble. It was just that he wasn't particularly good at anything and *that* seemed to cause trouble, not him. Always last to be picked for the wizard school illusion team try-outs, he knew this was because he was useless and ended up letting everyone down. But not today he vowed, crawling to his grassy bed and lying down, not on this quest. On this quest he would help, not hinder, and he really believed he could.

Jed's breathing slowed and his heavy eyelids started to droop, he smiled as his staff fell to the ground by his side and rolled towards him; snuggling its head into the palm of his hand.

From the top of a small knoll, inconspicuous, dark eyes watched Jed and everything else as well; dawn would come soon, but till then the group could rest. He wouldn't rest. Someone had to look out for trouble and that someone was normally him anyway.

The eyes swept over everything and took it all in, inexpressive, un-emotional…bored.

CHAPTER FOUR
Realisations

As the four suns of Mog slowly swept up into the sky, like large fireballs shooting to a target and finally reaching each other and merging as one large light, Dawn came. She came suddenly and without warning, one minute there was fading night, cool and dark, the next moment the day had started in a flash of heat and Small-light. You may wonder what Small-light is, well, on Mog Small-light is a flash that comes with Dawn, not exactly red, not particularly gold but those colours, mingled together and slashing across the open sky. Telric clambered down from his post, flexing his back and arms when he reached the ground and shaking the weariness from his body. Cracking his jaw and trying to ignore a yawn he moved over to the horses, all of them were awake but they moved slowly and unwillingly, still tired out.

Lance, however, was already up. He'd been up for a while, and seeing Telric up in his tree, and not wanting to have to take a turn on watch, he had slipped away quietly and run to the sound of nearby water. The little thief had found a stream and had a contented hour fishing. Now, whistling a bright tune with his silver-finned trophies slung over a shoulder, he jogged to the cart, (winking to Telric) and decided to play one of his favourite games. Wake the sleeping Eternal.

Telric watched as the boy lowered the fish to the floor and slid onto the cart silently. He moved to Karmas sleeping form, after going through numerous pockets on her to find any sign of money he gave up and blew on her nose. It twitched and she rolled over grunting. He stifled a giggle and put his mouth to her ear…

"WAKE UP KARMA!" his yell echoed around the clearing.

The Azale shot up and stood, promptly falling over again because of the heavy metal on her hands and neck. Lance grinned at her and was about to dash away, when he stopped. Karma looked up at him and then turned away, nestling her head into her legs and rocking her body back and forth. The thief's face was stunned and he glanced to Telric, but the assassin was already moving to them and sat next to his friend. After an awkward moment he sighed and patted her on the back, she unwound her arms and clung to him instead. Telric gave a sneer, unsure what to do in such a situation, and then Lance sat next to Karma and wrapped his small arms around her too. Hugging the woman fiercely. It was at this precise moment that Jed awoke from under the cart. Blinking sleep from his eyes he yawned and rolled over, his staff shook itself before jumping up and following its master. Jed got up and turned to clamber atop the cart when he took in the scene, Telric turned and beckoned him up. Moving to them Jed sat down, Karma raised a tear-stained face and looked at him, hope shining in those once bright eyes, now seeming dull and void.

"Can you get it off?" she almost whispered, her voice breaking. The Azale stretched out her hands, she meant the metal that was restricting her use of magic. Jed sighed and looked at it wonderingly. Metal bands that could stop you from using magic, how had some common seeming bandits got a hold of them? Unless some great magic-wielder had sent them after Jed and his group…

Forcing his mind back to the present question at hand, Jed caught his staff in mid-air. As he touched the metal Jed felt his skin turn cold. His face drained to an ashen grey colour, it was as though he couldn't hear…couldn't feel…couldn't speak…couldn't even see with a gasp of fear he wrenched his hand away and scrambled back from Karma and the metal. His breathing came deep and fast and his brow was dripping sweat, yet he felt so cold. Karma looked at him, desperately and pleadingly. He shook his head apologetically.

"I can do nothing for this curse-forsaken thing. I am sorry Karma"

Yet she had not heard his apology, having already replaced her arms around her drawn up legs and burying her face there, rocking again.

It was mid-day before the four companions started on the road again. They had un-hitched the heavy troublesome cart and were now riding astride the colossal horses that scared Jed beyond all reason. It had taken Telric and Lance an hour to persuade him to get up onto one of them, and then a further ten minutes to assure him that he wouldn't fall off. Karma had been completely uncooperative. Dragging her feet and seemingly unable to stare at anything but the metal on her hands and at times cautiously touch the band around her neck. She didn't seem to care about anything and her eyes, which had once shone so vividly and brightly with magic, were fading. Instead of the whole green colour, Jed could make out two dark black pupils. Using his staff to pathetically wallop his horse over to Telric he leant over and asked, "What's wrong with her? I've never seen her act this way…" Jed immediately wished he hadn't. Telric glared at him and his eyes burned.

"Don't you even know that magic is what makes an Eternal an Eternal? Do you not realise that their only true connection to this world is through their music and their magic? Its quite simple, the bands around her neck and hands are...cutting her off from her links to her own kind. She is starting to become a human and for the first time will know real age. If we don't get those bands off her...age will catch up" his tone was vicious and he snapped, "And if age catches up...Jed have you ever known an ordinary human being, who does not wield magic in some way, to live for two hundred and twenty four years?"

Jed shook his head with silent realisation.

"No, I didn't think so. She will crumble to dust before us and I will be able to do nothing about it" he hit his saddles pommel and pushed his beast into a trot. Lance followed, holding Karma's own beast's reins and dragging it along. Jed tagged on at the end, but the words still echoed in his head. I will be able to do nothing about it...

CHAPTER FIVE
New Trials

The party's path took them towards a river. At first Jed had clutched at his horses mane and clung to it shakily, trying not to look at the ground. But soon he became relatively at ease on horseback, his body no longer rocked about wildly and his hands un-clenched from the reins he now held loosely. They were all still deep in the forest and they were all silent, conversation had died a while ago and there wasn't much to comment on in this dark, muddy and humid area. Then Jed suddenly heard a sound on the edge of his hearing, water falling, a lot of water, falling at a great height. His eyes sought the sound and saw, at the very top of the treetops, just peaking out into a patch of blue sky, the start of a waterfall rushing down some large, un-shapely rocks.

As they moved onwards his view increased and he shortly saw the rest of the picture. One moment trees and forest grass was all he had to see, the next...they had stepped out of the foliage and into a large clearing, and at one end of the clearing was the waterfall. Huge, dark and with green vines and flowers of red and gold entangled on the slick black stone. At various points there was a space in the rock, no vines climbed over it and only one flower sat at its heart. It was light pink with white streaks and golden crests poking from its moulded shape, the Frayaia flower, rare and beautiful...the only flower that you had to ask to pick. And even then only for a good cause, the Frayaia cures all fevers and all poisons in the body, they have their own minds and choose to save someone's life on their own accord, a rare thing. From the days of old when the world seemed vaster and the people on it smaller. The rock formed the back of the clearing, dominating everything else by sheer size the rest was surrounded by the forest's thick green foliage and large, twisted trees. As the sun shone down on them from its peak, the rays fell across the water and glinted golden and spoke of hidden depths. The group slid from their horses onto the ground, their heads moving to take in all of the small paradise. Small birds spun downwards to fall into the pool and rocket out again holding wiggling fish in their beaks. Small animals known as Cochees climbed the vines on the rocks and peeked out from the ledges with huge, bowl-like eyes and bristling short, curling fur to scare these unknown predators from their home. Telric still led the way, with a look of regret on his face whenever he looked towards

Karma, who was still walking around unconcerned by anything but her hands and neck, trapped as they were.

They were led to the waters edge and Jed could see down into the clear depths, it was very deep and seemed to have tunnels under the water, the currents could almost be seen clearly, leaving bubbles in their wake. Fish inhabited it, small and silver, large and grey, darting and quick or hidden and slow. Jed looked up from the underwater world and saw that the rest of his group had disappeared. In a sudden panic he glanced around the clearing...nothing, no sign. He opened his mouth and then he saw Lance dart out from behind the falls. Jed's mouth dropped open and he followed the boy wordlessly. When he came next to the water by the fall he saw a large enough gap for them to get through, and the rock on which they walked just behind the onrushing water was dry. Jed stepped forward and would have gone on had Telric not shot out a hand, he was yanked into a tunnel to his left.

The tunnels were deep and echoed every sound loudly, Jed was in awe of the place, not daring to speak for fear it would break the magnificent spell it seemed to have cast on him. Huge gems were mounted in the walls, some the size of a fist and others as neat and perfectly shaped as a hens egg. White stones placed on high rock formations gave off a flickering light, like fireflies trapped in a jam-jar, marking the way through the endless twisted tunnels and large, smooth caves. The floor was made up of different rocks, set next to each other like cobblestones. But these rocks were all different hues of blue and grey, and they seemed to mingle together and twist the eyes. In some caves they passed Jed's roaming eyes caught sight of large pillars as thick as four men and crafted with beauty, elegant to a fine point. Carved statues stood in one of these rooms, placed next to a throne of marble, still draped in red silks, its beauty marred by thick layers of dust, and huge grey cobwebs swathed the walls. But soon the tunnels grew shorter and the caves smaller, till they stopped passing through them at all and were left only with a small pathway to follow, and follow they did. The entrance glared with the bright light of a fine summer day, which stung Jed's eyes after so long in the dim light of the tunnels. Blinking hard and shielding his face with a hand the wizard plodded on following his friends, yet felt sad to be leaving the place so soon...he could stay there for years and not tire of searching the chasms. They reached the opening soon enough and found themselves on a ledge of grass with a dugout path to the side of it. Telric led them down the path without a word, his face composed and his manner seeming to suggest silence. Yet when they reached the bottom a sight beheld Jed's eyes and he could not help but gasp, the caves were nothing compared to this.

He had heard of the Azale village of Faynar'Haye, how the houses were small but grand, how the trees flourished all year round and the fruit they bore was soft and tender and small children seemed to float as they ran in their games. How the folk there were named 'The Veiled' because they would do no harm to another being, they would run and hide rather then hurt or kill another. It was nothing compared to the real thing.

"Why have we come here? We don't need to restock..." the words came unbidden from his mouth and Telric answered calmly.

"There are some Azale here known as the council of the Elders, their leader is the Eldest. They are the oldest of the Eternal and can see something of the future; they are very wise. Maybe they know why those bandits had the glowing metal bands and maybe...maybe they can help her" he pointed to where Karma stood listlessly, her feet appearing leaden as she moved. Jed questioned further.

"How do you know so many things about the Azale, might I ask?"

The answer came with a half-hearted laugh "You can't traipse around half of Mog with an Eternal like Karma and not get to know about these things. She can barely keep her mouth closed without information pouring out of it".

At the bottom of the path stood a man and a woman, both shorter than Karma by a head and both garbed differently. Instead of tight breeches and her leaf-shirt, they wore loose robes, coloured in different hues and sewed with birds, so lifelike that you thought they would fly away if you tried to reach out and touch one. Both wore light fawn sandals on their feet and the woman had bracelets and bangles up to her elbows, rings on nearly every finger and a variety of necklaces. Most shone gold and silver, but here and there a wooden bangle could be seen, with mother of pearl or some equally desirable gem set in its side. The only decoration the man wore was a purple gem in his ear connected to a white chain that was attached to another darker gem higher up in his ear. They turned to face the companions, both smiling softly and bowing, hands on knees as they did so.

"Welcome travellers, to Faynar'Haye. What brings you here, to our small village?" their voices melded as one and they spoke together, never missing a beat, their eyes kind and smiling. Telric stepped forward and bowed to the man and woman as they had done to them, Jed and the Lance quickly followed suit. Karma did so too but had to be shaken out of her stupor before she blinked heavily and slowly bowed in turn. As the man and woman saw the metal glowing on her hands and neck they hissed as one and drew back, eyes never leaving it except to throw sympathetic looks towards Jed's friend...maybe they did know what to do?

"Thank you for your welcome Path-watchers, we come to rest and restock for our long journey north, we move to the Northern Reaches on a quest. Yet we would seek the Elders and their advice", Telric said grudgingly, though looked as if he was trying very hard to at least show some politeness to the two before him. The woman beckoned for them to follow as she started to walk, trees bowing and curving out of her way politely as she made for a bank by a river that stretched for miles. Putting out a hand and bending a finger forwards, she spoke some low words in Azale. Suddenly, from the blue depths, a wide stone path rose, stretching across the water to the other side of the river, the water on the stones seemed to slide off and they became dry; like the rocks by the waterfall. The woman stepped onto it and moved forward, beckoning for them to follow again. Once on the other side they moved through the village and Jed's eyes grew large with delight as he gazed at everything around him.

Children ran barefoot through the lush grass, their hair long and light, shades of gold and white-blonde; very few had dark hair as Karma did and they stretched out their arms before them in their play. Jed noticed an old man sitting underneath one vast tree, with a child on each knee and more children all around him. He waved his hands in the air over a small fire, making pictures of the smoke as he told them stories. The small homes of the Veiled were of marble and carved wood, different hues glistened out from the rock and seemed to make the depiction of people and animals on their walls come alive, like the bird on the Path-watcher's dress. The shops were mostly wooden and had rails that beautiful cloth hung from, the designs and patterns unique and shimmering. Men and women smiled to them as they passed and each bowed with their hands on their knees, Jed tried to bow back but found that there were too many Azale to bow to and that he kept being left behind. Karma smiled vaguely as she watched their faces though her eyes appeared cold and uncaring; forever looking past you and into a world of her own. Lance appeared as open as Jed in his pleasure at such splendour. Telric glanced at Karma cautiously from a corner of his eye whilst he watched everything around her at the same time. Observing her, Jed was reminded of a mother hen watching over her chicks.

The village was neither large nor small; it was perfect. It seemed neither crowded nor sparse; it felt cosy and secure. At the end of their walk through the rough road they came to a large tree. Jed gazed up at a canopy wider than several others stitched together; and then noticed the leaves. As he looked at them, flying to the ground in a swirl of patterns, Jed noticed that every single leaf was different. Not one appeared to be the same, and every time a leaf fell to the ground a new one appeared in its place moments later. There were boundless supplies of shapes and sizes, colours varied from rich autumn russet to light grassy knoll green. The leaves had different patterns on the veins too, interwoven here and crossing over there. Jed turned his attention back to their guide, smiling to himself; Azale were known for being ingenious. He had not realised how much so up until now, this was the sort of magic rarely touched by mortal man. This was ancient. He watched the Path-watcher woman as she took out a large key from the folds in her robe, her hand smoothed against the age old bark and she smiled at it, her eyes warm with affection. Her finger traced a line on the bark, as plain as the rest, and stopped halfway and brought the key up under her finger. A shimmer of pearly white light shone from the key and as it moved forward, a key-hole suddenly appeared and the key was somehow in it without seeming to move, turning with a sharp click. Stepping back the woman bowed again.

"From here onwards you must find your own way, it is my duty to open the door. Only you can decide whether or not to enter it. The hands of our Mother shelter you, Aria Mathar Cerentia."

The companions peered through the doorway and looked into the gloom, large webs hung from every corner and the floor was ashen and bleak compared to the bright grass on which they stood. Telric turned to them and spoke, his face scrunched up as he tried to remember.

"This is the way to the Elders of the village, it's a type of test. We have been asked to stay on the path, it is the Veiled's wish that we do so, we must show that we can do as we are asked and therefore ask a favour in turn. Its old magic, older then the Elders themselves even…they don't know why the test is as it is, yet they keep it intact for the next generation of their kind. Too much has already been lost from the last era; they strive to keep the memory of ancient things alive so do not question as to why we walk it now" his eyes pinpointed Jed and held his gaze for a moment before carrying on, "Temptation lies all around us and should your foot step off the path for an instant, the door will shut and we will wait in the darkness till the Elders choose. If we reach them you are all to step forward and give your name, loudly, these men and women demand the utmost respect as befits their rank. And we must show it to them, is that clear?", he glared at everyone in the group and tapped Lance's hand smartly as the boy tried to take the large and rather beautiful key from the door without anyone noticing. Both Jed and the boy-thief nodded their assent but from Karma, who still gazed at nothing, there was no sign that she had even heard the assassins' words. Telric sighed heavily and took her hand, leading her through the doorway and sinking into the shadows beyond. Jed rolled his eyes upwards and gave a silent prayer to any God's that might be favouring him at the moment before following them. Lance was about to step onto the path when the Path-watcher intervened, holding onto his arm.

"This is no place for children, go and play with the others, boy. You will find much amusement I am sure…and kindly return the crystal bangle that you have lifted from my person", she said, her tone smooth but severe.

"Ohhh!" an audible whine was heard and the sound of something been shoved roughly into a hand which jangled as it moved.

"Thank you child, now run along"

Lance took one more look at the path, at which point his guardian stuck his head out of the passage and said, "Do as she says Lance. And try not to steal too much", before turning and sinking back into the shadows and darkness. The boy looked around and saw two tall Eternal children gazing at him with vague interest; he bounded up to them and gave a wide grin.

"Hi! 'Ere, do you want to learn a trick I can do? All you 'ave to do is take yer 'ands out of yer pockets and I'll show you…"

*

Stepping further into the murky, foreboding tunnel, Jed tried to pierce the shadows surrounding him with his eyes as he sought to see into hidden corners.

The tunnels of the mountain had been magnificent; throwing

colour around in rays where light had caught on the corner of a gem here or a mosaic tile there. These tunnels were drab in comparison, dull to the eye and boring to boot. The tunnel walls were of dry, cracking mud and chipped rocks, their only decoration the long, silky webs of huge, brown, mottled spiders that scuttled hither and thither as they pleased.

Every now and then Jed spotted a small pair of eyes that shone blood red; but as soon as Jed blinked the eyes were gone and he was left staring at an empty space. After a while his eyes adjusted to the murk of the tunnel and he could make out large shapes in the dark. The red eyes belonged to huge bats, ragged and hairy with scars along their bodies. They hung from large roots, presumably from the tree above, which had broken through the walls and cemented themselves into the foundation; gnarled and twisted as a curse. To Jed the tunnel seemed endless and he thought he had been there for hours counting eyes and jumping at things that went 'bump' in the dark until, finally, as though the tunnel was grudgingly letting them go, they reached its end.

But what came after the tunnel was far worse.

The cavern that Jed and the others crept into was immense, its very presence echoing and powerful. Long stone spikes dripped in cones from the ceiling, in some places almost reaching the ground before they ended. The ground was littered with insects and bugs, crawling about to make an everlasting slithering noise. The bats from the tunnel had followed the group, and now swooped down to grab mouthfuls of the creepy crawlies before flying away to munch their prize. Every stride Jed took brought forth a squelch and a crunch as tiny lives were extinguished in a step.

Casting about he soon spotted the path that Telric had told them of, it reminded him of powdered snow and seemed not at all dangerous. Jed cupped his staff with a hand, whispering magical words to the gem so that it stopped pretending to be made of wood and lifted up. Shining brilliant white and green hued light into the darkness. The intricate patterns that had hidden inside of it shot out to claim their places on the staves side once more. As he moved the gem towards the ground, Jed noticed that its pool of light picked out ice crystals leading away from them like a carpet of purest ivory. The thing looked simple enough, but by now he had learnt that nothing was as it seemed.

No insects crawled on its surface, they all packed at the sides, when they had to move past the snow-path they moved faster...perhaps this should have been a warning for them all, but it went unnoticed.

Karma, Telric and Jed stood next to each other, on the very edge of the path, looking at it with wonder. Jed looked at with suspicion, ancient magic was dangerous and amazing he knew, and there were always consequences to using it; he did not want to go first. And Karma, standing in her still dazed state did not appear fit to even walk across the carpet, let alone battle with any magic that might spring from its depths.

Telric blanked his face and took it upon himself to go first. With an arrogant swagger to his step he moved forward onto the carpet of crystals turned and smirked at them.

"Come on! Its not hard, look, I'll do it again if you're all afraid. Watch", he raised a foot.

"Telric stop fooling about!" Karma's eyes were wide open now and they watched the assassin like a hawk, yet her cry went unheeded and as the assassin's foot hit the floor again, he froze.

His shoulders hunched and his mouth opened in a gasp, yet no sound escaped, his eyes widened and looked past everything else and in them, at the very centre of his pupils, a burst or colour...starlight.

His hands clenched and unclenched as Telric's temptation whisked by in his own minds-eye.

CHAPTER SIX
Temptation

Telric was eleven; his feet ran swiftly towards his small home on the edge of the village green. His mother would be there, waiting for him by the fire and he had something to show her. He couldn't wait, happiness shone from his eyes and his face lit up with joy.

Bursting through the door to his house his feet moved on there own accord, automatically taking him to the kitchen and opposite the hearth, to be swept up into a bone-crunching hug and placed upon his mothers knee.

"There you are dear, I was wondering where you'd got to. Did you run off and play with the boys today? I wanted you to come straight home!" Maya Zeal stood tall and slim and elegant; her hair was long and curled to the flat of her back where it shimmered a dull brown in the suns rays, with wings of grey at her temples. Her eyes were an ocean blue and her face, once lovely, now had wrinkles at the corner of her cheeks and creases on her forehead. But her hands were still young and soft as they flicked back her son's hair from his eyes.

"Ma! Don't be angry, I only played for a bit. I have something to show you" the boy said, excitement in his voice. Telric's fingers fumbled into the pocket of his jacket and brought out a necklace, a very small blue gem held on a scrap of leather that was tied in a lumpy knot to fit round his neck.

"Look, I won! I won the race in the schoolyard, Mistress Kati gave me this as a prize"

Maya took the gem and her fingers smoothed over the cold stone, lifting it up the light to see marks that reminded her of sea waves lapping against the shore.

"I'm pleased for you Telric, why not put it in the hall? When your father gets back he'll see it" she smiled down at him.

Her sons face fell.

"He won't be home early tonight then?" disappointment clouded his voice.

"No child, he must work late…the crops did not bring as much as they should have this year. He…he had to find a spare job again, only for a little while" she tried to look into his eyes but he turned away roughly, getting to his feet and folding his arms to glare moodily at the fireplace.

Moving to him Maya's arms wrapped around his shoulders and she leaned her head on his neck.

"Please Tel…its not often…you want to eat don't you? Please just…let it be, don't brood about it tonight I've got you favourite meal read-"

She was cut off suddenly as she heard the bang of the large oaken door at the front of the house being pushed open, hard. Her eyes widened and she grabbed the iron bar that lay next to her chair. Telric had his head up and he was already moving to grab his father's daggers; they were no strangers to bandit attacks.

Moving fast Maya was about to run forward and bring her weapon crashing down on the assailant's unsuspecting head when her husband entered the room, she dropped the bar and her mouth dropped too.

His short-cropped black hair was dusty from the road and out of place; his dark green eyes held fear and terror in their centres, his breath came in gasps and his left arm hung at an awkward angle. It was broken. She was about to greet and comfort him when he moved first, jumping to them with relief on his face.

"They haven't reached you! Lore be praised, your alright! Maya…Maya he's found us again. I was looking for a job today and when I went into Mayors office he was waiting there. A smile on his face and three of his bully-boys with him, we haven't the time to get away…I only just made it out the window and even then…" he gestured to his arm. Matthias watched his wife and saw her jaw set and her eyes harden…as they had done a long time ago when she had been young and they had both worked together.

"No, no my sweet, we can't run, there is no time - we can't fight either. We're both too old…but we can save him"

Telric's head whisked from his mothers face to his fathers, frustration painted his features.

"Mother? Mother what's he talking about? Pa, what's wrong? Who broke your arm?"

"No time…damn it! There's no time! Telric come. Now boy do as your told!" Matthias snapped and his son leapt to obey, he moved round the house collecting trinkets and clothes, a cloak here and a piece of jewellery there. When he had done Maya was in the front of the house opening the large wardrobe that stood there, thick and solid…large enough for a child to hide in safely. Pulling his son along Matthias shoved Telric into it, passing the pack through afterwards. His usually hard face threatened to cry and he bit his bottom lip.

*

Jed watched with anguish as he saw the assassin unfreeze his hands from his sides, his face still held in a gasp. Telric took a step towards the side of the path; the place they had been specifically told not to leave and Jed voiced a warning.

"No!"

One more step, Telric stopped, his shoulders hunched again and he threw back his head violently.

Karma grabbed Jed's sleeve, her own dilemma forgotten as, hands shaking, she watched the direction in which Telric trod.

"Jed, look at his eyes...lore! Look at his eyes!" her voice cracked and she coughed heartily before blinking her own slowly.

Jed looked gave a yell of horror and shock as he recoiled back in fright.

Telric's eyes, that had held such a deep blue colour, like the evening sky, were turning lighter. Shade-by-shade...then another explosion...starlight...

*

"Telric...Tel? Listen, something...something bad is going to happen in a while, we can't stop it and you can't either. Don't try, you'll just get killed, when they have gone...as soon as you can hear no footsteps, sneak round the back and get Bray. Ride him as hard as you can to the next village and then the next, it's not safe for you here. Keep running and don't stop, try to save the horse but if you must run him till he's dead and buy another. You've got everything of value in that little pack. You can sell some of it, you have my daggers too and you know how to use them. Lad, just keep moving, no matter what. Bye boy", the last line was said gruffly as his father pulled Telric into an awkward, one-armed hug, before shoving him back and moving to the door, he started to pile things in front of it.

Maya moved forward, tears leaked from the corners of her bright eyes and her hair fell in wisps. Kneeling she pulled her son into a fierce embrace, whispering in his ear.

"I love you Tel, remember that, I'm...I'm sorry this turned out as it did. One day, when your older maybe...maybe you'll find out why this happened, I hope you do. But don't think less of your mother and father...please...good...goodbye Telric", she pushed away and Telric moved after her, a hand rose in protest. But she shut the large wardrobe doors and he heard a click as they were locked. At the bottom of the door

he saw her push the key through the crack, her hand shook and Telric moved his eye to the keyhole. He heard voices...

His father and mother stood next to one another, an iron bar in hand and severe determination on their faces, jaws set and eyes hardened. The front door had a chest piled behind it, a few chairs, a rug; anything Matthias and Maya had been able to lift. Now the fortifications shook, harsh voices called from outside and Telric heard men laughing. The door shook again, a crack appeared and he saw an eye peaking through.

Matthias leapt forward, his iron bar slashed in the air once and a scream was heard from outside. Blood fell on the floor and dripped from his father's weapon. The men outside laughed harder and one roared...he hadn't liked having his eye gouged out. The door quivered violently, two chairs fell and the rug started to slide away. Maya shuddered in fright but stood fast. Then, with a yell, the door burst forth. Splinters showered the walls and the rest of the barricade fell to the ground.

A man raced in, his face streaming and his eye socket bleeding heavily. There were four altogether, huge men with arms like barrels and chests like tree-trunks. The bleeding man flung a hand out and Matthias hit the wall, sliding down it only to scramble back up, but his face was white and his nose streamed. All the strangers wore a type of uniform, grey and crisscrossed...the pattern twisted the eye. One man, the only one with grey at his temples stepped forward...a dagger in each hand.

"Maya, Matthias, its good to see you remember old friends. It's a pity we must meet under such circumstances, but you ran from the leader. He hates people running from him. We've been sent to sort it out..." his voice was deep and held a note of amusement in it, Telric watched, shock on his face and his fingers biting deep into his arms to stop himself from hammering on the door.

"You cursed idiot! We were friends! I...I was your teacher! We asked to leave the guild, he didn't like that and tried to keep us against our will, surely...surely you can see why we ran? We wanted a normal life, we wanted to get married, settle down. Please Raygar, please...friend", his mother had spoken with force and anger at first but now...now she sounded tired and weary. Old.

The man she had named as Raygar shook his head sadly.

"I'm sorry Maya...orders are orders...you taught me that a long time ago"

His hand moved, a blur of speed, and Maya gasped only once as the dagger appeared in her chest. Blood spread out in a pool on her dress *and her face fell as she toppled backwards. Matthias moved to catch her...but she was dead before she hit the floor.*

In the darkness of his wardrobe, a tear trickled down Telrics face, his hands were stuffed into his mouth and he bit down hard to stop himself from screaming. He tasted the sharp metallic tang of blood in his mouth.

*

"Maybe, if we shout to him...maybe he will hear us? It is worth a try surely?" Karma's voice echoed around the cavern, sounding tired.

"Yes, yes, we must try at least" Jed hurriedly agreed with her but noticed that she had already opened her mouth to start screaming.

"TELRIC! TELRIC IF YOU DON'T SNAP OUT OF IT RIGHT NOW I SWEAR THERE WILL BE TROUBLE! Lore! YOU STU-PID HEADSTRONG MAN! THINK OF LANCE, WHAT IF SOMETHING HAPPENS TO YOU...TELRIC! HE IS A CHILD! TELRIIICCCCC!" she exploded, her words angry in Jed's ears but there was a frantic undertone behind them. Her eyes shone with unshed tears, it was then that Jed realised there was more to her rela-tionship with the assassin than friendship.

He turned to see if she was having any effect on the figure cloaked in black that stuck out like a sore thumb on the white. Telric took another step, his hand raised before him this time...a trickle of blood fell from his mouth and dribbled down his chin. Jed watched his eyes closely, they were white now but he could just make out another explosion in them, this time it was black...starlight

*

Matthias stroked his wife's blood-matted hair and rocked her back and forth on the floor as Raygar shook his head.

"I am sorry, I really am. One time you were both the best and we would all be dead by now, but times change, people change. Bye bye...old friend"

His arm shot out again, a blur in Telric's sight, Matthias moved but the blade caught him all the same, this time in the gullet. As he sank to the floor his throat gurgled and black blood streamed from his mouth, mixing with spittle and frothing in a revolting mess. The men surround-ing Raygar grinned, cruel intent in their eyes and hands already moving to items on the floor and attached to the walls...pushing them into bags that were hooked by their belts. The man who had just killed Telric's parents however stood there, his eyes downcast and his shoulders drooped, as though a heavy weight had been placed on them.

Everything froze. The men's hands stopped in mid-air as they reached to fill their bags with loot. Telric found himself out of the wardrobe. He stood before Raygar; the man who had slaughtered his parents like sheep. He glanced to his side, dreamlike and unaware, a mirror stood opposite him and he watched his hand rise to his hair and touch it...it was smaller than he remembered...his hand. Childlike, his eyes younger and wider, he didn't remember being this short either.

But this was wrong, this hadn't happened all those years ago, he hadn't come out of the wardrobe. He had hidden till the men had gone...then he had run...he hadn't come out of the wardrobe.

Suddenly his hand held a dagger and the men around him were moving again. They dropped the bags and stood in front of him, Raygar looked at him with tears in his eyes.

"Telric, what have I done? I killed them...your parents, my teachers. I don't deserve to live. Telric. Kill me too, you have to"

Telric smiled, he had wanted to kill this man all those years ago, strived to. But he had never found Raygar; the man had hidden himself too well, Telric moved forward. Then stopped.

This wasn't right, this hadn't happened, what was going on?

He stepped back, letting his hand fall to his side, though it still clutched the dagger tightly, his features became suspicious.

"Who are you?"

The man fell to his knees, hands stretched out and a stray tear leaked from an eye yet he grinned strangely, he was mad.

"Who am I? I am the man who just killed your parent's, I am Raygar of the Secret Guild, and I...I...will kill you now."

Suddenly the man was on his feet again he also held a dagger yet he moved slowly, purposefully.

Telric once more found his arm rising, to throw the weapon in his hand, but he stopped. His ears twitched and he looked around at the walls, his home...it was bleeding.

No, not blood...words.

TELRIC! TELRIC IF YOU DON'T SNAP OUT OF IT RIGHT NOW I SWEAR THERE WILL BE TROUBLE! LORE! YOU STU-PID HEADSTRONG MAN! THINK OF LANCE, WHAT IF SOME-

*THING HAPPENS TO YOU…TELRIC! HE IS A CHILD! TELRII-
ICCCCC!*

His ears twitched again, he could hear Karma but only just.

The writing on the walls.

His mind woke with a jolt, as though it had been drugged before
and he had just regained conscious thought; moving to one side he
dropped the dagger to the floor. It fell heavily, point down.

This was a trick. The path, he had stepped onto the path…those
light-cursed Eternal were playing a trick on him! This was the test, he
had to get out, he had to push away temptation…Raygar stood
before him, and he had stopped moving when Telric had dropped the
dagger. He and his men were frozen once more, inanimate. But
Telric could see the mans eyes moving, watching, considering, weigh-
ing…Telric ripped the dagger from the floor and moved towards him.
Raygar had killed his parents! He had set Telric on the path that was
now his life, never loving, never feeling, only killing…if he wanted
Telric to kill so badly why not see how he liked being killed by him!

*TELRIC! YOU NEED TO STAY ON THE PATH! YOU'RE A
STEP AWAY FROM THE EDGE MAN STAY ON THE DAMN
PATH!*

He stopped mid-stride, watching the words. But what did she
know? Had she been there when he needed comfort? No. Had she
been there when he needed someone to help him choose? No. Had
she been there, when he had built up the guild? No. And then, at the
back of his mind, piercing through the white-hot rage that filled his
head came a small voice…

*No, she wasn't there then. But she is here now…,doesn't that mean
something?*

It did, It meant a lot. Telric turned to face the man before him
slowly, his chest heaving and his jaw set; much like his father's had
been moments before. His mouth curled in a contemptuous snarl and
his eyes, his emotionless eyes…burned. He brought his hand up with
the swiftness of a viper striking and slammed it into the wall, yanking
his hand away from the hilt and stumbling backwards. Telric looked
at the walls where the writing stood and again at the men standing
around him and finally at his parents. The blood still pooled from
their bodies and trickled forth to lap against his boot.

Jerking back from the sticky liquid he glared at the walls and his mouth opened, yelling his anger.

"There! I've played your game, and I have won, you let me out! I know the rules. I've passed the temptation, its gone. Let me out noowww!"

Light faded, his eyes grew dark, he felt himself falling and wondering why…braced himself for the jolt that would wrack his body when he hit the hard floor, yet it didn't come. His eyes felt as though they were glued shut, unable to move them, his voice frozen in a never-ending yell. Telric fell.

*

Jed watched as Telric stopped suddenly, a foot rose in the air…just about to move off the path, it froze and Telrics body turned limp, he swayed for a moment and then fell backwards with a crash that echoed around the cavern and made the bats take flight. Their piercing screeches faded slowly, and then Telric lay still. It was too much for the Azale beside Jed; regardless of the danger the white carpet might hold for herself she charged forward, light and fast, almost flying. Yet when she reached Telric's side she stumbled and Jed watched with wonder as the white powder moved away from the metal on her hands, blowing fiercely to each side of it and leaving a shining floor underneath. Blinking heavily the Eternal was about to move back to check Telric when she caught sight of her hands, her eyes shone once in the darkness, then faded, scrunching her face in confusion. Jed heard the echoed words that rung from her mouth.

"Why hasn't it happened to me? Why haven't I faced my temptation, what did I do wrong…*will the magic ever come back?*" the last words came out as a frightened whisper, but Jed was concentrating on her hands. The white powder that formed the perilous path seemed to be trying to move away from it and he saw that underneath the carpet was a bright metal. Karma sat back on her heels, head cocked to the side, watching the now intensely glowing metal earnestly…as though it would jump off suddenly and she would be free; but nothing happened. Instead Jed did a very, very stupid thing, made from a very, very small mistake.

The metal is taking up the Azale power from around it…the carpet won't work on me now!

Jed stepped forward with a sigh of relief; he made his way towards

Karma. However on his fourth step...he froze.

It was then that Jed knew that the metal bands that Karma wore were taking the power out of the carpet around her. But *she* was the one wearing them.

A very small mistake can lead to a very big consequence.

CHAPTER SEVEN
Foolish Thoughts

Jed was the first up in his dormitory on Seventh-day; in fact he was always the first one up, the first to be ready to go to classes, the first to be waiting outside a professors door and the first to answer any question asked in class.

But today Jed was up for a good reason. Today was his sixteenth birth-date. It was the day he was to receive the magical staff that signified that he was now a Dedicate Mage. And today was the day that the guild chose new members for its illusion team. The newest, most admired and most imaginative entertainment that was available in the whole of the west isles. Jed had tried to gain a place in the team ever since he could remember and ever since he could remember…he had always failed. But not today, today he would be confident, today he would have his staff…and today he would be part of a team. A real group of friends, not just 'the loner', not just 'the bookworm', he would be 'part of the team'.

Pulling his algae green, fraying tunic over his head and tying it loosely with a length of dull brown cloth, Jed yanked on a large pair of socks and a pair of thick leather shoes that were four sizes too big. Then, after grabbing his hat and book-satchel, he looked towards the large tan door at the end of the long room. His small, rasping bed was right at the back, crammed in between bags and boxes, he had to pass eleven other beds of snoring fellow students without waking them. Birth-dates only ever had one downside to them and that was birth-beats.

Jamming his hat onto his head and pushing the bent glasses that were sliding down the bridge of his nose back into place, Jed quickly scurried forward. He watched the floor beneath him and told himself where to go.

Right, he thought, second floorboard on the left for five steps, move to the exact middle of the room and creep forward two steps, go back to the left and forward one step, over to the furthest floorboard on the right now…got it, forward seven steps…

The words in his mind directed his feet and not one floorboard creaked or groaned to give him away. Ten steps away from the door now, his dormitory mates slept on, unaware.

Seven more steps…four…three…and…
RIP!
THUD!
CLUNK!
Jed froze and turned around, ever so slowly, the satchel over his shoul-

der now had a large rip in the bottom. His books had fallen to the floor and the eleven boys behind him were wide-awake. One was grinning maliciously and the others were already throwing off bed covers and coming to stand in front of him. Jed dropped to his knees and grabbed two battered, leather-bound volumes of 'Magic and Mayhem, history in a new light' and started to stuff them into his bag, already muttering a repairing spell on the confounded thing. His spindly fingers scuttled across the floor like a large spider as he groped for the last book. They had just reached it when a foot stepped on his hand, making him wince with pain. Looking up, his watery eyes stared into the round, harsh eyes of Hassid, the boy who had grinned and the little leader of Jed's dorm. Hassid took his foot off of Jed's hand and yanked him upwards by the back of his cotton tunic with a large hand.

"Well! Looks like Jeddy here was planning on leaving before we got a chance to give him a happy birthday, eh lads?" the strong boy glared around the room and his cronies laughed faithfully. Jed cringed and folded long, lanky arms over his face; he knew what was going to happen next.

"And how old are we today Jeddy?" sneered Hassid, Jed muttered that he was sixteen, wanting the thing over and done with. Hassid cupped an ear and gave a fake confused look.

"What was that? I didn't quite hear you…"

"Its my sixteenth birth-date"

"Oh joy and the Gods and Goddesses be praised. Line up lads, Jed's going to receive his present from us all, and since he's sixteen and I'm feeling generous…lets say he gets sixteen 'gifts' from us all, fair?" Hassid dropped Jed to the floor and balled a ham-like hand into a fist, drew it back and then forced it down in a throbbing, jolting blow.

"One…" he chuckled.

Jed clasped his hands tighter over his glasses and clenched his teeth from the pain.

*

Karma stopped gazing at her hands to look towards Jed, she came out of her daze enough to realise that he was doing the same thing that Telric had done before he had fallen. The mage took a step forward, his hands were raised above his head and his eyes clenched shut, his face a mask of pain and his head flinching every now and then. His staff was moving about him, for some reason unaffected by the white carpet. The Azale maiden crawled towards Telric and checked his heartbeat, smoothed the trickle of blood from his mouth with a soft finger and then sat back against him, watching the mage through tired eyes. She couldn't help him, Telric might have been able to...she could do nothing without her magic, she felt useless. Worse than useless, she felt as though she should have died years ago, but she wasn't, her body was tired and her brain exhausted. Karmas eyes closed and a tear ran down a perfect cheek. She couldn't help Jed now...

*

The huge hall of the mage guild was the largest room in the whole place; it held a long, ink-stained dais at one end where the teachers sat in a long row of deep purple-velvet upholstered chairs. At the other end were row upon row of students. The oldest sat at the very back; proud and tall in long, dragging robes on wooden chairs. The newest members of the guild sat at the front on the floor in a shy, slumped huddle. The hall itself was decorated deep amethyst edged with silver trimmings. And it gave off a glow of good health and warmth, everything seemed to have been made to compliment each other and the only thing that stood out was the high-backed, bright white ivory seat of the Archmage. The man who sat in it had long white and grey hair that was neatly parted and draped over his shoulders like an extra cloak, his beard was trimmed short and oiled to a point and was a dark, iron grey; it had once been black. He had deep brown eyes and wrinkles in every fold of skin, his nose was straight and noble, his cheekbones high and his fingers were old and scarred. At first the Archmage appeared strict and imposing, but the brown eyes were warm and deep and comforting, a small smile lit up the formal face into a welcoming grin.

Jed didn't sit with the older students at the back; he didn't sit on the floor with the younger ones either, instead he stood in line with his dorm-mates. Pulling his floppy hat down low to cover a brilliant bruise on his cheek and a bust lip that was red and swollen. Soon the doors of the huge hall were shut and the Archmage stood slowly, he held a yew-wood staff in his left hand and his right one lay atop a pile of the beautifully crafted instruments at his side. The line Jed stood in suddenly started to move forward and he jumped up to look over the shoulders of his peers and see what was happening on the dais. Every time a student stood before the Archmage the old man gave them an odd look and then sud-

denly plucked a staff from the pile. Sometimes dragging one from the bottom to place it into the palm of the young figure before him, then he would lean over and whisper something into that students ear, and finally each student would walk down the steps leading off the platform and stand in their rows again, this time facing their fellow students and holding their staves out proudly.

Soon it was Jed's turn to step forward, he gulped and his Adam's apple bobbed up and down, he stumbled his way forward and almost tripped over his large boots. Only managing to save himself from the fall by grabbing onto the Archmage's shoulder. As soon as he was righted Jed pulled his hand away as though a red-hot poker had burnt it, chuckles came from behind him and he blushed bright mauve. But the Archmage only shook his head with a slight smile and gave him an odd look, as he had done with the boys before him.

Jed's eyes roved towards the waiting staves, some shaking with excitement and others calmly waiting to be chosen a master. However one was pushing its way up from the bottom of the pile, it was more exceptionally carved than the others around it…meaning that it held great power for someone, Jed would love to have such power. To show everyone that he was good for something and that he wasn't so useless after all. But he also noticed that the staff was turning around, seeming to glare at everyone and never staying still for long…it was hyperactive and Jed instantly put all thoughts of the power out of his head. Everyone knew that hyperactive stave's were a nuisance, intelligent, too strong-willed for their own good and at times uncontrollable. It would take a lot to handle.

His eyes flickered back to the Archmage and he gulped again, tugging his hat down over the bruise on his left cheek and hoping those keen brown eyes wouldn't notice it. Then the elderly mans hand shot out and brushed along the pile of staves beside him…it brushed past nice, easygoing staves and excitable yet subdued staves…and when it reached the hyperactive staff, it stopped. Jed bit back a groan as he was handed the thing. It had a white gem set into its top and as soon as Jed's fingers were wrapped around it the flaming thing tried to shoot off into the air. It dragged Jed forwards for a few, panicking moments and then dropped back, letting its new owner fall to the floor with a painful thud.

Howls of laughter erupted all around him and the young, newly appointed Dedicate Mage, scrambled to his feet muttering an apology to the Archmage but the old man just leant forward and put his hand on Jed's shoulder, whispering "Stop hiding yourself in the boy, he needs you now…and he will need you in the years to come, he does not seek you out so you must seek to be let out!"

Jed gave him a look of confusion and opened his mouth to question, when he felt his own magical power flare up in a temper inside him. His eyes widened with embarrassment and he soothed it gently, making a mental note to let some of the excess power out. For now it would have to be good and stay inside him, he refused to let it discharge and explode around the room. And he refused to let his mind break down and give in to its flaring…there was nothing more humiliating at the guild then losing control over your power. The Archmage's words were soon forgotten as he was half-dragged off the dais by his staff, that seemed to want to go over to other boys staves and…well, he didn't know if staves…gossiped, but he had the strongest feeling that his wanted to. Hassid glared at him from another row, his own staff shook nervously at his side and had few carvings. Jed was positive he wouldn't have minded having a staff that was hyperactive as long as it could hold the most power of the bunch; Jed remembered the beating he had received that morning and winced. But suddenly he had a thought, one that had never occurred to him before.

Don't dwell on it, he's just jealous. He can't touch you now, now you have a staff to help you and he doesn't know half the things you do about magic. You could wipe the floor with his face in a magic duel any day.

He smiled, agreeing silently with the notion…then he noticed that his staff had grown quiet and its carvings had formed into a face. It was smiling at him. Without knowing why Jed smiled back and fought down the urge to pat it on the head.

*

Karma wiped her tearstained face and watched, mouth open, as Jed's staff moved towards its owner. Jed opened a hand and grasped it firmly, then struggled forward with it for two steps…as though it was trying to break free from him but, no…it was dragging him nearer to the centre of the path and Jed was fighting it. He was moving towards the edge. He got a step closer and his eyes opened, they were black, as though the pupils had spread out like some out of control disease and sucked up everything in its path. The Eternal shut her mouth with an astonished snap and watched.

*

Jed sat outside in the sunshine, beneath a vast tree, lurking in its shadow with a bulky and tattered book on his knee. Both of his scrawny hands gripped its sides and his eyes seemed to tear down the pages hungrily, flickering so fast that anyone watching would swear he wasn't taking half of the words in. But he was, and he was taking them in clearer than most and adding his own ideas onto the ends of them, enhancing them and improving them. His staff lounged idly by his side, half asleep and half bored, so far Jed hadn't 'tried it out', he hadn't dared. So much power could be drawn into the thing and stored and then unleashed. Power was an amazing thing to all wizards, it made their world a little brighter, lightened the darkest days and shed light on life's problems. Jed was afraid that if he used the staff, the power would be too overwhelming to stop and he'd hurt someone. It was true that most of them deserved it, they'd hurt him after all…but that wasn't right, he'd sink to their level, be like them and he'd hate himself for it.

He lifted a hand and looked at the miniature sundial that was strapped there, holding his hand straight he saw that it was noon, the time the illusion team would come and watch the people who wanted to join their team, and time to get ready. Jed shut his book ('Mystical and Magical Myths') tied its leather thongs together at the side. Slipping it into his book-satchel Jed cocked his head to the side and wiggled his fingers a bit at the staff by his side. It rolled over obligingly and drifted up into his hand, he smiled and gave a chuckle; the thing reminded him of a dog in some ways, companionable, happy to please…but not always obedient to its master's wishes. Standing up Jed heaved his heavy bag onto a bony shoulder and used the staff as a walking stick as he made his way towards the outdoor gymnasium. His mind thought of different illusions, he had three thought out and all were brilliant, with amazing effects if he could pull it off. His magic might not be that enhanced though, he might not be able to call all the effects and use them as he should. Jed pushed the contemplation away. The very thought of failure or uncertainty could cost him the chance to get onto the team. He had to store up all his luck for this one day, these few precious and nerve-wracking moments…

Soon he had taken his place beside his fellow competitors, last in the line as always; Jed watched as the boys before him conjured up dancing snakes and miniature worlds that evolved quickly before his eyes. Small rainbows that showered down coloured rain underneath its arch, a large meteor shower that shot towards the ground and then dispersed and one boy even did an illusion of the illusion team! Finally it was Jed's turn he gulped as the team's captain turned to stare at him and raise an eyebrow, looking bored already. Jed moved forward a few steps and then sat on the ground, legs crossed and hands on the staff that lay across his lap. He closed his eyes and flung his head back, up towards the sky, a low buzzing noise filled the gym and the chatter of earlier contestants faded and died as they looked to the sky.

It had been a beautiful, sunny, summers day but now a black veil was being pulled over the sun and the sky. As though night had fallen, stars flickered everywhere and a full moon shone brightly a few hundred yards away…the stars started to move, faster and faster, a blur of colour against the midnight black night-sky. Then the sky stopped moving and one, very large star came into the middle of the onlookers circle. Jed had sweat beaded on his forehead and he was trying to keep the staff on his knees still as it shook up and down wildly. The star grew bigger and bigger and soon it was larger than the moon. Its bright white colouring started to change, light indigo and deep midnight blue entered the mix, a blood red and a vivid aquamarine, a shimmer of silver and a dash of gold. The colours swam in circles inside the star-globe; they melted into one another and flecks of bright light started to spin out from the star…it swirled, faster and faster. Gaining speed all the time and throwing out more beauty and radiance in its wake, the faster it spun the larger the flecks grew, till they were no longer flecks but small stars themselves. The illusion team clapped and hooted, thinking that Jed was done, but he had not yet opened his eyes.

His breathing was unsteady now and his hands shook from the weariness that clung to his body from holding so much power for so long. His head came down and rested on his chest, his hands he now forced onto the staff, clasping it hard and willing them not to shake.

It was time for his finale.

The small stars sunk back into the globe and spun in opposite directions from each other, whirling and unfurling like flags in a strong wind…and then they burst.

Smallest globe first, bouncing off the next and starting a chain reaction. When the outer wall of the globe burst it threw light and handfuls of colour like shining gems catching the sunlight as far as the eye could see, some seemed frozen in a beautiful burst, the scattered lights making tiny thread bridges towards the stars centre. It was like a spider-web, and instead of early-morning dew shining in blobs along the lines, jewels and gems and precious stones seemed to glitter instead.

It was magnificent.

When Jed opened his eyes again it was to see the clear blue sky. And it was to applause.

Boys who had scorned him all his life and teased him and jibed him and pushed and poked him…were pulling him up and clapping him on the back, almost fighting to pass him a handkerchief to wipe the sweat from his brow. The illusion team were smiling and clapping harder than anyone their eyes were bright with eagerness at having such an illusionist in their midst. Jed smiled faintly as he shook hands that were offered to him, and realised that his staff hovered a little ways off. He pushed forward through the admirers and went to stand by it, his hand slipped around its middle. When his fingers touched the wood though, a growling, almost angry thought exploded in his head.

This isn't right you know, this did not happen all those years ago, you just wanted it to. It's the path; that's what's doing this, and the Azale! You failed these tryouts fourteen years ago! You were disgraced and laughed at…think Jed, it may be what you want…but could you live with this lie? Could you live in this false world just because you wanted something so badly so many years ago?

Jed creased his forehead, the path? What path…and why was he suddenly thinking of the colour white? White shining crystals, like snow…powder almost…a man a woman…no…a female Eternal…

His head swung round to stare at the staff in his hand, usually so bright and almost never still…now it lay as quiet as a lamb in his hand…the path…

His head swung again, this time to see the illusion team stand before him the captain had his hand out in a friendly gesture.

"Well done Jed. Well done. How would you like to become a member of the team?" the older boy said, smiling and kind-heartedly.

Jed's head leapt with those words, 'Member of the team' finally! After so long it could be his, he would have friendship! He would have joy! He would have…he would have a lie. Jed's hand had been moving forward as he had been thinking of friendship, had squirmed with excitement. Now it shrank back and Jed felt unsure. A white carpet…he remembered a man that seemed to be half-hidden by shadows. An Azale whose eyes shone with unshed tears as she tugged at a glowing metal around her hands and neck and a small boy who laughed and joked with a wheedling voice. Names came slowly and unwillingly, Lance…the boy? Yes. He remembered a sulking face as his small hand pulled out a silk *handkerchief and dropped it into Jed's larger one…yes he was a thief, the boy.*

Members of the illusion team were looking at him with eagerness, their mouths working words of compliments and flattery, their hands all out and waiting to be shaken. Jed's head leapt again and this time he actually moved forward a few steps before his staff tugged him back and dragged him away. Jed scowled at it as he turned back to go and talk to his soon to be team-mates and tell them that he would join, how dare it stop his happiness like that? He moved forward a step when the staff dragged him back with such force and stopped so abruptly that Jed's head hit it hard. The wizard fell to his knees and two long fingers went to the front of his head and came back red and sticky. He should have felt dazed after the clout; he should have felt woozy and tired…but his head felt clearer and less clammy than before. He looked at the team around him, expressing their concern at his fall and would he please consider their offer? He looked at the staff in his hand, quieter than usual…and then he remembered.

Telric.

Karma.

The quest.

The Elders.

And the carpet.

Jed cursed himself as nine types of fool; of course the carpet would still work on him! He didn't have any metal bands as Karma did! Fool, fool and stubborn-headed ignoramus, the wizard berated himself and then stood up. The captain smiled brightly at him and offered his hand again, it was so tempting; friends…almost like family. Perhaps he would lead a better life in this fake world?

But it would be a lie and you couldn't live with it, not when you know…

True, the thought was right…again. Jed looked around him and after another debate with his thoughts, feelings and common sense, closed his eyes and walked away. He bit his bottom lip as he moved away and winced to himself. He might have been happy here. And suddenly his world changed, the guild vanished, the grass beneath his feet withered and died and his breath caught in his throat as he fell towards the ground.

He felt like he was falling forever.

*

Jed woke groggily and slowly, he lay on the carpet and his glasses had slid to one side of his head. Righting them he gave a startled yelp as Karmas face came into view, she was leaning over him with a worried expression.

"You're alright! Lore, Gods and Goddesses be praised! I thought I'd lost you both and...oh Jed...he won't wake up. He just lies there," she pointed with an elegant finger to where Telric lay, Jed groaned as he sat up, stiff and covered in white dust from the floor he had fallen onto. His staff lay next to him and when he went to touch it with a hand it shot up and started to drone like an angry wasp. Jed was helped to his feet by Karma and when he was righted she frowned as she caught sight of the glowing bands around her neck. When she looked up her eyes reminded him of a frightened child's. Telric was still flat out on the floor; Jed shook his head, and then knelt by the assassin's limp form. His fingers went to the back of the man's head and found a lump, standing he sighed and waved his staff in the air, making a circle and a line across Telric's unmoving body and then saying.

"Arise, arise,
Float and flair
Be free and breezy carried by air"

Telric moved up into the air and Jed put a guiding hand atop of him, letting his staff zoom about dizzyingly, and leading the once more listless Karma by the arm. Feeling very alone Jed walked forward, pulling Karma along beside him and floating Telric before him.

The three companions made their way to the end of the carpet without any further trouble, at the other end was a large cedar door. Varnish that had once shone brightly on it was now faded and peeling away. The heavy brass hinges were the size of a man's head and had rusted, been covered in heavy dust, along with layer upon layer of cobwebs. The only thing that seemed new or un-neglected at all was a huge gold doorknocker that stood in the middle of the door. It had been fashioned to look like a face with large ears, which were furry and seemed to stick out like crazy tufts of hair; its nose represented more of a snout than anything else. Thin whiskers protruded outwards from its long, sweeping eyebrows and the hideous thing had a large hand that seemed to hang from a chain around its neck; it was so lifelike that liver spots were softly imprinted by its head. Jed shook out a skinny hand from his voluminous sleeves and reached forward to lift it up and bang it with an echoing crash on the door. His hand, however, quickly leapt away when it sneezed. Jed gave a shriek and promptly hid behind Karma. When he had recovered sufficiently Jed turned back to the doorknocker and watched as it twitched it's nose, a small cloud of dust appeared as it shook its head and then its eyes turned to sharp slits that glowed softly as it gave them a suspicious look.

"Whadya' want?" it demanded, in a voice that croaked and creaked angrily like old leather. Stepping forward once more, Jed spoke.

"I have to see the Elders...please?"

The knocker gave a hearty yell of laughter, which ended in a coughing fit; and when it spoke again it wheezed.

"Ack! You's lot been on the white path, ain't ya? Ha! Ahahahahaha!" it stopped to breathe heavily and cough again, it sniffed, revoltingly, and gave them what could only be called a spite-fully evil grin. Revealing sharp rows of teeth, like pins.

"Hey! It gots one of you's an' all! Ackhahaha! Awww, if I could only see wor happened, ack! I'd laugh meself to death I tell you's!" it told them all rather cheerfully. It was then that Telric decided to come round, he groaned and coughed then blinked his eyes a couple of times.

"Why am I floating in the air?" came his arrogant and silky voice. Jed waved a hand vaguely and Telric was righted, he instantly brushed himself of imaginary dirt, without a word of thanks. He looked around and seemed to take everything in at once. Then his jaw set stubbornly and he pulled his broad-brimmed hat down hard on his head, he gave one quick, rather puzzled, look in Karma's direction then he folded his arms and sneered with contempt.

"Well. That was unpleasant" was all he had to say before shutting his mouth with a sharp click and raising an eyebrow at the door-knocker, which was now laughing so hard that its eyes appeared to trickle golden tears down it's cheeks which dribbled down the door. Jed glared at it and with one hand grabbed an ear. It's cries of laughter changed to those of pain.

"Owwww! Hey! Le'go me, it's not my fault I find stuff funny! Ouch! Yowowowowowowwww! Alwight! Alwight! I'm sorry, jeez..." it frowned as he let go of its ear, and the hand around its neck moved up and rubbed the offended part.

"Right. Now. We would like to see the Elder's please" Jed let his tone become one that would be used to speak to a small, slightly dense child. The Knocker sneered and then sniffed rather haughtily.

"If you's lot wanna go see the Elder's all you's hav' ta do is shake me hand. Simple pimple. Easy peasy. Can't ask fer fairer than that can ya?" it looked at them all with what passed as honesty on it's golden face, the hand hovered in the air in front of Jed (who looked around the group to see if anyone other than himself would like to go first). Sighing, he held his carved staff firmly in his left hand and, taking the cold metal in his right, gave the thing a large shake up and down in the air. He was about to let go of it when he realised that he couldn't. His skin slowly changed colour from his fingertips before spreading swiftly up his arm. He opened his mouth to give a girlish, high-pitched scream, but his tongue had turned to lead.

CHAPTER EIGHT
Omens

Jed watched in horror as the goblin-headed knocker laughed and his own body turned the dull grey colour of metal. And suddenly he felt a tug and his own lead hand melted into the gold one. The rest of him followed at an alarming rate. As Jed's face was sucked in he felt the sensation of rushing through the air, faster and faster. His eyes watered at the speed and barely noticed the flashes of colour, red, yellow, blue, green, indigo, violet…every colour under Mog's sun, as he was dragged down a long silver chamber with many twists and turns. Looking straight ahead his eyes now widened as he saw the wall coming up fast. He was going to hit it. He'd be squashed, mangled, painfully hurt…he would be…

Through it!

Looking around Jed found himself crouched on a large platform, his hands held protectively over his head and his staff whizzing around him, yet again radiating all the malice of a watchful guard-dog. The room in which he found himself was dark; he stood on a high grey platform that was surrounded by nine grand chairs, on even higher platforms. Looking over the edge of the dais he tried to search for the bottom. There was none. His neck craned further and further and as he strived to look deeper he felt something bump into his foot, blinking he turned back and caught Karma before she stepped over the edge, pulling her away and forcing her to stay still. Then all of a sudden Telric gracefully landed on the floor and immediately whipped out a dagger in each hand, twirling them in his fingers expertly. On his left palm, in the little light given from nowhere, Jed could make out a tattoo of a wine red rose on the assassin's hand, one thorn stood out and dripped black blood.

"Good day travellers"

The airy voice was gentle and soothing, like the lap of water against a boats hull. Looking back at the seats Jed could now see that every one of them was filled, the woman who had spoken stood and as her eyes flashed once, light filled the area and Jed could clearly see each Eternal in a chair. Every hair on their heads was either grey or silver or white, yet each strand shone out, like thick wire, reflecting the soft glow that seemed to shimmer around each figure. The women wore their thick braids to the floor, in some cases it trailed behind them like a brides train; men wore their hair just as long, but with beards to match, some tossed over the shoulder and others over their arms. Each pair of sharp eyes shone a different colour and each face seemed almost ageless, apart from the light wrinkles under eyes and vein-covered hands with long, claw-like nails painted silver and blue. Telric instantly hid his daggers as though he had never drawn them, bowing jerkily with hands pressed against his chest. Jed followed suit, though rather clumsily, his staff nodded in the air and then jumped into his hand. Straightening again he watched as Telric took two measured steps forward and placed his fingertips together.

"Good day Elders, and thank you for receiving us Eldest" he made the last comment to the woman in the middle of them with hair longer than the rest and who also had a large gem set in a ring on her finger, the size of a small hen egg.

"I am Telric Zeal, of the capital of Torath'Danar, I come to seek answers and help" again he gave a jerky bow yet this time with his fingers outstretched above his head. Someone nudged Jed in the ribs and the mage realised it was Telric nodding towards the Elders.

"Er…Good day Elders and thank you for receiving us Eldest. I am Jed the wizard, of the wizards' guild in the west islands. I…I also come to seek answers and help" he tried to place his fingertips together and bow again but for some reason his hands were shaking. The Eldest nodded to him and he waddled back to the others on unsteady legs. She stood and her voice echoed around the cold room.

"And why have you come to seek our aid and help?" she asked.

Telric nudged Karma a step forward.

"This is Karma Lanoelin, a few days ago we were set upon by bandits, not the ordinary way-laying type, and these bandits had some glowing metal bands. They placed them on my friend and since that time she has not been able to touch magic and she has gone into a sort of…coma, for lack of a better word. Jed, the wizard, cannot get them off and I didn't know where else to go…" he trailed off at the last words and looked up at the shadowed figures on their chairs. The old Eternals glanced at one another from side to side, it was almost impossible to make out in the gloom, and then each stood simultaneously and held their hands upwards to the sky. Nine sets of eyes flashed, fierce, intent colours and murmurs filled the room, the murmurs of the Azale language that flowed and filled the ears like a sonnet. And suddenly a sweeping white staircase appeared leading from Jed, Telric and Karma's platform, up to the Elder's. Each man and woman stepped down from their seats and slowly walked down the staircase towards the travellers, finally forming a half-circle around them, hands folded neatly inside long sleeves and heads cocked to the side in curiosity. The Eldest strode forward and graciously nodded her head towards them. And then she moved to Karma, laid her hands on her shoulders and pressed her forehead against the younger Azales, her eyelids closed in concentration.

A buzz filled the room, starting low and gaining depth as it rose in pitch, Telric and Jed watched avidly, willing whatever she was doing to work. But, just as suddenly as the buzzing had started, it stopped.

Jed watched as the Eldest's face drained of what little colour it held, her skin became dry and withered, stretching across a gaunt face and showing the skeletal features beneath. Her hands' became thinner and the long nails stretched outwards before curving in. Her hair grew and became ragged around the edges, her breath became hoarse. With a cry of warning Jed leapt forwards and pulled the Eldest off Karma. As she was pulled away a light filled the area, blinding and magnificent. Jed pulled at the Eldest's hands; they refused to be prised away, as though melded onto the glowing metal. As he finally yanked them free the light went with another flash and as the last spark of it disappeared, a force, like a wall of air, pushed Jed back throwing himself and the frail woman beside him to the ground. When he hit the floor, dust flew upwards in a great cloud, settling on and around Jed, making his beard appear white, his eyes water and his nose sneeze. Elders hurried forward to help the Eldest and two of them pulled the wizard to his feet and dusted him down. Then, after seeing that he was perfectly fine, left to make a fuss over their leader. Telric watched it all in silence, then his eyes turned to observe Karma and Jed saw, for a fleeting second, regret in those hard eyes. Would he rather have Karma free and the Eldest dead?

Yet he was not allowed to linger on his thoughts long for as soon as the Eldest stood she shook off her helpers and moved back to Karma, her words were kind but Jed noticed that she avoided touching the other Eternal like a man avoids being bitten by a venomous snake. Instead she shook her head in a mixture of wonderment and sadness.

"This is bad magic, older than us, deeper than our minds and beyond our reach. Yet at the same time it is tinged with something new, some evil that would seek to catch and kill and destroy..." she shivered and pulled her shawl tighter around her bony figure, rubbing her arms and looking cautiously at the three, now standing by each other and listening intently. She flung out a hand dramatically and pointed a quivering finger at them.

"This thing, this darkness...you quest to destroy it, yet it seeks to annihilate you first. It has one of you in its grasp already, who will be next? The child? An innocent who has yet to be tainted by the world?" her hands weaved in and out and a picture of Lance floated past them, smiling and running, laughter pouring from his mouth. Telric shook his head fiercely at the idea and muttered some quiet vow to himself. The Eldest carried on, the finger pointed at Telric and as she weaved a picture Jed saw scenes from the man's life.

"Or would it be you? You who lives his life in the shadows and hungers for the death that took your family's life?" A man and a woman lay dead on the floor, a child ran past them and out of a broken door.

"Will it be you, who would deny love and friendship for the danger it might bring to those you seek to protect?" Another picture, Karma put a hand on Telric's arm and he threw her off, shaking his head and backing out into the night.

"Will it be you, who would hide his true feelings away in a box and throw it into the darkest well...just to gain a reputation and a wall to emotion?" Another scene, Telric leaning back in a dark chair, speaking with a man, garbed in black like himself and a red rose flashing on the palm of his left hand.

Now the Eldest turned to Jed, the finger raised, yet it was not quivering anymore and her words seemed sad.

"Or would it be you? A man that has not yet learnt half of what he could yet hunger's for more each day?" A picture, a scene; of a small bony-kneed boy with wisps of hair and thick glasses, pouring over books with a hungry look in his eyes whilst others outside were playing happily.

"Will it be you who has so much to give, yet still needs to come out of his shell to give it?" The scene this time was of an older Jed, his hair to his shoulders now and the beginnings of a beard on his face, he was sitting in a classroom, surrounded by other boys. The teacher had just asked a question and Jed was about to answer, then hesitated and stopped, slumping back into his seat, averting his eyes to the floor as the other students glared at him.

The Eldest's hand dropped and she sighed heavily, still looking at Jed. "There are not many like you left in this world, mages as powerful as you could become. Your Archmage hides you all away on the

West Isles where your guild can be found, how many of you are left? Withering away in some rotting schoolroom, how many will ever get a chance to leave as you have? A soul needs to be free Master Jed, without freedom, there is no hope, and without hope...what is there?" she turned, as if to go but Telric moved forward "Wait! You haven't helped us!"

The Eldest turned back with a look of regret on her face.

"You cannot be helped against the darkness that seeks you four, yet I can give you guidance for the girl, it was written once, by The Oracle, that anything that is made can be destroyed. You just have to trace it back to the source, take Karma to the creator of these bands that bind her, and then she can be set free" she went and stood with the other Elders, who had once more drawn into a semi-circle around Jed and his companions. Here the Eldest gave one more look to Karma and, shaking her head, raised her right arm and moved it in a circle three times, then she pushed forward with her palm. A light shone and mist was pulled up from below the platforms and spread around them, thick and fog-like; a door appeared before Jed and then, just before they were hidden by the mist the Eldest gave a few last words.

"Go through the doorway questors, tonight you will be given a feast due to the honour you do for the Azale. And on the morrow you will be given the finest steeds, worthy gifts, good food and you will continue on your journey. Farewell for now"

And Jed heard, just as he stepped through the doorway, eight echoing voices give the same words "Farewell for now"

*

When Jed stepped through the doorway, he was immediately outside again, beneath the canopy of the huge tree with the ever-changing leaves. He blinked in the bright sunlight and wiped his thick glasses on his robe, as they had grown dusty from the tunnel. And suddenly Karma was next to him and Telric appeared next to her, he also blinked in the bright sunlight, squinting his eyes and creasing his face in displeasure at his own discomfort. Karma however gave one; long and heavy blink and then stared around aimlessly, as though everything was boring and dull. As though she had given up, her will crumbled and the only reason she was carrying on was because she was being made to. When she turned to look at Telric though, her eyes focused for a moment, he was a lifeline. Something to hold on to whilst she was being swept away in a fierce storm, something that was warm and near against the cold reality that was forced upon her by her bounds. Yet as soon as she looked away the light died and the eyes drooped heavily, returning her to the stupor like state.

Telric nudged Jed and pointed to the roof of a small house with a tree next to it; on the roof sat Lance, a smirk on his face and his eyes flashing with amusement. Below, on the ground, three tall children were shouting up to him and sounded angry. They were about to climb the tree to get at the small boy when an adult intervened and put out his hands, as the three drew nearer they heard his words.

"No children it is dangerous, the boy will come down when he is hungry and you may have your things then, but for now..." his sharp eyes picked out Telric, un-missable in his dark clothes whilst everyone else wore light garb, the man gave a sigh of relief and moved to them, shaking his head in frustration.

"Maybe you can get your charge off the roof? It seems that he was playing a game with the children and picked their pockets whilst doing so, they are angry and want their things back and he refuses to come down."

The last words were directed with a frown at the stubborn thief, as he watched them all with caution. Jed was sniggering into his beard and trying very hard not to laugh out loud, even Karma gave a sad smile, Telric grinned...proudly. But he did go over to the tree and lean on it whilst looking up slowly at the child, when he opened his mouth to speak everyone was listening.

"Lance...are you going to come down and give these kids their things back?" the words were quiet, yet had a disinterested air about them, the assassin examined a fingernail. Lance crept to the edge of the roof and dangled his legs, grinning, obviously very pleased with himself.

"Nah, why should I? I can sell these things for a bucket load when we get 'ome, they 'ave more too, I didn't steal everyfin', honest to the Gods!" he put up a left hand and gave them an angelic look.

Jed's shoulders heaved with amusement and he stuffed his hand-kerchief in his mouth, Telric gave a half-laugh and shook his head, tipping his wide-brimmed hat back.

"And what did I do to you the last time you said no to something I said Lance?"

The thief hooked his teeth around his bottom lip and his face paled a little, worry starting to creep into his features.

"You 'ung me upside down by me left ankle fer 'alf an 'our and didn't let me eat nothin' fer an 'ole day..." his face settled into a reassured look and his voice was calm, if taunting "...but you can't get me whilst I'm up 'ere, so that's alright" he finished with a grin and a chuckle.

Telric shook his head and made as if to walk away before turning back, hideously fast. The dagger flew and before Lance could scrabble away it pinned his cloak to the rooftop, whilst the boy tugged at the sharp weapon and tried to move it Telric climbed the tree with deftness, then wrenched the dagger free and lifted the squirming Lance over his shoulder. Placing him before the burgled children the boy huffed and moodily thrust out his pockets, spilling the objects to the floor. Telric raised an eyebrow and Lance took off his cloak, unbuttoning the hidden pockets in there and shoving the pile of shining objects into the Eternal children's waiting hands, he replaced his cloak, folded his arm, stuck out his bottom lip and gave a tremendous sulk. It was at this point that Jed let out a loud laugh and had to bite his tongue to stop more from pouring out of his mouth. Lance stalked up to him and kicked his shin. Jed fell over, his laughter forgotten, and found himself wrapped in his own long cloak.

It was Telric's turn to laugh now.

*

For the rest of that day they were left to amuse themselves, and in truth all they did was sit under the shade of the huge leaf-changing tree and either doze or watch village life as it went past with interested eyes. But now it was dropping dark and two more Azale stood in front of the four 'Questors', there was a woman and a man, each wore deep purple robes with golden scrolling and long sleeves, their hair was a fiery red and braided in intricate patterns alongside their sharp ears. Bowing they helped Karma off the ground and beckoned for the group to follow, which they did.

After a few minutes of gliding silently through the town the guides stopped at a wooden house and opened the door, here the man entered whilst wordlessly beckoning Jed, Telric and Lance followed, but not before they knew that Karma was in a house just across the street from them, accompanied by the woman. Once inside the quaint cottage Jed was fascinated by everything, the walls were the colour of golden sand and had flying white doves painted across it. The doors were carved from ebony with white ivory handles and the floor was polished redwood. Apart from a few delicately carved chairs there was no other decoration. The man stood before them and gave a quick nod to each.

"These are the rooms you will sleep in tonight," he said, pointing to three doors across from them.

"For now I would ask you to enter them and change into the feast clothes that are laid out for you on your beds. As soon as you are ready come out here and I will show you to the feasting fields" he gave a polite smile and then stood to one side. Jed found himself glancing at Telric, who shrugged and moved towards one of the doors, as he touched the handle he looked up suddenly. On the door his name had appeared in mother of pearl, bright against the black background. Lance went to another and after a moment of trying to pry the gem letters from their frame, sighed and entered the room. Jed shuffled through the doorway in more or less the same fashion and was pleased to find, in the right hand corner of the small yet cosy chamber, a small pool, big enough for one person to bathe in. Next to it stood a glass bowl of soap and scouring sand. He was about to slip into it and have what promised to be a soothing soak when he realised that he had only been asked to change clothes. Jed's spirits dropped slightly at the prospect of another late night but nevertheless he went to stand beside the large four-poster bed that stood in the middle of the room. On it lay a selection of fashionable robes, stockings and boots. He slipped the fresh stockings and boots on without hesitation but his fingers lingered over the robe, it was stunning. The material was silk and coloured a deep emerald green, with gold stitching and flared cuffs, the belt was plain black leather that gleamed and smelt new and unused. The buckle that adorned it was an attractive and delicate design, a staff...curiously like his own, twisted together with different metals, stars in each corner. After a slight hesitation he tugged the robe over his head and tightened the belt at his waist. It felt good to be in fresh, clean clothes and the fine weaving of the silk was a luxury he had never felt before. After curling the end of his beard into a point Jed hooked it into the top of the belt and raised his hand from his side, the staff flew into it instantly, twitching slightly before settling. Moving towards the door Jed watched as the carvings on it copied the design of the robe. He smiled to himself before stepping out into the hallway where he was greeted with a smile of delight by the waiting Eternal. Jed blushed at the attention and shuffled into a quiet corner to wait for the others.

Lance was the next out of his room, swaggering, grinning from ear to ear and flourishing the short cloak he wore with every step. He was dressed in a red and gold velvet shirt that had gems sewn into its cuffs and collar, his cloak was black and the underside the deepest of purples, his own little belt was black and the buckle flashed a dagger on it, most lifelike. His breeches matched the underside of his cloak apart from the two golden lines that threaded their way to his shoes. These were black ankle-boots that shone in the lamplight as he turned for them, waving his cape to show off the rich lining. The boy looked handsome as far as small children go; already there was a line to his chin and a lilt in his eyes that proclaimed he would grow into a striking youth. Jed himself was sure that he had never cut such a dashing figure yet when Telric sauntered out, all hopes of ever appearing anything but bookish fled his mind.

The assassin was dressed from head to toe in black, not the dusty, travel-swept black he had worn minutes ago; but a deep sky-black that shimmered slightly as he moved and reminded Jed of long, cold winter nights where he would just sit and gaze into the night. The only other glinting colour that could be seen was the silver of his cuffs, collar and buttons. Every item of clothing was of the finest cut and weave; the designs were so simple as to be almost plain yet to have added more would have made him look foppish. His belt was made up of metal links and held a sheathed dagger, neat leather gloves and a small leather purse. Telric had somehow found time to sweep his short hair back into a neat yet fashionable style and his dark blue eyes shone out from his pale complexion. Had he not possessed so many small scars he would have looked majestic, instead he was exceedingly handsome. Fitting a long signet ring to a finger he waved to the door and said, "At least they know my favourite colour, shall we go?"

Lance laughed and Jed rolled his eyes, the Eternal shook his head and all moved towards the door.

*

The trio were led yet again by the Azale, who seemed content to smile quietly as he walked along, hands hidden inside long sleeves. They strolled past the huge leaf-changing tree, through the woods and out onto the fields, it was clear which the 'Feasting Field' was. It was in the middle of the crops, the largest of all, and the decorations had just finished being laid. And what festivities! Jed had never seen tables so exquisitely carved, and had never seen such food! There were huge fish and water-shrimp dishes, drizzled with melted butter and shredded fresh herbs. There were at least several different salads, ranging from red onion and horseradish to freshly cut sweet corn and peppers. Every type of vegetable imaginable was laid before them, diced and sliced carrots and sprouts cut and arranged beans and turnips, different steaming pots and bowls were strewn about the place and mountains of magnificent pies and cakes covered several of the immense tables. There were treacle-cakes decorated with fresh honeycomb and sprinkled lightly with candied nuts, citrus scones, blueberry muffins, a multitude of different tarts and jellies, and a six-layered trifle. A huge chocolate slab (that the children were 'helping' with) an amazing variety of decorated wafers and biscuits, to name only a few of the delights spread before them. There was freshly baked bread that still steamed from its time in the oven, with glazed crusts and studded with nuts and herbs and spices and apple, baked in different amusing shapes, the many aromas that Jed's nose caught were new and exciting, he had never eaten such food at the guild. There was every type of stew in every shape and size, there was cheese of every complexion; some studded with hazelnuts and others apricots and grapes and many more. And there was a whole table dedicated to different vintages of wine and drinks, brewed by everyone in the village. With fruit cordials for the children and ale and mead and fruit-wine for adults, even flavoured milk. The decorations were superb, with streamers trailing from overhanging tree branches, flickering in the light breeze, garlands with material of the finest embroidery and latest style were draped on the back of every seat and along the fields surrounding fences with complicated designs of far off lands neatly sewn into them. A huge fire stood to one side and children ran around it laughing, at times stopping to throw something on it and watching as the smoke changed colour and made silhouettes to entertain them. Women and men seemed part of the decoration themselves, like the figures on a bridal cake. Each wore long flowing robes, with the occasional set of breeches on younger men and adolescent boys. The dance beckoned and pulled others into its fray, each step executed perfectly and each twirl making outfit shine as the firelight caught the shimmering fabric and fine thread.

And the music, Jed had never, and would never again, hear such melodies. Complimenting each other and seeming to stream from the heavens above. No words were voiced to the tune; the refrain was enough in itself. As their guide left them Jed felt his feet start to tap as he moved towards the dancers. Telric caught his arm and shook his head.

"Watch yourself Jed, the Azale's music enchants us too readily and we get pulled into things too easily. Anyway, I think we have to go and see the Elders" he pointed to a table; Jed had missed the long silver hair in the blur of other, richer colours. Lance looked at the bonfire and the children running around it, his eyes bright with joy and wonderment; obviously wanting to join in, but with a glance at Telric he followed silently.

The Eldest sat at the head of the high table, the Elders seated next to her and the musicians behind them, knowing nothing but the music they made, eyes closed and fingers dancing faster than the eye could see sometimes and at others floating like a feather to the strings. When the three drew level with them the council rose in their seats, nodding swiftly and smiling. The Eldest stood last, hands clasped in front of her and her own feast clothes plain compared to those around her. Yet as soon as she stood the music stopped instantly and the dancers took seats, looking at their leader expectantly. The old Eternal raised a hand and pointed to Jed, Telric and Lance.

"These three...among with one other who seems to be late-" her tone repressed agitation but she stopped mid-sentence and looked across the field, in the direction that Jed and his friends had just come from, other heads turned. The Azale maiden who had taken Karma to the cottage was leading her across the field; Jed's friend wore the purest white and crème chitin. Strands of silk decorated her dark hair, the material floating behind and around her in imitation of delicate wings. Her face had been painted, her usually soft, pale lips were now deep blood red and her eyelids reflected the deep green of her eyes. Karma's feet were clad in snowy slippers, her arms were bare despite the chill of the night, part of her dress trailed behind her on the floor and Jed could pick out a silver necklace around her delicate neck. The gem set in the metal was cut to look like a dove and (as in all the Veiled's work) seemed on the verge of flight. Half of her long hair had been swept up on top of her head, delicately twisted and curled around the silk, the rest swung from side to side over her shoulders as she was led. The only thing that spoilt the effect was the fact that at times she would stumble and hardly blinked at all, gazing past everything, unseeing and uncaring. Jed turned in time to catch Telric's reaction, a hopeful smile lit his face when he first noticed her but then, after a closer study, he took in that frozen face as Jed had just done. The smile went and his face fell, but his eyes refused to leave her, and a small frown appeared on his lips.

When she reached them, the Eternal maiden dipped a low bow to the Eldest and stuttered "I apologise Eldest, it...it would not have taken so long but...but we could not touch her hands or neck and it was difficult to make her co-operate..." she trailed off and gestured to the still softly glowing metal that trapped Karma. The Eldest just nodded patiently and motioned for her to go and sit down, and then she gave a glance at Karma and resumed her speech.

"These four are honoured here tonight, as they will be in every Azale village, town and city they pass. Tonight we throw them a feast, for tomorrow they will restart their perilous journey and who knows what dangers it may bring?" she held up a hand and shrugged, before carrying on.

"These unlikely travellers seek to help us in our time of great need and trial, for they go to kill Ragea Atia to save the Azale race. They go to destroy the bounds that Atia would use to kill us, as he has done with one unfortunate already!" she gestured to Karma and her audience offered muttered sympathies. Then the Elder held out her arms for silence once more.

"They seek only friendship as they go along their travels, yet not all will welcome them. They may seek help along their journey, but it will not always be given and times will be hard. And they may not seek shadows and darkness, they may not seek death and corruption...but that is what they will find in the end, for at the end of their quest they will find Ragea Atia" she turned to the group and shook her head "and you will be remembered as our saviours. Not many men are left in the mortal race that are prepared to do as you do, to risk all to save a small part. You are of a different breed; though you may not see it, though some of you may not want to see it...you have noble hearts. I for one thank you deeply and give my blessings to you in your quest" and then she took her skirts and bowed deeply before them.

There was a moment's silence in the clearing and then, as one, every Eternal stood, even the children, and bowed towards the small group. An absolute hush fell upon them and it was a while before they raised themselves up and sat again. By the time they were all seated again Jed felt the heat of a blush rise in his cheeks, Lance looked slightly shocked and Karma was actually smiling; yet Telric remained unperturbed and sat with the others in silence. Soon the music resumed and dancers were returning to the floor, though most stayed to eat first. Jed ate all within reach, never could he remember a day of such gluttony and as soon as he had steadily chomped his way through one pile he moved onto the next plateful. Lance ate quickly and simply, stuffed some bread and cake into a pocket and rapidly threw down a drink. Finally running off to join the other children around the fire, grabbing some of the powder they were using to make shapes and laughing excitedly. Karma picked at her food, yet at least ate something unlike Telric who ate sparsely from what was placed in front of him before concentrating on the wine. Soon Jed had satisfied his newfound appetite and looked to the dancers, trying to hum the amazingly woven tune behind him and failing to; instead he stood and hovered on the edge of the dance-boards. His staff kept him company until Telric had had his fill of alcohol and came to stand next to him. Jed was surprised to find him by his side, let alone upright and in perfect control of his speech. After all he had drunk he should, by all rights, be on the floor. The assassin rolled his eyes and sighed.

"If you want to dance go and ask someone, don't just mope about please!" his voice betrayed the impatience he normally hid well. But that was easy enough for him to say, all he had to do was flash a smile at a pretty maiden as she drifted past and he instantly had a partner, flowing into the pattern as though he was one of the Azale himself.

Jed frowned, tugging his beard and folding his arms, he'd get a partner. It was just a case of…well…he wasn't quite sure. Jed had read about dancing often enough, just because he had never actually tried it didn't mean he was incapable of doing so, did it? He shrugged the thought off and was about to go back to the dining table when Lance floated past…an Eternal maiden on his arm smiling as he tried to act old and educated.

That was it.

If a small boy, with a reputable reputation as a thief could get a dance, surely he could? He was about to boldly go and tap someone on the arm, when Telric came back; someone new was with him.

"Ah Jed, just the person I wanted to see, this is Rose. And sadly she has no dancing partner yet, I knew you didn't and she seemed overjoyed at the prospect of dancing with a wizard. Rose this is Jed, don't mind him if he blushes and falls over a bit, that's just his way of showing he likes you…" as Rose looked at Jed, Telric gave a smirk, but Jed was stopped from retaliating when Rose grinned and fluttered her eyelashes pointedly whilst taking his arm, stepping towards the dance floor.

"Well then Jed, I must say I've never met a wizard before, but then Telric told you that. I've always been fascinated in the working of mortal magic, maybe after a dance we could speak with each other?" her voice flowed, as Karma's had when Jed had first met her.

"Erm…yes…yes of course we can, will you wait just a moment, I…er…I need to ask Telric something" he gave her a wary grin, as though she might bite at any second or rush off, and was relieved when she only nodded politely. Jed moved back to Telric and glared, dropping his voice a fierce whisper.

"I told you I could get my own partner!" he berated moodily.

"Yes but I want to dance with someone else and she wouldn't leave me alone, have fun" Telric gave a wink and was about to dart away when Jed grabbed his arm. Curiosity getting the better of him once more.

"Who do you want to dance with?"

Telric didn't say anything but his eyes flickered to Karma, who was watching the dancing longingly, and then wrenched his arm free and made a beeline to her.

Jed watched as Telric leaned down and offered Karma an arm, saying something to make her laugh a little and pulling her up into the dance. Then Rose took his hand and pulled him back to the floor, laughing quietly when he missed steps and grinning as he blushed at his own clumsiness.

Before that night Jed had wondered what it must be like to dance with a beautiful woman, and when that night ended he wondered how on Mog other men put up with it…

CHAPTER NINE
Enemies

Jed woke slowly, he was sure that there was not an inch of him that did not ache. Groaning he wondered if he had been drugged, why was he so tired? Blinking his eyes hard and brushing sleep from their edges he fumbled his glasses into place, sitting up slowly with a wince. He took in his surroundings, still feeling dizzy from last night and sure that he'd feel the twinge of pain from dancing for many nights to come. The bed he sat on was made of fine wood, and the covers were decorated with soft maple leaves and perfume beads, giving off a heady yet pleasant fragrance. His staff lay against an intricately decorated wall, full of strange scenes of life with unreadable writing underneath each picture. He hadn't noticed it the night before. Looking up Jed noticed that the ceiling was painted a deep blue and that every star drawn onto it shone a brightly lit, sky-blue day, with the four suns of Mog positioned as one in the sky. The sun peeked over the top of a cloud and even they moved around, bumping into one another almost playfully.

Jed wrenched the bed sheets aside and was about to go and dunk his head into the small, bubble filled pool to clear it, when the muscles in his legs suddenly forgot how to work and he fell flat on his face. Growling angrily he realised that he still had his feast clothes on and one shoe looked as though he had tried to tug it off before giving up.

Sighing Jed crawled the rest of the way, stripping swiftly and sinking into the water with a smile…then came back up, pulled his dripping hat off and threw it into a corner.

It was at this moment that the door handle turned and Telric strode in, already fully dressed, looking as though he had washed only a few moments ago and full of energy. Jed sank as far down into the water as possible, hoping the pools frothy top would hide him. Then Jed glared at Telric, he could at least have knocked before barging in and the man had no right to be so cheerful at such an ungodly hour. The assassin just rolled his eyes skyward.

"I don't know if you've noticed Jed but we're both men…I'm sure I have nothing you don't unless it's a horrible and disfiguring disease"

Jed ignored the snide comment and asked, grumpily, "What now? Surely we aren't leaving so early in the morning!"

Telric smirked and shook his head.

"Nope, we're not leaving just yet, we have another hour, and if I were you I'd hurry up. We still have to get our things together, gather food supplies and then get to know our mounts for the ride"

This was going too far. Jed was tired, still blurry-eyed, slightly hung-over and someone was telling him he had to talk to a horse.

"'Get to know our mounts'? What on Mog are you talking about?"

"If you hadn't noticed the Azale do things differently to mere mortal men Jed, their horses are different to ours. They speak mind to mind and only carry you if they like you. They are intelligent, fast, and have awesome stamina…if you want to walk the rest of the way because you missed a chance to get to know your bearer and possible friend then it's your fault, now hurry up!" he snapped angrily, and abruptly stalked out of the room. Presumably to go and converse with the four-legged creature he had just mentioned. Jed shook his head at the oddity of it all and reached for a towel.

He definitely didn't want to be left behind if it meant staying with a herd of talking horses as well as mystical immortals.

*

Stepping out of his room and into the dusty street he wondered if the whole town had come to see them off, a few hundred faces turned to greet him. Jed glanced to the side and waved shyly, then his eyes pinpointed Telric's wide-brimmed hat in the crowd. Shuffling towards him, muttering apologies to those he nudged out of the way, Jed could already see the 'talking horses'. They were tall, elegant, and reflected the Eternal somewhat, with their lengthy legs and prancing nature. Shaking their manes from side to side and occasionally blowing at someone's face in a comical manner. Telric had a hand on the neck of a tall black stallion, whose mane and tail curled wildly and who arched his neck proudly. Karma was back in her usual garb, adorned with her weapons. She already sat atop of her beast; who looked as though she had been left out in a snowstorm, so light was her colouring. The mare's mane and tail stood straight and she was the smallest of the four horses. Lance was being lifted onto his horse, a dappled grey gelding with a large head but seemingly a sense of humour…he kept trying to blow Telric's hat off and Lance was finding this extraordinarily amusing. And then Jed found himself standing next to his own mount, a bright chestnut with white markings on his face and back legs, and he was huge. Jed looked up, and kept on looking as his head tipped right back to stare up at a set of pink nostrils, he put a finger in the air and kept his face carefully free of expression.

"Er...hello...sir?" he ventured.

What came next shook Jed's brain against his skull.

"Ah wizard! Good day, I have been asked to come and meet with you to see if you are worthy enough for me to carry across the miles of land that stretch out in this world. I am Autumn-Wind, might I know your name?" the voice boomed and Jed felt like holding his hat to his head lest it blew away. Yet looking around, no one else appeared to have heard the exchange; he turned back to Autumn-Wind and gave a bow watching as the beast curiously snuffled his shoulders.

"I am Jed and...er...it seems that I have been asked...to talk with a horse, not that that could be a bad thing...not at all..." he had added the last words when the huge stallion pulled back his head and tossed his mane, perhaps in anger.

"You have never conversed with my kind before?"

"No...not lately at any rate..."

"That is a great shame; my great grandsire told me stories when I was but a colt, of how wizards would come from many miles to stay in the Azale villages and converse with the horses there. He spoke with great fondness of mages Jed, he always told me of their great wisdom and how they were the only mortals that ever seemed to take time with their words. Others speak so hastily and with such speed...as though they were foals themselves. I have often wondered at his tales and am glad that I can finally meet with such a great mortal being"

Jed squinted with confusion, "You're not mortal then, like...most animals?"

Autumn-Wind gave a shrill whinny of laughter, showing his teeth and shaking his head up and down.

"Mortal? We beasts are far from it! Why Jed, my great grandsire still lives after many passing seasons, it is true we die...but time seems to have slowed down for me and my kind. We live long lives, spanning out hundreds of years more than mages, gathering wisdom and roaming the free fields. Yet we keep our strength and all the vigour of youth until our dying hour!" he said shaking his head matter-of-factly and pawing at the ground with a hoof, Jed just nodded and listened, open-mouthed. When it became obvious even to his stunned self that Autumn-Wind wanted an answer or at least an implication that Jed was listening he spoke.

"That seems to be a great gift; I wonder…has it always been like this for you?"

"A good question! And the answer is nay, we have not always lived like this, but the story goes that our ancestor, the great Fleetfoot, rescued the Archmage Balseener when he needed to escape a deadly foe and his energy was utterly spent. In return as a gift he wove a spell, proclaiming that every blood relative of Fleetfoot would live long and keep their strength and their intelligence would increase tenfold. It is a great tale and one that requires many hours for a thorough telling; therefore I will not tell you of it now, perhaps later."

"You've decided to carry me then?" Jed asked, no able to keep the excitement from his voice, here was a creature of words and tales! Of stories of the old world! Here was someone he could relate to…even if he did have four legs and a tail…

"Yes, it was my decision from the start, it will be an honour to bear one who is about to make the ultimate sacrifice of death to save the Azale. You will be a hero in these lands and I will tell your story to my own foals someday" he nodded and even managed a smug look on his long face. Telric had secured his pack and saddlebags and was about to mount up, Jed realised they would be on the move soon but he had to ask one more question.

"Tell me, please, who carries my friends?"

Autumn-Wind pointed a nose towards Telric's large beast.

"That is Nightfall, his name means deepest of the dark and he is the favourite to become the herd's leader next fall. Till then he would travel with the Deadly-Man" Jed gave a chuckle at the name given to Telric and then watched as his new friend swung his head towards Karma's mare.

"That is Winter-Sky, the one who carries the Swan-Like-Lady, her name means the time of day that is not quite morning and not quite night, it also means the sharpness in the air that proclaims that winter has come. She has a fiery temper and strong will, yet she is so beautiful too" Autumn-Wind snorted sadly, his head hung to the ground, lip dragging, then he raised it again and lastly looked at Lance's mount, who was now turning his head to nibble at the boy's boot. When the large chestnut spoke of him it was with a disapproving tone.

"That is Jester holding the Smiling-Child; I think you can guess what his name means by his ridiculous actions so far. The youngest here, but we figured that a young boy would wish to speak with someone near his own age and maturity" he gave a sniff and raised his head regally *"I*

think you'd better get on me now, everyone's starting to stare..."
Autumn-Wind mentioned and laid his ears back as Nightfall glared in
his direction. But his ears pricked and he gave a happy snicker as
Winter-Sky shook her head at him and tugged part of his mane gently.

It was then that Jed realised that not one of the horses had bridles
and they only wore a very lightweight saddle. He groaned and hitched
up his robe, grabbing the front of the saddle and trying to pull himself up. He failed miserably and in the end Nightfall reached over
with his long neck and nudged his backside till he was capable of
swinging a leg over.

"Thank you" he told the large horse with a nod.

"Don't mention it Stork-Man" came the hard, dominating voice. Jed
disapproved of the name he had been given, but who was he to
argue? After slotting his staff through a hoop of leather at his side,
awkwardly Jed looked out at the sea of faces that watched him and
the others, there were so many. Young and old together, smiling happily. He looked towards Karma, his face drooping into a sad frown,
and one dark Azale, one greedy, selfish, evil being wanted to turn all
that happiness and compassion into this? This painful shell, this life-
less husk of a body? He shook his head; how could someone become
so involved with himself and his own plans that he would destroy
hundreds of lives without a backward glance? Hundreds of bright
stars in the night sky, blown out forever. What could Jed do to stop
that from happening?

He was shaken from his deep thoughts by the sound of the Eldest's
voice, the crowd surrounding the 'Questors' moved to let her and the
eight council Elder's through. The aged woman stood before them
and for some reason gave each a proud and satisfied look before
speaking to them for the last time.

"If you ride hard for the next four days, keeping on the woodland
pathways that move towards the northeast, you will reach the great
road and be well on your way to becoming the hero's and heroine of
this era. We ask you to go to the source of evil and destroy it, we give
you fine steeds and worthy friends, good food and..." she raised a finger and four of the council members drew level with her, carrying
oddly shaped parcels wrapped in silk, the Eldest carried on "...we
also give you a weapon. A weapon that will not break for any force
brought down upon it, which will not bend in the strongest heat and
will not rust. They were forged from lighting, fire, magic and metal

fallen from the skies, please accept them as a gift from the Veiled and the village of Faynar'Haye" she smiled once and nodded her head.

One council member went to stand beside Nightfall and passed a package up. Telric looked down at his and twitched the folds of material back to reveal a curved and delicately decorated blade, with faint misty-white patterns running along it in light lines and dark slashes. It was set in a carved hilt of ebony and rosewood, with an eye delicately glancing out from each side. He smiled and his fingers lightly traced the white designs on the blade, then he slipped the dagger into his belt and nodded with appreciation.

"Truly a great gift, Eldest"

"What weapon could we give one whose greatest weapon is himself? Only something as perfectly balanced and well-made as this dagger" she answered with a smile and a shrug.

The next council member moved to Karma, who took the gift with unblinking eyes, her fingers fumbled the silks sheets revealing a golden necklace, shaped in the style of a sword. The tip looked very sharp and shone a dull black, Karma smiled at it and then wrapped it up and placed it in a pocket, she did not give thanks for the gift but the Eldest gave her a sincere look and said,

"Sometimes the smallest prick of a poisoned blade can end ones life as surely as a dagger to the throat, and at such times secrecy and tricks are always used to cover your opponent's eyes"

Again, a council member lifted a package towards Lance, who eagerly pulled its covering away and grinned at what he saw inside.

A large silver medallion hung from a golden chain, in the centre of it was a gem of tiger's eye and around that a ring of amethyst. He yanked it over his head and gazed at it around his neck, the Eldest gave a small chuckle as she explained its use to him.

"And at times the best weapon we can have is protection, no spell or magic charm will ever find its mark on you my small friend, if you wear that Protector" she went to stand next to the boy and gave him a grin, he grinned back and reached down to hug her around the neck, then sat back, very pleased with himself. Finally a council member moved towards Jed, passing up his gift, he unwrapped it with excited fingers. Inside he found a silver flute with the ruby etchings of a dragon, Jed traced the picture and smiled as it glowed softly, then turned to listen to the Eldest one last time.

"My friend this gift has been at our village...longer than any here can remember we only know that a wizard left it with us. Telling us that we were to chose whose hand it would go to and I and the council have decided that it should go to yours. What we give you is no weapon, for the simple fact that, at times, the pen is mightier than the sword, and a pen is made to write words and words flow into song. And at rare times, song flows into creation, make music and see if your words have the same effect as that pen...you would be surprised at what magic music can have in the right hands, and I think your hands may be the right ones for this Magic-Maker" she gave a bow of her head and turned silently, moving back through the crowds and away down the village streets and alleys, and towards the Leaf-changing tree.

There was silence for a while, in which time Jed looked once more at the flute in his hands, he then un-strapped his saddlebag and slotted it neatly into the folds of his new robes, making sure it was tightly packed and then placed his hands at each side of Autumn-Winds neck. Telric broke the silence by asking Nightfall to start the journey, his shod hooves echoed in the silent street as he set out. Jed looked at the faces all around him as he followed on. Hopeful and pleading, desperate and sad...he felt as though something was missing...and heard a small nagging voice in the back of his head...

What did you expect? Cheering, a great shout of joy and huzahs for their saviours? No, they will watch until you are out of sight and then they will wonder desperately throughout the following months, have they done it? Have they finished their quest...or have they failed? Will I be caught and bound too? What will become of me? Where will I go...and can I hide?

*

The group travelled hard that day, sticking to the paths that would lead them to the great road and speaking little to one another. When Telric finally decided it was time to camp, the horses looked tired and as soon as they were unsaddled they took water and went to grass, chomping away steadily and suppressing their large appetites. Karma dragged her bedroll into a corner on the edge of their campfire light, refusing to eat and staring at everyone in a dazed fashion. Telric put his back against a tree and slid to the floor with a yawn, pulling his small rug up to his shoulders he lifted one arm in the air, Lance dove under it and was soon snuggled up against his guardian's chest. They fell asleep like a father and son on a lazy, sunny afternoon, smiling contently. Shortly after that Karma closed her eyes and laid her head against her arm, she too slept peacefully...and it seemed that Jed had been left to take the first watch.

He muttered, remembering his first failed hours of alertness, his foolish ponderings were responsible for the state his female friend was in now and he couldn't help feeling at least a little guilty. After a while Autumn-Wind came and sat with him, calm and peacefully watching the fire with a drowsy eye, but Jed still remembered his promise.

"Autumn-Wind? You said that you would tell me of the Archmage Balseener and how he was rescued by Fleetfoot and therefore received the gift of long life, strength and higher intelligence. I know it is late, but it will help me pass a few hours whilst I keep watch for my friends...will you tell me of that tale now?" His words were little more than a whisper yet he still sounded too loud in the quiet clearing.

"Indeed Jed, I told you I would tell you the tale and I will tell it now...I cannot sleep anyway, I need to digest my meal first" he said in an off-hand way, then he shifted slightly, stretching his neck and legs out and shaking his head and yawning, when he had done he blinked a few times and then turned to Jed.

"The Archmage Balseener was known as the youngest wizard ever to take the mantle of Archmage. Being only seventy eight years of age, he was renowned for his wisdom and spell knowledge of Dragons and other magic wielding creatures. He was brought up in the country of Turth and at the young age of eight he was found by a Mage and taken to be taught the ways of magic and the mysteries of the future that evade most mortals eyes. At the wizard guild he was much loved and gained many companions, yet he gained a powerful enemy. Nazirr, who was born on the Wizard Isles themselves. He was jealous of Balseener, seeking to better him at every possible event. Hating him for his many friends and admirers and despising him for becoming the youngest ever Archmage. Petty things that can burn a man up if not dealt with from the very beginning. He left the guild and all it stood for far behind, he travelled the lands and seas, seeking dark and ancient wicked spells, perfecting them and becoming one of the greatest known evils of that age. Soon people were seeking help and refuge from the monster that Nazirr had become, many challenged him and hundreds sought to kill him...yet in the end none prevailed. And one day Balseener would take no more. Ignoring his advisors and closest friends he stepped off of the island he had come to

reign over and sought Nazirr out, following his destruction and holding his anger barely in check..." Autumn-Wind stopped for dramatic effect, Jed urged him on like a small child to a grandparent, impatient and curious. So the horse resumed the tale.

"He found Nazirr on a large island, past all civilized world and far beyond the dragon lands. The great beasts whirled around him, cunning of tongue and sharp of eye, and quick to strike a death-blow to any living thing...yet they could not strike Balseener, so powerful was he that the first mighty beast that threw flame at him from his mouth was ripped to shreds in the air. Its wings becoming tattered and not able to hold its large bulk, dropped to the sea and drowned with a heart wrenching shriek. The others pulled back then, and let him enter their domain unharmed...as they had let one other man do so. Nazirr waited in the mountains, on the highest pinnacle and in the coldest of weathers. There the two enemies fought, dealing vicious blows to mind and body alike, pulsing brightly like two suns locked in a heated battle of fire and blood. They were unaware of the huge bodies of Dragons strewn all around them having come too close to the mages magic and catching the feather-end of such powerful spells. Nazirr brought dark beasts from other lands and plains to attack Balseener, who in turn defended and struck back with powerful spells and the Gods on his side. They battled for three whole days without seeming to tire and neither looking away from one another or turning a cheek. Yet finally someone had to give way. Balseener stood with his back to the west on the fourth morning, and as the sun rose it struck him fully in his eyes, blinding him for a moment...giving Nazirr a chance to kill his hated foe. The evil one struck out, having only enough strength left from the duelling to push Balseener off the mountain pinnacle and down to the rocks below. The Archmage cried out as he fell from such a height, knowing he would never be able to save himself, he called for help once, twice...and as he was about to hit the rocks and become no more than a smear of blood, a beast rose up out of the sea. At first he thought it was a wave, sent by the winds to soften his descent but as he looked closer he saw the foam and swirl of water to be the likeness of a great white stallion. He rode on the back of Fleetfoot! Fabled creature and sea dweller! It took three days to reach land, and when Balseener was standing on the beach he saw that Fleetfoot was so exhausted from his long and fast trip that he had been left behind by the tide. Already he was sinking into the sand and would soon be gone. The Archmage refused to accept this and his staff rose in the air, with a great cry and the last ounce of his magic he tapped

Fleetfoot's forehead and watched as the great beast took on solid shape, becoming whole and real before his eyes, then he turned and threw his staff down. He had used the last of his power and would have no use of it ever again, then it is said that he left Fleetfoot and hid in one of the caves on the beach, some say he still lives there, others say he has died and gone long ago...and as for Nazirr...well, no-one knows what happened to him, but I have always believed him dead...surely he could not have fought off the dragons after being so tired from his magical battle..." Autumn-Wind finished his tale and bowed his head in silence; Jed went through the story that had just been told and the truths behind it.

"I know of Balseener, every mage is brought up to know of the great wizards from past years...yet no-one has ever known the full story till now, how can it be that you know all of what you say is true?" he questioned. His friend raised his great head and shook it, rather sadly.

"I told you that Fleetfoot originally came from the sea, did I not?"

"Yes you told me"

"Well, the great sea horse sired five great colts, each colt reflected a different element, one reflected fire and when he ran he left a blaze behind him and he could withstand any heat and no harm would come to him. Another reflected darkness and it was his duty to run across the sky and drag the night behind him, and throw shadows across the land. One of the colts reflected spirit and he is the source of Hope in our world, and at times the Gods will send him to those people who are noble and are on a journey To help yet others who are faltering and tired and lonely in the dark night, and when they see Hope they set back on their journey with new vigour and a fresh heart and mind. One of the colts reflected wind and any breeze you feel, any mighty wind comes from his breath, and the last colt reflected sea as his father had done. Amongst my people they are known as 'The Horse Lords'.

And each of these foals took on a herd and their children like them had their own special abilities, but soon, with the watered blood of many generations, the herds stopped having such grand powers of the elements. They yearn to be back where they originally came from. For example, Winter-Sky and myself are both descendents from the colt who danced in the wind and we long to jump into the sky and be carried along by a storm, yet we cannot. The gift that Balseener gave to Fleetfoot also became his entrapment, he wanted to return to the sea again after a few years. He was tired of the land and wanted to feel the spray on his face again…but no one could lift the spell and he died an unhappy beast indeed. Nightfall is a descendant of the darkness colt, he dislikes the day verily and prefers the calmness and coolness that come with the night. Jester is a crossbreed, he is of the hope and sea herds, he has a light hearted nature and though he isn't exactly the symbol of hope he can lighten most moods…and he swims very well. But you asked how I knew of this story…"

"Yes, please, go on"

Autumn-Wind sighed and yawned again.

"All the herds of the element colts know the story, it has been passed down from each generation as has all our history. Horses cannot write so we tell our history in tales, a very enjoyable way of going over what can be a boring event…now please, Wizard, will you finally permit me to sleep? The sun will be rising soon and I have not yet laid down to rest!"

Realising how rude and perhaps how pushy he had been on the subjects of the tale Jed nodded and watched as the huge horse stood, locked his knees and hung his head low, closing his eyelids he was soon sleeping. Jed also felt like dropping off to sleep where he sat…and was about to go and wake Telric to watch over the group so he could sleep…when he heard a noise.

It was little more than a shake of a few leaves, yet Jed pricked his ears up and grasped his staff, then moved towards Telric. He put a hand over the man's mouth and watched as the assassins own hand moved with viper-like speed, the dagger stopped short of plunging into his neck and Jed nodded towards the trees warily. Telric listened and then he nudged Lance from his deep sleep, whispering quiet instructions and unsheathing another dagger, balancing both carefully in his hands and quickly settling into a fighting crouch. The horses woke then, ears pricked and eyes showing white around the edges, hauling themselves up they moved their heads from side to side. Watching everything and pawing the ground cautiously…they knew something was hiding from them too. Jed moved over to Karma and found that her eyes were open and she was shivering, shaking her a bit Jed pulled her silver short-sword off her back clumsily, pulling her up and wrapping her fingers around the hilt, Karma gazed at it for a bit and then her hands firmed and her jaw set. As Jed turned in the direction that the others were facing he caught another sound to his left, and another still, this time to his right, and was able to give a strangled cry.

"It's a distraction! They're all around us!"

As soon as the words fell from his mouth Jed found himself with his back against the others and facing outwards in a circle.

Just in time.

A glint of gold against the green foliage was the only other warning given, and then four stout figures leapt…however they didn't leap very far, for the small fact that they weren't more than four feet or so in height and their legs weren't all that long.

The dwarves came from all sides of the forest and each seemed to have a target in mind for their axe, they wore the same leather armour as last time and three still had their beards in braids. They struck as one in a mad berserk rage and when Jed saw the ugly, angry, ruddy-red face of his opponent he was about to drop to the floor and cower when his staff jerked into life, moving on its own and dragging Jed along with it. It blocked the blow from the axe that surely would have split his skull in two as easily as a ripe melon and then thrust downwards with a twist. The dwarf yanked the half-moon blade free from where it had struck the ground and gave a maddened yell. Lunging forward he kicked out with metal-capped feet, trying to trip his enemy, whilst swinging the axe expertly over his head and dangerously close to Jed's long neck. Jed jerked backwards, away from the blade and felt air rush past his face; the staff swung him forward again and was trying to move right. Jed let go and the thing caught yet another blow meant for its master, bringing its other end into play and placing a blow on the dwarf's bulbous nose. He dropped the axe and it fell to the floor blade down, inches away from its owner's foot, pressing stubby fingers to his now streaming nose he tried to stint the flow of blood and failed miserably. As the staff pulled back for a final blow to the head, he made a half-hearted effort to fall to the floor and roll out of the way, only to be obstructed by his own axe, stuck into the ground as it was. Jed closed his eyes but still heard the sickening crunch of heavy wood slamming against bone, skin and a mess of veins. When he opened them again, it was to find that his foe was still alive, that much was obvious from the hoarse breathing, yet unconscious. Jed's staff was upright and its carvings resembled a face, an angry glaring face, Jed shrugged and put up his hands in a defensive position.

"What? You were doing fine on your own; I would have just got in the way!"

And that was all he had time to say, for as soon as his own life-threatening battle was over he had become aware of the ones going on around him.

Lance seemed to be faced with the largest of the ambushing dwarves, and he had to dodge and jump back from powerful blows directed at him. He held a dagger in each hand and his face appeared serious and worried, completely out of character for the little lad. Yet he was holding his own far better than Jed had been moments before and seemed to be coping, but he kept throwing looks over his shoulder in Karma's direction.

A thought in Jed's head clicked.

He spun and saw the Eternal barely managing to get her blade up to block blows, she was stumbling too, her feet dragged and her breathing was rough, her pale face was that of the un-dead. And as Jed moved towards her, he saw her fall back, tripping over a tree root and crashing to the ground. Her short-sword spun away and her fingers scrabbled for it in the dirt whilst she looked at the oncoming blade, moving down, down, towards her elegant neck.

He turned his head again and saw Lance clutching to the back of his foe, one of his small childish hands was scratching at the dwarf's eyes and the other held a small steel dagger, his fingers found the eye sockets of the dwarf and dug down hard. The dwarf flung his head back in pain and Lance's other hand slashed outwards...leaving a crimson line across his throat. Jumping off the ground before the corpse crushed him as it fell, the thief gave Jed a quick grin and then his head whipped around to see if the others were all right.

A shout.

Jed turned to his right to see Telric fiercely kick at his own opponent, shouting towards Karma and already running...but he wouldn't make it in time and the dwarf jumped. Grabbing the assassin's middle and pulling him down into a scuffle, which exploded in a flash of steel and a gush of blood, the assassin scrabbled back up and left the carcass on the floor to the worms. Jed heard a whirr of air past his ear, making his robes fly forward and his beard and hair stick up stupidly, the staff strained to get to the fallen Eternal. Jed could feel the strain, shared the pain as wood knots creaked in its frame and the air practically sanded it as it flew.

The dwarf heard the whirr of air too and looked up, stopping inches away from his deadly deed, saw the staff, his eyes widened and he let out a yell just before the long, hard piece of magical wood hit his neck at full speed, crushing his windpipe and carrying him into a tree, sliding down it in a heap. Jed felt something nudge his back and turning around he saw that Nightfall was holding the dwarf that Jed's staff had knocked unconscious in his teeth, shaking him from side to side and waking him abruptly. The little man clapped his hands to his head and groaned loudly, gingerly touching the bruise that was already forming on his swollen forehead.

Telric helped Karma to her feet and as soon as he was positive she was unharmed his eyes locked on the dwarf hanging from his mount's mouth. Jed winced as the assassin grabbed the injured man and shook him, making his head bounce back and forth wildly.

"Who sent you?" the words held as much emotion as ice and his face could have been carved from stone. The dwarf looked up at Telric through bushy eyebrows, and shut his mouth with a click, shaking his head slowly.

"Tell me and you can go now, refuse my question and I will take you back to my guild. You know who I am?" Telric was smiling now, it was not a nice sight and Karma was watching him, worry on her face.

When the dwarf spoke his harsh voice sounded like grit being rubbed against tree-bark.

"Ye be Telric Zeal, 'ead o' the assassins guild...and ye dinnae frighten me none mister, I do nae care what ye do to me. 'E'll do much worse..." his mouth shut again and he folded his arms stubbornly. Telric glared at him and walked over to his saddlebags. With one hand he unlaced the ties and pulled out a length of coiled rope, he tied it round the dwarfs hands and feet, and he tied it tightly...so tightly in fact that Jed could see blood around the small mans wrists, he had to intervene.

"Telric, be reasonable and tie them looser he's bleeding for lore's sake..." he put out a hand to loosen the rope and instantly wished he hadn't. Telric moved like a snake and Jed was flung to the floor, his wrist paining him. Karma moved forward and tugged the assassin's arm, shaking her head; Telric glared at Jed and flung the dwarf to a corner where he watched him.

"Don't tell me what to do wizard, you haven't dealt with this sort of thing before and I have...we are going to take a slight detour to Torath'Danar. Once there we hand this creature over to some friends of mine, they'll get something out of him. They always get something" he smiled slightly at the last and gave a chuckle, then clasped his hands together and his dark, brooding eyes watched the little figure in the corner as he tried to roll onto his back. Jed watched the man carefully, his own eyes thoughtful and considering. Sticking out a hand he felt magic surge through him, he stood shakily and looked down at his wrist, there were bruise marks around it where Telric had dug in with hard fingers. Sitting cross-legged on the floor he lay his staff across his knees, weariness gone from his body now that he held onto magic. The power seeming to make his senses sharpen suddenly as though he was truly alive for the first time and felt and saw everything in its true form, not just the dull pictures he had known beforehand. Jed concentrated with his mind, eyes squinted he rested both hands on his knees and he brushed a hair-fine strand of his power onto his wrist, wrapping it around the bruise marks loosely and tying it off tightly, no-one else could see the strand...unless they were a mage, and then again only certain mages could see it. Jed dealt in all magic, though in some areas he did not excel there were few like him, other mages had one specific power, always from one element, fire, earth, water, air, spirit...all were significant to the world and those who lived on it. Jed reached inside his mind now and grasped two of the five elements that swam there, spirit and water, to his own eyes a slender, translucent shimmer had now surrounded his form and was shooting up and through the strand of power that was about his wrist. This was the spirit, then another shimmer, this one with hints of aquamarine in it and a rippling. The effect was instant and the bruise started to fade and his wrist soon forgot the pain, but Jed did not forget who and what had caused it.

Rolling up into a ball on his bedroll the wizard sent a silent prayer up to Mother Weaver, Goddess of Dreams, for a good night, then Jed's lids sank slowly, flickering up every now and then...and finally staying shut. His breathing became smooth and his mind dreamt of past, present and possible future.

CHAPTER TEN
1 Spy

Ragea Atia watched the scene around the campfire and then ran his large, calloused fingers across the small hand-held mirror, the picture faded and the figures melted from it and left him staring at the shining surface. He smoothed the coloured wood and his fingers traced the metal patterns that ran around its handle in a swirl. The warlord leant back in his huge, carved oak chair with cruel, twisted and sharp antlers slotted onto the top, his fingers bridged together roughly and his large round eyes holding the pupils of a snake.

He was a huge, hulking man, his chest was a barrel and his arms and legs were as thick as tree-trunks and muscle-bound to the limit, his hair was a dark, almost dirty brown and hung in fraying strands to his shoulders. His face had once been handsome but now held a broken nose and a jagged scar across his left cheek, and his skin seemed patched, as though it was made of scales...and it was, he had experimented with his new magical powers. Dragon-scales were much greater protection than ordinary, flimsy human skin. His fingernails were long and pointed and hooked downwards, like a cat's and his teeth were chiselled into sharp points. Standing quickly and quietly his huge mildewed pelt cloak swung around him and made him look half hidden in ragged shadows. The epitome of a powerful warlord who held all his might on a tight rein. His long legs jolted into sudden action and took him out of the cold, dark chamber he had lingered in. But not before he had securely placed his Scrying-glass in a belt loop, they took him past other large, cold and empty chambers, past scurrying servants who threw themselves to the ground before him and kept their eyes hidden long after he had gone. After many snaking staircases, dreary and near lightless rooms, twisted corridors and carpeted halls, Ragea reached the centre of his newly acquired stronghold. It had fallen easily once he had reached its heart...the doors before him were large and unyielding, with heavy iron hinges and colossal ebony planks. His hefty, strong hands roughly grabbed a brass handle and pushed forward, the hall he stepped into seemed abnormally bright after the dimness of the other dull rooms with huge stained glass windows that portrayed epic scenes of Eternal life and history and dazzling glow-stones in each corner. Runes were on everything and shone a soft turquoise, some reflecting a thread of light to one and then to another, yet in the end everything reflected back onto a small disk that lay on a marble pedestal. The disk was only the size of a large playing marble and seemed plain enough; it was made from ancient bone and had one half-chip of black pearl in its core. Though there were many more ornate and jewel inlaid things in the room, this small disk caught the eye and held it with an un-nerving gaze of its own. Ragea pushed back some long strands of hair, revealing pointed ears that reached past eye-height, his hand moved towards the small disk, it beckoned him…it beckoned all, mortal and immortal, wielders of magic and common men and women of the earth. He watched it longingly, almost lovingly…but before his fingers could reach it he pulled away, the disk must not be touched, must never be nudged out of place in the slightest way. It held a world of magic in its shell, it held the Azale's magic to be precise. Every rune, every magical fibre of reflecting light was placed perfectly and the marble pedestal had been forced into its perfect position. If the disk were to be moved out of place, even a millimetre out of place, the magical world would close. Its dimension sealed from use for a long time, and the hundreds of thousands of Eternal folk all over Mog would fade and die for lack of their powers, would want to die without it, would yearn to die…no…Ragea took a firm step back. It must never be moved from its place. He was an Azale now too, the same fate would befall him and he could not allow that to happen…not when he had immortality in his grasp! Not when he danced magic on his fingertips and certainly not when his brilliant plan was coming together in such a masterful way. Those worthless worms the Scrying glass had revealed to him, those…those children! They sought to eradicate him? He had more dark power in a fingernail than they held in their whole bodies! The dwarves had proved useless to him, not able to bring the children to him and not even able to put up a good battle before they had died revoltingly. But it was of little matter to him, they would come to him in their own time…would face him and see how hopeless their pathetic plight was, and how little fruit their 'quest' would bear. He knew their weaknesses, had seen their minds and how they worked…the assassin almost matched himself for intelligence and guile, for cunning and deceitfulness, for well laid traps and rather glorious tactics…maybe even matched him in well hidden madness…but no…no…Ragea knew true madness. The little voice in his head that would not go away, the annoying, cunning, horrible little voice that giggled and shouted and shrieked and planned…it had been the Eternals fault…they had tricked him with the pact. Tricked him and left the malicious little voice and he would make them pay, he would make them all pay in the end…

Ragea had taken the high Eternal's home. He had killed many and enslaved many more and soon they would all wear his beautiful inventions, the lovely, shining metal bands, the 'Col'ars' and the 'Brakel'ets' as he had named them. He would forge hundreds with the aid of his Seer's and dark armed forces and as one they would clinch them into place and confirm the doom of all Azale magic wielders. Only he would use the magic meant for thousands, he would keep it all and grow to be all-powerful. His armies would rake the lands and he would rule everything, everyone would bow to him and everything he had ever worked for, ever planned and intended would finally be his and no one else's…Ragea stopped and realised that he was now right next to the marble pedestal and his fingers were groping towards the disk before him, he snatched them back in one swift movement and forced his legs to move backwards. He liked this room, it was the one place where he could truly feel his power and his gifts of magical influence…the one place he felt truly safe. It was a dangerous room, only he stepped though the doors, only he would ever enter this room and live…no-one else but himself. He looked at his hands again, they were flexing and starting to stir; he turned on his heel and almost flung himself from the hall he loved so much. Forcing the doors shut with a crash he leant against them, his snake-eye-pupils widened as he adjusted to the dim light around him, his fingers still squirmed…they needed work to do, he had to make them forget, had to make himself forget that small disk. His mind was suddenly filled with an image of the Col'ars, yes, he'd make some of them…he had to make enough to trap them all, had to force one around every Eternal neck and it was work he enjoyed, it was work that brought him ever closer to his goal, step by step. He jerked forwards into a walk again, powerful strides that betrayed no sound and flashing eyes that took all in, Ragea slunk off down long dank hallways, ignoring the damp sandstone walls and slimy coloured fungus's that seemed to have taken root in his home, forgot the sodden banners that appeared tattered and disintegrated next to rusting iron holders with green algae dripping from their sides. Rotting wooden shutters covered low windows to block out the freezing weather, on rounded corners a few battered looking soldiers huddled around small fires that stained the walls black with soot and threw ashes up in the air to float down and grind into the granite floor. His men bowed to him as Ragea moved along, he made for the huge converted barns outside, once they had held livestock and crates but now they held forges, potions and slaves.

It was snowing heavily outside, the large, downy particles drenched anyone who dared to step out of a door, laying forty centimetres deep in some areas and turning to grey slush beneath churning feet. Inside the barns heat struck Ragea like a heavy blow to the head, he yanked off his heavy outer coat and flung it at a man who had stopped in his tracks as soon as he had seen his lord walk through the doors. The lord in question lurked in the shadows and watched muscled men sweat and burn as they worked, a Seer stood beside each forge and every now and then he or she would take a smidgen of...something...from one of the many different pots set before them and hurl it into the fire, creating shrill bangs and bringing forth heavy smoke, as they did so they chanted illegible words and sheltered their eyes with a hand; as though weeping. The forges, smiths and Seers were kept in a strict line to the left of the barn, at the back and to the right stood cages, the metal bars steamed from long exposure to the heat and the people inside them huddled in small groups, straining so as not to be pushed against them. Ragea watched as one of the smiths looked up from his work and gave a gruff yell, two soldiers in plain, soot-stained woollen tunics stepped smartly towards the cages and unlocked them. With firm hands they reached out and pulled a woman from one of the huddling groups and dragged her, kicking and screaming towards the smith. They pushed her to the floor and held her arms and head still as she frantically shook herself from side to side and screamed. The smith took up his tongs and lifted something from his forge, the Col'ar glew white-hot as it was carefully opened, the woman had stopped screaming now and her eyes were open in shock and dread, the smith moved forward and in one smooth movement had clapped the metal around her neck and stood back. His Seer quickly stepped forward and threw a handful of herbs over the woman as she sobbed in what could only be throbbing pain, then stopped...her hands came up in the air, their palms facing outwards, her eyes flashed a brief black colour and smoke streamed from her mouth. The smoke coiled around the Col'ar and then seemed to sink into it...and as suddenly as she had stopped screaming, the woman fell dead to the floor. Around Rageas thick neck lay a thin set of silver links, attached to a tiny key at the end, which gave a bright flash and then dulled to look like a normal everyday charm or necklace. But if you lifted the key to your ear you would hear a hundred thousand screams from tortured souls. The Seer reached down with unprotected hands and took the Col'ar off the corpse, instead of its white-hot glow it now shone a metallic silver and then started to shimmer, the man placed it on a workbench, next to five other Col'ar's and two sets of Brakel'ets. As soon as he had finished one the smith started making another, the woman's carcass was dragged outside and flung into a cavernous pit that would be filled in later on. Ragea stepped out from the shadows and grabbed the nearest smith in a strong grip, pushing him to the side and yanking his tongs out of his hands whilst pulling on a leather apron, the Seer was replaced by Rageas own personal Seer and advisor. Her name was Mysticism…a chosen name of course, not her birth one, and she held the second highest rank to Ragea in the entire castle. She was wise, cunning, devious, beguiling, coldly beautiful and ever observing…any amount of gossip running through the fortress always reached her ears first. She always made the best reports and her foretellings always came true…so far. She wore a sweeping black suede dress and a dragging purple cloak that she always pulled up to try and hide in the shadows of her cowl, her indigo eyes were bright and intelligent, her face regal and composed. She worked as fast as her master at the forge, and waited to be spoken too, her battle tactics were such that she could outmanoeuvre most and she was always two steps ahead of anyone but himself. If he were not a smart Azale then Ragea would trust her entirely, but she hungered too much for power and he wouldn't put it behind her to plot his downfall and her own uprising, all in all worthy of his notice. As he worked the metal with his hammer, beating it out and heating it, then beating it again, he asked "What news of the hunting parties?" in the cruel, half-hissing whisper that was his voice. She gave him a half-bow before answering, "They caught three Eternal today my lord…four less than the day before, it seems our enemies grow ever more cunning…" she trailed off lightly, her voice both soothing and flattering at once, wheedling and pleading yet wise and contemplating. She looked up to meet his gaze and half opened her mouth before halting and raising an eyebrow at him, Ragea grunted and waved, impatient for any advice she would surely have.

"My lord, you know that my Goddess has gifted me with the true sight…you think yourself powerful and untouchable but I have seen the Gods world. They play with us like chess pieces on a board, and at any time a player might be removed from the board forever...yet I see only half of the game, and am always near blind when it comes to our enemies turn...majesty. If you would just allow me to become an Eternal, as yourself, they would surely let an immortal see more-" her clever words stopped short as Rageas hand grabbed her delicate neck and pushed it down onto the anvil before him, with his other hand he pressed the warm metal from his hammer-head onto her cheek...to the woman's credit she didn't scream or struggle.

How many times had he heard the same words? How many times had he had to argue his point? How many times had she still tried again...she was clever...had he not told her twice before that he meant the Eternals power to be his alone. Had he not made it clear that the main reason he was capturing and trapping the others of his kind was so that he could be the soul wieldier of their magic and one of the most powerful forces the world had ever seen? With that sort of power he could sweep the land and rule it all, everything, every-one...he would even go towards the dragons land and conquer them, making them bow before him and serve him as his pets. Rageas eyes burned with the joy and anticipation of that moment...then he turned back to Mysticism and the fact that she had annoyed him.

Digging his hooked nails into the back of her delicate neck he put his lips to her ear and hissed, "I have already given you an answer to your question...yet I will tell you again as you appear to be too stu-pid to be aware of it yet...no, you cannot become like me. I will be the sole wielder of such powerful magic and you, along with everyone else, will be my faithful and devoted servant. You will do as I say with-out question and you will not ask your question again...I can always find another with your talent, you are expendable...are we clear?"

She nodded and pressed her lips together tightly, whether from fear or anger he did not know, nor did he care. The warlord sneered at her and then let go, Mysticism smoothly slipped back into her for-mer place before the herbs, taking a pinch from a bowl and giving a harsh cry as she tossed it into the flames. Ragea turned back to the metal lying on the forge side and started to shape it...

He did not see the angry glare of indigo eyes that flashed hatred at him, he did not see the pupil's contract with rage and he did not see the devious mind that had plans of its own...

And if Ragea were a very clever Azale...he would have killed her.

CHAPTER ELEVEN
Homecoming

The Eldest had been right when she had said that after four days of hard riding Jed and his companions would leave the woodland tracks and enter out onto the 'Great Road'. As they went past the last of the trees and Jed caught his first sight of it he gasped, it was immense…he had only ever read about it in books back at the guild. It had been made hundreds of years ago, when all the peoples of Mog had worked side by side, hand in hand and as one to build it. It spanned hundreds of miles and had taken many years to build but it was a wonder to behold. Thick specks of red-clay dust that whipped up from the roadside caked Jed from head to toe, as it did the others, and soon he had taken out his handkerchief to tie around his nose and mouth so he could actually breath…the horses took it all in good faith, not complaining and keeping their eyelashes down, protecting their eyes. Telric seemed to have forgotten the incident with the dwarf and Jed and, as they topped a rise in the road, he pointed to what appeared to be a hill in the distance.

"That is the largest mountain in the whole of Mog, and it can be found in Torath'Danar…my present home and secretive stronghold. We should get there soon. That is if weather doesn't catch us, if the horses don't become lame and if we don't get set upon by yet more bandits. But when we're there, ha, when we're there nothing like that will happen. You should see it Jed, it's like a game you can play, every person is a piece on the board and I'm one of the players, moving the pieces how I like. If you ever get a game going, invite me and we'll see how far we can take it"

Telric gave him a grin, pulled his hat down low and asked Nightfall to carry on. Jed winced when he had spoken about playing with other's lives as though they were just part of a game…he hoped he would never 'get a game going' and hoped he wouldn't get picked up as a playing piece.

Lance had tied a long strip of cloth around his head and mouth to catch the heavy dust in the air, leaving only his eyes showing, dancing and joyful as they caught sight of the mountain. Jed wondered if he was a playing piece as well…or even a player. Shaking the thought from his head. The wizard sighed and stretched, rubbing an aching back and yawning widely. Whatever happened on the road, whatever happened when they reached the country of Torath'Danar he hoped that once they got there he could sleep in a proper bed.

*

The 'Questors', their prisoner and their mounts rode for three more days, becoming tired of travel and extremely snappish when it came to mealtimes as all they had left from their supplies was stale and flavourless. Borrowing Karma's set of wooden pipes and blowing out fast, happy jigs that he jumped about to, Lance was the only one who didn't seem to be affected by the gloomy mood that had settled over them like a blanket.

The mountain in the distance had steadily become larger and very vast as they moved closer towards it and by noon on the third day Jed's watery eyes could make out a large wall that stretched for miles and held a fortified gate in its centre. When the group of nine finally drew up to it, Jed could understand why Torath'Danar was named as Mog's greatest defensive country. Made from smooth grey stone the walls sheer height was admirable, the gate was made of hardened oak and ebony. A large dagger design had been laid into it and large black flags flickered in a light breeze overhead. Telric covered his eyes from the sun's glare as he looked up at the black-metal clad guards that stood atop the wall. One of them leaned over and yelled down, "Who are you and what business do you hold in Torath'Danar?"

Telric reached into a pouch that hung from his belt and pulled out a blood red rose, tying a small silver knife to it with a length of wire he took aim and flung it upwards towards the other man. The guard jabbed out a hand and caught it with ease and after giving the strange device a quick glance he gave the group a cautious look, and then disappeared from view.

Jed looked at Telric, who smirked and fixed his eyes on the gate, then sighed impatiently...dreaming about that bath he had promised himself earlier.

A few minutes later the guard had not returned and Jed was about to suggest asking nicely to be let in, when the huge gates started to open outwards with a groan. It took several men, straining side by side on each door to open it; their shoes had long spikes on the soles, which they used to dig into the ground and help push forward. When they were opened; twenty men on a range of black and grey horses rode out of the gates and made a beeline for Jed and his friends. They all appeared to be in a type of uniform, black metal armour and short black capes that held silver markings on the shoulder. The man leading them wore no armour, though his clothes were black and his cape was long and sweeping with silver edges. His head held a mess of golden hair and a large sandy moustache; he drew up alongside Telric and reached out with a left hand. Before both men shook, Jed saw the same tattoo on his palm as he had seen on Telric's the day they had met the Elders. A dark red rose with a thorn that dripped black blood.

"My Lord, we expected you to return sooner...and in slightly different company" his eyes flickered towards Jed and back to Telric so quickly that Jed wasn't sure they had moved.

"Well Urat, I choose my own company...and so far it has been fine," the guild leader answered and then pushed the dwarf strapped behind him to the floor. "This here along with his friends, tried to attack us in the forest. I want to know why, take him to the guild and ask him...nicely" he said, Jed had never heard a man say such words with so much menace.

The man he had called Urat put up his right hand and balled it into a fist, stuck up two fingers and then waved them forward, two of the soldiers behind him dismounted and grabbed the dwarf who sprawled and groaned on the floor. Together they turned and walked swiftly back through the gates, prisoner in tow. The other soldiers had formed two straight columns on horseback and as Jed, Telric, Karma, Lance and Urat trotted past them, the men filed behind in a protective stance. As they walked past them, Jed noticed that the walls by the gate were at least two horse spans deep and a portcullis with vicious spikes and well-melded steel creaked above them. Beyond the wall Jed could see for miles and ahead of them, by the roadside was a small village...he had expected a great deal more.

Telric had stopped talking to Urat in quiet, mysterious hushed tones and came up alongside him. He opened his mouth to say something and then stopped...as though he didn't see how he was to go about asking something...Jed made it easy for him.

"What?" he asked grumpily, who had hoped to spend a night in what had promised to be luxury.

"By the look on your face I can see you're not exactly impressed, but this isn't the heart of Torath'Danar, or where I live, this is just a small village made up of useful farmers. I live at the mountain." He pointed to the huge, hulking grey slab in the distance, "and it's a three-day ride to get there...unless you can help," he added the last almost cautiously as Jed groaned then sighed heavily. He felt physically and mentally exhausted from the journey they had just undertaken and he wasn't thinking straight.

Rubbing a temple with two fingers he asked, "And what do you think I could do?"

The others strained their ears to listen as they leaned forward to hear Telric ask.

"You could...transport us..." Telric asked, for once almost hesitantly.

Jed forgot to be tired as he eyes contracted into sharp slits and he fixed Telric with a withering glare.

"How do you know about that? No-one but a mage is told about it...and even then only a very few are allowed to actually use that method of travel, its guild regulations and its dangerous, tell me how you know," he demanded, shocking even himself with the icy edge that tinged his voice. He might not stick up for himself but his guild was different. It had a reputation, it had secrets, for those secrets to be given away by one mage...the disgrace would be intolerable, Telric shrugged and pinched the bridge of his nose.

"I'm the assassin guild leader Jed, I know lots of things...it comes with the job. I am the one who has to decide, I'm the one who has to keep over five-hundred men and women busy or else they might get bored and decide to overthrow me...and I'm the one that all the nobles in the world would gladly like to get rid of. Knowing about mages being able to transport their matter from one place to another is a minor issue compared to that," he answered and then folded his arms, "if you think I've been too serious and watchful on the road you're wrong, that was like a holiday for me. As soon as I step back into the place I call home, a hundred and one different problems will crash down onto my shoulders and the more I take off the more will come. Please, I need to get back as swiftly as possible...it will help a lot and we can follow up the quest sooner than I had hoped."

At his last words he glanced towards Karma and then back to Jed, Urat smirked knowingly and then it seemed that everyone went back to staring at Jed.

He clucked his tongue impatiently and put a finger on his lips...there were consequences to certain types of transport travel...if he were to transport them using time then they would all knock off a week from their lives...but there were other ways. Turning back to the waiting group Jed nodded his head.

"I can transport us, but I'm going to need to be touching water while I do so…a lot of it, very cold…in fact almost freezing. It will help believe me, and I'm sorry but I can only transport myself and eight other humans and our own horses…they will have to travel normally" he jerked a thumb, indicating the soldiers behind them. Telric gave a nod and Urat went over to his men, after a few brief instructions they all turned as one and started off at a fast-paced trot towards the horizon, apart from Urat, two soldiers and the dwarf. When they rejoined the group of Questor's, Jed asked Autumn-Wind to make a move towards the village as fast as he was able. The horse obliged and set off at a bouncy trot that made Jed's teeth rattle and his voice box waver up and down as he answered questions.

"Why do you need water? Can't you just transport us here and now?" Telric asked as he managed to stay still in the saddle whilst Jed managed to feel sick.

"Normally I would," he replied, "but I'm tired. In the morning when you wake up and you're sleepy, have you ever splashed cold water on your face to feel more refreshed and less like going back to bed? It's the same with magic, when we mages get tired, we aren't strong enough to keep a hold of our power when we use it, if we're touching water we wake up and it helps. And when the water ripples it's just like a message tower that sends out signals to neighbouring cities, making us faster and more precise. After all transporting has its ups and downs. What if I were tired, what if I made a miscalculation, we could end up ten miles in the wrong direction and that could mean in the air or underground…you understand?" He finished, realising he had been partially babbling…but he couldn't help it, this was magic, this was educating someone and that meant learning which meant he was having fun.

When they reached the small village Jed was quite astonished to see how well the simple farmers lived, their homes quite large and their fields well laid. Crops grew high and men and women worked alongside each other to get the last of the harvest in before winter set in. He was also surprised and pleased at the short time it took to get a bucket of water to him…that was after everyone had come to shake Telric's hand and call him "My Lord" whilst smiling and offering cups of homemade soup and wine up to them all. As they ate and drank Telric went over instructions of the place he wanted them to get to. When the fussing was over and done with most of the villagers gathered round in a circle, eager to see the magic they had been told about in stories. Jed got off Autumn-Wind, asking the others to do the same and telling the horses what was going to happen so they wouldn't take fright and bolt off in every direction. Then he sat on the ground in a tailor position, legs crossed and hands on his knees, his Staff across his lap. After a moment of calm he reached out and draped his long fingers into the bucket before him; as soon as his fingers touched the icy cold water his head shot up and his magic turned into a livewire of excitement. Keeping his hands in the bucket; Jed closed his eyes and looked into himself, finding the chest inside his mind that held his power. In his own head he seemed to take out a glowing key and place it atop the chest, it opened up and light shone out of it, bathing him with warmth…as though he had stepped into a bubbling, balmy pool. The first thing he did was to dab an index finger into a pile of spirit and touch the metal around Karma's hands and neck…he watched carefully as they slid to the floor. Well at least he knew it had no impact on mortal magic. He reached out and grabbed a handful of glowing magic from each section within him, fire, water, earth, air and spirit; then he took part of each element and moulded it together to make the shapes of his companions, Urat, the two soldiers and the dwarf, adding layer after layer until they were thick and filled out, finally he grabbed a handful of magic for himself and wrapped it around his body. Now came the tricky part, Telric had told him that the place they needed to be was ninety eight miles away. It was the main city centre and they should end up in front of a large black flag with a silver dagger slashing across it diagonally that dripped red material at its point,a white border edged it and it was mounted on a carved wooden pole that looked like the tip piercing the flag's corner. Jed let his mind drift over the miles of land, faster and faster, nearer and nearer, he could see the flag fluttering from a distance and strived to meet it, he could now make out the design. He slowed so he wouldn't pass it. Twelve shimmering ropes came from the way he had come, one for each horse and person, grabbing each rope in turn and tugging he pulled hard, standing each person and beast beside him. Jed opened his eyes…

He, his friends, the man Urat, the soldiers and their prisoner were standing in a busy town square, blinking and looking around smiling. Women wearing stout woollen skirts in dark colours with deep necklines and their hair braided to their backs jumped out of the way in shock at suddenly seeing a large group of people appear out of nowhere. Soldiers that patrolled the streets raced forwards, swords drawn and angry shouts coming from their mouths. Telric and Urat reacted instantly by holding up their left hand palm up, showing them all the tattoo of a red rose with a long thorn dripping black blood from it, and telling them quite calmly and coolly who they were, and wondering why were they so surprised, had they never heard of magic before?

Jed stood shakily, the cool refreshment he had received from the bucket of cold water had vanished and he had to hold onto his staff to support himself. Whilst the other men sorted out the groups right to be in the city Jed took the time to take deep breaths and look around him. Men wearing short jackets that tied down one side and long breeches that were stuffed into the top of their knee-high boots glared at him as they shouted out their wares to others, telling them to come and see as they competed with neighbours nearby.

The houses rose to three stories in height, all made of stone with slate roofs and all looking strong and stable and hardy, as though they could easily withstand a small siege. Other men, obviously not merchants from their lack of products, hung around shadows in twos and threes; they all wore deep blacks and blues and greys ands greens, and when Jed and his friends had appeared all of them had watched with amused interest. Now and then one or two caught Telric's eye and each man exchanged a nod. Some men caught Telric's eye and gave a low bow that made their heads almost brush the pavement. Jed was able to take all this in whilst hearing Telric talk in a voice laced with amusement and cold humour, his air and body language holding a commanding presence. Lance grinned at some children, who sung a tune in the streets and joined in under his breath,

> *"Stroll down a dark and lonely street,*
> *Who do you greet there and whom do you meet?*
> *If you're a noble count to four,*
> *Hear the assassin at your door,*
> *If you're an innocent turn your head,*
> *If you don't then you'll be dead"*

Then the boy saw a group of street urchins, skinny and dirty, wearing rags that hung in tatters with their bare feet wrapped in strips of cloth, their eyes were large and hungry, their mouths fixed in a stubborn line and their gaze defiant and tired. There were eight of them all together, young and old and as soon as Lance gave them a wave they grinned, showing a gappy flash of small rotted teeth, then they ran off down a side alley laughing. As the last girl turned to scramble after them, her white hair in ragged curls to her shoulders, Jed thought he saw a flash of light surround her skinny, nimble form...but then it faded and she ran off. The wizard opened his mouth to call after her and then shook his head...it couldn't have been magic, he must just be tired and anyway he'd never heard of a female mage before.

He would have thought more about it had he not been bone weary, and suddenly a soft hand touched his arm and Karma tugged at his robe, the others were already starting to move away. Together he and his pitiful friend caught up and Jed found out that they were going to the assassin guild...via the palace gardens.

The palace was quite close to the city centre and it was magnificent, it had painted gold gates surrounding it and white marble and coloured mosaics glittered beautifully on its outer walls. Behind it, looming and overlooking the country like some giant guardian lay the mountain. Jed's eyes felt like they would pop out of their sockets as he stared around at everything, they rode past the gates easily, with friendly nods to the guards there. Jed hoped to go through the front doors that had carved people on them, noble kings holding swords high above their heads and women that had fish's tails instead of legs playing harps and beckoning people to enter. Instead they circled past the doors and round the palace. Telric lead them on Nightfall, through large training yards where warriors exercised with wooden practice swords and poles, sweating and breathing hoarsely as their superiors walked amongst them correcting a hold on a sword here or a thrust with a pole there.

Jed watched it all with a half-hearted interest, he was now too tired to do anything else and he hardly realised it when the party reached the foot of the mountain. They dismounted and Autumn-wind, Winter-sky, Nightfall, Jester and Urat's beast were led away, back towards the palace stables. They stood before a door carved of stone, at one side, halfway up, was a slot...an almost shapeless keyhole. Telric moved forwards and from the back of his belt he drew out an intricately designed dagger, it had a solid brass handle with a silver snake curving around it that had red jewels for eyes. The assassin put one finger on either side of the hilt and placed his thumb on the bottom of the pommel, then pushed upwards. The blade slowly slid apart from the tip and opened up to reveal a diamond key inside, Telric pulled it up and out of its secretive case, placed it in the slot and twisted three times to the right. Replacing it carefully he then took hold of a shapeless lump of rock by his left-hand side, that had seemed no different from the rest, and yanked downwards.

The door stood still for a moment and then slid to the side with a rough groan as stone slid over stone, a gap was left, big enough for a man to get through and not a centimetre more. Telric smiled, almost happily, and stepped inside, the others followed and their eyes met darkness.

*

A light was struck with a piece of flint and stone that lay on the floor, there were five wooden torches and Urat picked one up, and almost dropped it again when Jed reached out a hand to grasp a spark as it flew from the flint and drop it onto the torch-head. With a "whoomf!" noise the torch lit up brightly and Jed could see what looked like a narrow tunnel cut from stone that led away before them. His Staff shuddered when he had held the spark and now hid behind him...magical it may be but the thing still remembered that some staves could burn quite easily. They moved up the tunnel, the eerie quiet that had settled over them since leaving the town centre was broken when Karma gave a smile and said to Telric, "I remember this place...how long ago has it been since I last came here?"

The assassin grimaced, "Too long, for two whole years you went off, gallivanting about the world, trying to fight bandits and learn from others. That was until you grew lonely and asked me and Lance to come along for a while...I should have been back here months ago" he muttered with fake grumpiness, whilst smiling slightly, Karma laughed a little at his answer and then went quiet. Lance chuckled merrily as Urat winked to him and then tried to look innocent when Telric raised an eyebrow. Jed smiled weakly at them all and then looked up the tunnel, before them stood a small black door with a sliding hole at the top and no handle or keyhole, when they reached it Telric knocked three times and then waited. The hole slid open and revealed one bloodshot eye and a hooked nose. Telric pushed his left palm through the hole, once more showing the tattoo that was imprinted there. The eyes bobbed up and down as the man it belonged to nodded, the hole slid shut and there were numerous clinking, clunking sounds as locks were unbolted and keys were twisted. A minute later the door stood open and the small group were striding through and into a dimly lit box-like area, another door stood before them but this one had a handle and Lance jumped forward to push it open and run through into a vast hall decorated in deep, richly coloured mahogany and ebony, pictures of outstanding apprentices and assassins with a plaque over each (telling how they were killed in the line of duty and carelessness), were hung above a set of sweeping staircases that held plush red carpets running along them. Men and women moved through the halls quickly, some even carried book-satchels and looked only to be sixteen, it was just like the guild back home with the exception that everything seemed rich and expensive, and the feeling of death hung in the air overhead, they all gave a nod to Telric as he past them and they all smiled at Lance. The assassin turned around and opened his arms with a wide smile, "Come into my parlour said the spider to the fly" the assassin said, as though he was speaking to himself, then in louder tones he added, "welcome to my home Jed"

They were all lead to separate rooms and Telric told them that they could wander freely as long as they didn't go through doors that were guarded, he also showed them his study and said that if they needed him he would most likely be there and if he wasn't they should wait for a bit and he'd surely turn up. The halls of the guild seemed endless, with too many twists and turns to count. Karma was placed in the capable hands of the guild's maids and taken to her room, Lance shot off through an open door and into the mess hall to be greeted with cheers and laughter. He was soon heard playing a set of pan-pipes with enthusiasm. Jed saw Telric grin with fatherly affection at that, and Jed was put in a room that was two doors down from the guild leader, he wondered if Telric was being polite or cautious...

Stepping through the solid wooden doorway he was immersed in a warm red atmosphere, the floor was carpeted in a cushy, velvety material that had twisting eye patterns on it, the walls, which were carved from the mountain stone, had tapestries hung over their bare surface with pictures of legends sewn into them. Jed was amused to see one tapestry with a wizard on, shooting magic out from his fingertips, then his amusement faded, had mages really been away from the mainland so long that people thought they were nothing more than stories? He sighed and fell heavily onto a large four-poster bed with black silk sheets and the last thing he remembered seeing was the red rose that had been carved into the wooden headboard above.

CHAPTER TWELVE
Secrets

When Jed woke he had no idea how long he had slept, looking to the small desk on his left hand side he saw that someone had left a meal of citrus fruits and nut-bread on it, along with a small pitcher of wine and a cup of what seemed to be juice. Someone had also taken the time to put his glasses and hat on the bedside table and pull off his boots before shoving him under some sheets, Jed didn't care who that someone was but he gave a silent prayer of thanks to them anyway. A beaded doorway, which he had not noticed before, had steam coming out of it; tottering over on legs that were still half-asleep Jed peered into a room with white stone tiles and a tub with hot water that still steamed. Grinning happily Jed quickly shed his clothes to the floor and hopped in quickly.

After he had washed and taken the time to trim his beard and long hair neatly; with a pair of scissors that had been left alongside some soap and a washcloth, Jed got out and dried off. Wrapping a towel around his middle he went back into the main room and after putting on his glasses he spotted a brand new robe draped over a chair. Pulling it on he wrapped a black leather belt with a silver buckle around his waist and retied all his pouches and his purse to it, he also tugged on a pair of warm stockings and dark brown boots that fitted snugly and were immensely comfortable. The robe, which had a round golden collar that was attached at the back of the neck and seemed to be almost like a wide necklace, was a metallic green with gold blobs running down the long sleeves and around the edges of numerous pockets. His hat was the same dull green it had ever been (and Jed was glad of that) and his staff was also the same, plonking the hat on his head he sat down at the table to fulfil his ravenous appetite.

*

After finally finishing the large meal, Jed left his room and made his way down the hall to Telric's study. For once he wanted to be filled in on how long they were staying somewhere and how much time he had to explore...with the added hope that there would be a room in which he could exercise his magic. He had used it yesterday, that was true, but keeping it locked up for a week on the road hadn't helped and if he didn't let some out soon it would force a way out. Magic was like a well, it filled easily and from time to time you could bring buckets of it up and drink some. But at other times, when you hadn't drunk from it for a while, it overflowed and created a small flood that could cause large disasters.

When he reached the door to the study he knocked, waited then knocked again. No answer. Poking his head inside Jed saw that no one was there and he remembered Telric's words the day before, … "if I'm not there, just wait and I'll surely turn up within the hour".

Shrugging he went inside and shut the door behind him. Turning back round he gasped, the study was twice, if not thrice as big as his chamber had been and it was magnificent. A large black desk stood at the rooms centre, with piles of paper and writing inks cluttered around it. The floor was inlaid with red flagstone and on it, outlined in small ruby gems, were little dragons that breathed out painted fire and hid behind fake rosebuds. The walls had every sort of weapon imaginable hooked onto them, one wall seemed completely dedicated to bookshelves and glass-jars holding powders and pellets and liquids, the back wall, behind the desk, had Torath'Danars flag imprinted on it. The ceiling was a dispersal of silver pieces, placed around jaggedly and scattered amongst them were amethysts and snake sculptures with coloured eyes. The chairs were wrapped in soft black leather and were large enough to seat three children easily, the oil lamps and lanterns that were placed around the room refelcted off the silver on the ceiling to shine down on the floor below.

Jed's roving eyes went back to the desk in front of him, piled high as it was with what seemed like clutter, paper lay about in heaps, packages were sprawled on top of them and under Telrics chair, half-peaking out from behind the cushion, was a little black book. Jed's curiosity was piqued and his fingers twitched as he reached for it, slipping it out easily and flicking through the pages.

The book kept falling open in one place, as though someone had read it over and over again and the paper had become creased. Jed sat down automatically and started to read...

Lori Allan- aged thirty-eight, killed in the first year of the guild's revival, daughter of rich merchant, ransom was not received.

Tomi Farspread- aged twelve, killed in the first year of the guild's revival, son of nobleman in Morad'ead, did not change vote for head of council.

Jason Draft- aged twenty-four, hunted down for crimes against the guild, killed after several days of torture.

He soon realised that it was not a book, nor a diary; it was a ledger. A way to keep track of the dead and the deeds done to them, it was full. Page upon page of names and deaths and descriptions, he shuddered as he thought of them all.

Jed would have read more, but it was at that exact moment that the handle on the door leading to the study started to turn…

*

Jed's eyes widened and he did three things at once, he shut the book with a snap, shoved it back underneath the chair he had been sitting on and took four strides towards the other side of the room, managing to put a thoughtful finger on his lip, as though he was interested in the flag he faced.

The door opened and Telric came into the room, laughing to someone over his shoulder, when he turned he saw Jed and raised an eyebrow in surprise.

"I expected you to sleep for longer, seeing as how you were so tired yesterday, what can I do for you Jed?" he asked, coming to stand next to him. Jed flushed, feeling guilty at having read the ledger and also curious and intrigued. Were there other such books? Why had they been written at all? What was to gain from the names of those listed except the memory of what had been done to them? He coughed and quickly remembered why he had come to the assassin's office in the first place.

"Err…yes, I…I was wondering if you could tell me when we'd be off again?" he muttered, Telric didn't seem to notice his extra edginess or blithering and replied.

"We're going when we can, it may take a week or so…"

Jed's staff froze in the air and turned, *"A week? A whole week maybe even more? Karma could be dead by then! The high Azale could be overrun!"*

Jed opened his mouth to agree when his jaw froze in shock…Telric turned to look at the staff, the assassin was the first to react.

"It can talk? Gods, Goddesses and the Lore we live, that lump of wood can TALK!" his normally cool composure melted, he was staring at the staff as though it would turn into a deity to smite him. Jed's jaw unfroze and he let out a high-pitched, girlish shriek.

"ArgghhhhhhhHHHHHHHH!" he then promptly hitched up his robes to the knee and ran to hide behind Telric. The assassin pushed him away with disgust and they both listened in shock as the staff spoke again.

"Yes I can and I'm not a 'lump of wood' I'll have you know, I am a magical instrument...we have feelings too!" Then the carvings on it flowed into a face-shape and it turned to Jed, *"You know for a wizard who has just found out that his staff is intelligent enough to have a mind of its own, you seem very much like a housewife who's seen a dead rat in the larder"*.

Jed's eyes were fixed on his staff as he managed to squeak, "You have your own mind and you never even told me? I've carried you around for fourteen years...of course I'm shocked!"

Telric slowly sunk into a chair and looked on in amazement as Jed and the staff proceeded to argue.

"Well you never asked me whether or not I could speak to you, you didn't even bother using magic through me the first month you owned me...so I decided to keep a few secrets of my own" the staff shot back and then floated slowly forward.

"A few secrets of your OWN? Listen here staff...I was already upset that I had such a hyperactive and overly powerful wooden contraption as you. Lore, as soon as you were placed in my hand you tried to drag me into the air. I was upset, only just turned sixteen and not in control of my actions. Besides, I didn't want to draw attention to the fact you were so powerful, Hassid might have tried some nasty trick" Jed's voice now took on a note of fear as he once again remembered that day. He suddenly fell silent and scuffed a shoe, looking at the floor. He knew he should be thankful to have such an intelligent staff, they were supposed to be of immense help and good friends to their owner. Glancing at it he blew out his cheeks in confusion.

"You really kept it a secret for that long? Without even an inkling of suspicion on my behalf?"

The staff gave a nod in the air, *"Mostly, there were times when I did speak to you. I helped you out...but I did it so that you would think that you were thinking the words. Lately however you've been wondering about my little side-thoughts...I knew I couldn't keep it away from you much longer, better to get it out in the open"* it turned to regard Telric and its carved eyebrows were brought down as it frowned.

"And what about the original question, a week is far too long, be reasonable. A few days are all we can afford to be here"

Jed nodded in silent agreement, it wasn't until later on that he realised that his staff had changed the subject quite effectively, yet at that time he was too worried about what would happen to Karma to think otherwise.

The assassin put up his hands in self-defence, "It can't be helped, the king is raising an army, and I'm sending half of my guild members up there. Ragea's going to have a huge number of evil beasts at his command; we need time to prepare. You can't expect me, Karma, Jed and Lance to go up there on our own and face a few thousand dark Azale single-handedly"

"Lance? Lance is going? Telric how old is he, ten? He's a boy for Lore's sake, see reason man," Jed frowned, but Telric was already shaking his head.

"I can't leave him here, I have too many enemies who will use him as leverage on me and in my business I need no ties. If he's with me I can protect him and keep a watchful eye, nothing will happen whilst I'm at the guild. My members already know what I do to deserters and those who bungle too many jobs. They can hardly fathom what I'd do to someone who hurt that kid" his eyes glinted coldly as he said it. Jed felt a headache coming on.

Rubbing his temples with shaking fingers he moaned, "What did I do to get mixed up with assassins and boy-thieves and evil warlords? All I had to do was find a nice quiet quest to go and complete and I'm stuck trying to overthrow a mad-man whilst talking to someone who's five steps ahead of me and finding out I have a talking staff that likes keeping secrets. Tell me, where did I go wrong?" At the last words he threw his arms up in the air dramatically, Telric shook his head and chuckled quietly.

"What you did was catch Karma's eye by starting a brawl in a tavern, and you ended up with us because every man I know has a weak spot for her smile. I'm one of them" he stood and sighed, two fingers pinched the bridge of his nose and he blinked heavily; he had dark bags under his eyes and his face was pale and gaunt. Steering Jed towards the door he asked, "Is there anything else, because I am terribly busy and terribly tired and the sooner you leave me alone to finish my piles of work", he indicated the hulking heap of paper strewn across the desk, "then the sooner we can actually go and finish this quest and you can go back to your little guild and be admired and remembered in the eyes of all Azale everywhere as a hero"

Before he was practically shoved out of the office alongside his staff, Jed thrust a foot in the door.

"There was one thing actually" he went on quickly as Telric groaned, "I was wondering if you knew of anyone who could show me around town. I've never been off the West Isles before and I would like to explore...if that's alright" he ended pathetically.

The assassin thought for a moment and then grinned, almost evilly. "Work can wait, I know someone who can help you out..."

*

Telric led Jed through the winding corridors of the guild and into the mess-hall were most of the assassins spent their spare time, Lance seemed to spend all his time there and loved to entertain the older men with a set of pan pipes for money and puzzles and riddles. He also made it a point to practice charming any available woman within a few metres; one glance from those bright, innocent wide eyes was enough to find him on a comfy lap to be spoilt for hours. It was a large room, with a high ceiling that held timber crossbeams and a huge fireplace that was of carved marble. There were black and blood red tables everywhere and men and women alike sat in shadows with fine wine placed before them in silver chalices as they chuckled quietly among their fellow killers. When their guild-master appeared they gave shouts to tell him to come and join them. Telric was also informed that he appeared to have a second-shadow (Jed dare not stray too far from his friend in the dangerous atmosphere). The guild leader gave a small smile and waved them off with a hand. Lance gave a grin and followed them, chattering away about how he had won at dice and cards and how many new riddles he had to add to his collection, he also whispered that some of the members were restless and bored. They needed something to do or they might think of something themselves...and he hinted that Telric would not like that something at all. The man nodded and went to sit in a tall backed chair, Jed and Lance were left to stand next to him as he called out, "Where's Jay? He's normally fooling about in here by now, someone go and get the useless sop"

Two youths, apprentices by the eager look on their young faces, jumped to the task and set off at a run. Telric turned back to Jed, "If you want a guide around here the best man you can find is Jay, he's a court bard and jester for King Saia...in his spare time he's a gambler and a courtesan. Always on the lookout for a pretty smile and a glass of good wine, he's witty, clever and hilarious. He's also a spy for me and does a damn good job. Jay is everyone's friend, he can weasel into the tightest circle of cutthroats and discover their deepest secrets within a few hours…you can't help but like the man," he grinned and shook his head in a wry chuckle. Jed secretly moaned to his staff *"Great the exact opposite of me then."*

It answered back, *"Stop being such a spoilsport and for once try and live a normal life. Go on, get your nose out of your books and learn how to play a tavern game…you know what game means, yes? The thing where you actually have 'fun' for a change"*

Finding no sympathy Jed moaned to himself, *"Brilliant, I have to be shown around by a madman and that I have a talking staff that is sarcastic all in one day, thank you Gods".*

The two lads who had run off promptly returned with a tall man in tow. He wore an array of eye-wrenchingly bright material, of golds and reds and blues and silvers, all made of silk. His collar was long and had spikes at its end and bells on the spikes; he wore a long, flapping cloak that had what seemed to be hundreds of different pockets sewn onto it. His eyes were chestnut-red, his hair was light auburn and he had perfectly tanned skin with even, white teeth. Jed disliked him instantly. Hearing this remark his staff butted in again, *"Now you're just being childish"*. Jed didn't care and lurked by Telric's chair as the over-enthusiastic boys unhanded the jester and he turned on them in mock fury.

"An outrage you young cads! An outrage I say! Touching one who is superior in wit, intelligence and loving charm," he gave a grin to a woman who was sitting at a nearby table and then turned back to the boys, "in such a crude manner…aren't you lucky that I'm kind and modest too? Here," he tossed them each a gold coin from a hand that had been empty a minute ago and then told the boys to be off. Turning he swirled his cloak, made a huge, overdramatic stride to Telric and gave a stupidly amusing bow, much to the delight of his audience, when he straightened he dropped the act and gave a sidelong grin.

"Well now, didn't expect you to be back for some time you useless gallivanting twit who dares to call me a friend. How have you been?" Telric was about to answer when Jay's attention shifted to Lance (who had been trying to steal the jesters juggling balls that hung from his belt). Picking him up by the back of his shirt he gave a grin, Lance grinned back and put on an 'innocent little boy' face.

"Don't try that on me Lance lad, I taught you it!"

The room burst into laughter as Lance objected heatedly.

"Na ya didn't! I learnt that on t' streets mate!"

Jay raised an eyebrow, put the boy on the floor, whisked out a pipe from his pocket and blew a sombre note.

"Is that a challenge me boy?" he asked, eyes sparkling with life and laughter. Lance was about to answer when Telric clapped a hand over his mouth and rolled his eyes.

"Why is it that whenever you two get together you end up playing silly boys games?"

"I object strongly sir, they are anything BUT silly...and anyway I am a boy, or didn't you notice you crippled old man?" Jay cried out in a young child's voice.

The cape whisked again and when it settled Jay was partially hidden underneath it. He was on his knees and had stretched his face to resemble that of a young street waif, tugging his sleeves to pull out more material, making his arms look as though they were too short for them. The room burst into laughter once more with a scattering of applause and Jed found himself smiling along with them, Jay seemed to be bursting with energy and a need to entertain. Yet again he had jumped up, tugged his clothes back into place and was gripping Jed's hand in a firm shake.

"Nice to meet you sah, I'm Jay the magnificently marvellous man and joyously jesting jester, among other things, how do you do?"

Jed was allowed to pull his hand back and replied, "Erm...well I'm Jed the mage, I'm fine thank you...and yourself?"

He was clapped on the back and told, "Never better old chum, you know they say you can't keep a good dog down? Well the same goes for me...Telric why on earth did you get two of your little lackeys to pull me over here if you weren't bored? Goddesses help you if you did it just to show others you could...I was having a wonderful conversation with a female friend of mine" he sighed, Telric laughed openly.

"And we all know you have many of them. No, I didn't get them to yank you over here by your ear-hole just to prove something. I need you to show Jed around the town, and hopefully keep him out of trouble and out of my way whilst I do a little war-waging, think you can do that for me friend?" he asked with glinting eyes.

Jay put up a hand, "Say no more sir, if it's a night out that needs to be planned you've come to the right man. Drinks, games, sight-seeing...that sound good enough?"

Telric nodded and sat back in his chair, Jed was about to call his staff (which was floating around the ceiling beams) to hand when his power poked him. He needed to let some of it flood out of him before it decided to force a way out itself, and who knew what trouble that would make? He was already feeling a trickle escape from his control, turning back to Telric he blushed when the man sighed and frowned.

"What now?"

"I need to let some of my power out...otherwise it's going to push itself out. Have you got a room I can let it go in?" he asked quietly, Telric waved an arm around him "How about here? I'm sure my members would enjoy it"

Jay grinned, "Wot? Magic show old man? Excellent, I shall inform the ladies and gents eh?" and without another word he strode into the middle of the room.

Jed glared at Telric, who shrugged apologetically, and followed the fool to stand on a dais. Jay swaggered around until he had caught everyone's attention and then threw out a hand whilst announcing the wizard.

"Masters, mistresses, ladies and gents...and Lance" he added the last when the boy jumped up onto the stage to follow him around and mimic his moves, making the most of the assassin's laughter.

"Today you are about to behold a wonder that fled from Mog's mainland aeons ago, well...to be precise only ninety years ago, but well before my lifetime anyway. A sight that will shock and amaze, stun, startle and flabbergast you all. For today my friends we have magic amongst us and mystic mayhem for the mind to devour. It is my overall delight, my jumping joy and the pinnacle of my pleasure to introduce for you...Jed the mage"

He finished with a bow, bounded off the stage, catching Lance who jumped off after him and grabbing his juggling balls from the boy, then went to join Telric at his table, leaving Jed under the scrutiny of a hundred or so faces that were half-hidden by shadows. He gulped audibly and froze. His staff came to hover beside him and nudge him mentally, *"Remember the illusion team tryouts? Give them some illusions; make a few things move. Wave your arms around mysteriously and no matter what keep your face straight. It's quite simple really".*

Jed nodded and smoothed his face, making it wise and foreboding, he raised a hand and shot it out, then pulled it forward...a chair behind him slid forward with a groan and he sat on it. Closing his eyes for a second he unlocked his chest of power and dove into the well that lay beyond, he opened his eyes again...this time to see what he could use his power on.

Jed remembered seeing the snake and rosebud design on the fireplace that was behind him, grinning he put both hands together and rubbed them fiercely. A drone of noise filled the air and his hands got hotter and hotter, after a minute of this he yanked them apart and held them palm up...a small, flickering fireball rested in each hand and suddenly rose into the air. They hovered for a split-second and then raced off towards the captivated audience, zigzagging from side to side and 'whooshing' past people's heads. Abruptly they flew back towards Jed, moved around his body and jammed into the red ruby eyes of the silver snake sculptures behind him. The eyes glowed softly and the snakes began to move...

They slithered along the fireplace's ledge and there melted together into one large reptile, leaving two smaller ones on either side of it. They hissed with a lifelike essence and swayed and watched carefully as the rosebuds decoration around the fireplace started to grow. The grass green vines wrapped around walls and along the floor, up chair legs, springing up in clumps on tabletops. The snakes slunk forward and all of a sudden their heads came up with a sharp hiss.

The fireplace flickered and went out. Torches around the room died instantly and shutters unrolled over windows. The room had been flung into a dark, cold world.

And as rapidly as they had gone out, the torches burst back into life, shutters folded up and the fire gave a roar as it flamed again.

The roses now covered the entire room, it was like sitting in a chamber built from leaves and flowers. The three snakes had curled around Jed's chair and staff, hissing softly, looking deadly beautiful.

Lance reached out a hand to pluck a rosebud from the wall, and the illusion sunk into itself in an instant. The snakes were once again just sculptures and the roses now only decorated the fireplace, and they were carvings...nothing more. Jed stood and his chair floated back to its original place. he grasped the staff in his left hand and gave a small bow. When he straightened he felt worried...nothing had happened...did they not like the illusion? Had it been that bad? He bit his lip in confusion and was about to try edging away towards the door when Telric stood up and clapped. Lance and Jay joined in with enthusiasm and everyone else there practically jumped to their feet, some men and women actually came forward to clap him on the back and compliment him. But before everyone in the room rushed forward to try and do the same thing, thus creating a small stampede, Jay bounded forward and pushed Jed from the hall, calling out apologies and farewells as he went.

Jed didn't care, he was grinning, and feeling immensely proud and he had a talking staff.

Life was starting to take a shine to him.

CHAPTER THIRTEEN
A New Magician

A few hours later Jed found himself in the heart of Torath'Danars capital, Hidden-Heights, in a tavern with a tankard of something very enjoyable in front of him. Jay had been playing a lyre for everyone in the tavern to dance to, but now he stopped for a rest and to take a huge gulp from his own glass chalice, filled with rich and spicy smelling wine.

"You know for such a powerful country, you must have a rather stupid king" Jed slurred after throwing the rest of his drink down his throat and sniffing loudly.

The jester raised his eyebrows in surprise, "Why do you say that?"

"Well, so far I've seen at least a hundred assassins hanging around the streets in clumps...the guards ignore them completely and they seem to be able to get away with murder, literally. Lore, if I was king of this country I'd have sorted the guild out years ago" he waved a hand with a nod of his head, images of himself sitting on a cushy throne with a golden crown and decent haircut floating around in his mind. Jay gave him a sincere look and then (after calling a barmaid for more drinks) he looked Jed square in the eye. "And what if Telric sorted out the country instead of the king sorting out the guild?"

"Say what?" said Jed

"Listen, a huge operation like the assassin guild could not work in a...a decent well meaning country. Here it's different; Telric tells the king what to do. Heck, he runs this place single-handedly because he can't trust anyone else to do it. I've heard tell of his sleepless nights and most days the servants find him asleep at his desk with piles of papers still to be signed and sealed. He has a hand in just about every other country in Mog as well. He has information that some spies couldn't dream of getting, he's got all the nobles of this world on edge and in his favour for fear of a dark dagger in the night. He's a tactical genius, let alone a scholar of notable depth. Lore! He can pull off any act twice as well as me, if I had his sort of mimicry talent I'd have full coffers by now. He's invented poisons; diseases and antidotes no one else would dare think up, in short he's a genius, this country's lucky to have such a man like him running things behind the scenes." He finished with a prideful smile and a half-smirk, Jed looked into his new tankard wondering how many he had already had of...well, he didn't know what it was...but it was nice. It made him feel tingly and happy. His staff sulked next to him, propped up on the wall, as it was the thing was not very happy because he'd been instructed not to talk...it'd scare too many people. Jed ignored it and went on asking questions.

"But...it makes no sense, if the Tor'Dans have such a 'hidden leader' that sneaks about and manipulates everybody so much, why don't they rise up and overthrow him?"

Jay chuckled and shook his head, "Because Telric has them on his side; he gets the best from other countries for the people and himself. They like the way things work out, he rules and they get a decent price for just about anything. And they get it all for being good and agreeing with the man who's helping them. It's the best deal they've ever had in their lives!" he gave another laugh and clapped Jed on his back, making him cough and splutter the mouthful of ale he had just gulped.

Jay then stood and went over to a maid, after a sly grin and a few words he slipped a coin onto her tray and came and sat back down again.

"What was all that about?" Jed mumbled, still coughing and whacking himself on the chest.

"Since you're in the best tavern I know and since you wanted to see the sights of Hidden-Heights...I thought you might like to try one of our delicacies here, caught fresh every day and cooked up within minutes" Jay answered.

Soon the waitress he had spoken with came back holding a steaming dish that smelt divine, plonking it onto the table in front of Jed she smiled to Jay and then rushed off to see to another customer.

Jed's nose thought the food smelt wonderful, his eyes did not. The thing before him had tentacles, was covered in a thin, watery soup and was purple and red. He picked up a fork and poked it, a tentacle bobbed up and down on the soups surface. Jed poked it again. Jay gave him an odd look and laughed, "What are you waiting for?"

He replied in a sincere and honest tone, "I'm waiting for it to move, I'm sure this thing is still alive," he poked it again and made a face, oblivious to the peals of laughter that Jay was desperately trying to repress. In the end the jester had to wheedle and plead for Jed to even try a mouthful...and though it did taste delicious, a mouthful was all he would eat...because as soon as he'd finished it, the drink he still slurped kicked in and he slumped backwards in his chair.

Jed woke again when his nose was filled with a disgusting scent, opening his eyes and shrivelling his face with displeasure he noticed that the stench came from a vial that Jay had thrust under his nose. Jed tried to clear the smell from his head by waving a hand about whilst shakily getting to his feet and asking, "What in the name of Lady Luck is that?"

The jester tucked it away into one of the numerous pockets on his cloak and then replied, "Potent-Drifter, a bit like smelling salts but with more kick to it...very handy to have when your friend inconveniently slips into unconsciousness because he can't handle his drink" he gave a roguish grin to Jed and then dropped it when Jed almost fell backwards whilst holding his head between both hands and groaning. He'd never felt so strange in his life.

"Here now, are you alright? Can you stand or do you need carrying?" Jay asked. Jed muttered an unintelligible answer and suddenly felt as though he was drifting along easily. Looking down he saw that his staff had caught him from falling onto the floor and was now floating along, carrying him.

"Did I know you could do that?" said Jed.

"No you didn't, I wouldn't get used to it mind...this is only temporary," came the reply. Jed didn't care and nodded whilst he, his staff and Jay went back to the guild. He'd had quite enough of sightseeing for a while...even if all he had really seen was the bottom of his cup.

*

As soon as the group of three were outside in the main entranceway, Lance appeared at the top of the stairs; spotting them he slid down the banister and ran towards them. His chest was heaving and his brow was covered in sweat, he panted as though he had been running for a long time. When he reached them he gulped and placed his hands on his knees. Between trying to draw deep breaths he managed to say, "I've bin looking fer you lot everywhere...I went...all...over...town...Telric wants to see you in his office Jed, right now...he says its 'portant and involves...the quest." Then he stopped heaving and coughed heartily, groaning he fell onto Jay (who rolled his eyes at the boy and then lifted him up onto broad shoulders). After a quick glance at Jed he pulled out a small packet from yet another pocket and thrust it into his hand. "Here, swallow that before you sleep where you stand, it'll keep your lids open for an hour or so...can you remember the way back to Telric's office?"

His staff replied for his master whilst Jed opened the packet and gulped down the small green pill that was inside,

"I remember, all he has to do is hang on, goodbye Jay", and with that it took off up the stairs, leaving the stunned jester to glare at Lance who was chortling at his friend's shock.

"Did you tell me that thing could talk?" said Jay.

*

A minute after Jed had swallowed the tablet, the weariness that gripped his mind and body slipped away and he felt refreshed. The drug left him feeling as though from a good nights sleep. His staff had stopped outside Telric's study. Half-falling and half-sliding off his trusty steed Jed thanked it and gave a knock on the door, he heard a voice cry from within, "Finally!" and then Telric was dragging him in by the arm and pushing him into one seat and carefully propping his staff against the other. The assassin gave them an excited smile and sat in his own chair, leaning forward he asked.

"Jed...do you know anything about the Forbidden Realms?"

The mage nodded, he remembered reading and learning a little of them when he was younger.

"Yes, it's where all the magical creatures, faeries and sprites fled to aeons ago...the unicorns sealed all the land's boundaries and no human can enter unless one of the creatures brings him or her through...or unless they have amazing strength in their magic." He would have gone on for a while except to Telrics right a faint black, misty substance was forming in the air.

It frothed and bubbled down to the ground and then up again, all of a sudden it dispersed and in its place was a huge tiger...but it was not like the usual orange and black striped tigers Jed had read about in his biology and healing-help classes. This one had a black coat and silver and white stripes, its eyes shone golden and it was at least ten feet long from nose to tail-tip. It gave a massive shake of its shaggy head and licked its lips...then, quite clearly, it said "Actually that is not entirely true, for a start we magical beasts did not 'flee' to the Forbidden Realms, we went there of our own accord. Secondly not all of us live there the other...darker creatures amongst us live in the Northern Reaches."

Jed's face twitched, frozen in fear, his throat was too tight to scream and his nostrils were flaring for air...his staff sighed wearily and told him to stop acting like a girl-child and answer back politely.

Telric gave a smile and said, "Don't scream, this is Zeta...a Stalker from the Forbidden Realms, Zeta meet Jed...a cowardly lump who has the advantage of being a powerful mage. Jed, he has information that we can use." Jed was clearly excited about meeting a creature of legend and was doing his best not to burst out with questions. Turning back to Zeta, Telric said, "Please, would you mind repeating to my friend what you have just finished telling me? It would be a great help."

The huge beast nodded and stretched luxuriously then turned to Jed (who had now gotten over his fears and was itching to get his hands on pen and paper so he could start writing answers to questions there and then) and said, "A couple of weeks ago an Eternal runner came down from the High Azale with a message that he was meant to give to a group known throughout the land as 'The Questors'...but he was followed by a handful of northern warriors...me and my kind can only presume they were sent from Ragea Atia, that mad-man who rules over the Dark Lands. He reached the furthest boundary of my homeland and would have been killed if a passing Stalker had not pulled him through and into safety. As it was he died from his wounds a handful of hours later, but he asked the Stalker to get this message to 'The Questors' so a meeting between my kind was set and I was chosen to bring this to you, being the fastest there." Zeta smirked at the last sentence and had a decidedly smug look on his face, and no-one can look as smug as a cat. Then he continued "So here I am...I must admit that I'm quite shocked from your appearance and initial reaction at seeing me, the last wizard I ever knew was worldly wise and well travelled...you seem...different somehow" he creased his velvety forehead and cocked his head to the side in puzzlement, Jed blushed.

"Well...that's because no wizard has travelled away from the Western Isles and the guild for over ninety years. I'm the first and I got out...sort of by accident" he winced remembering being shoved out of the guild door, bags tossed after him and the Archmage's face purple with anger, shouting "And don't come back till you've finished a quest. By the time you're done, mayhap I will be able to get some work done instead of having to get you out of mess you've concocted!"

Shaking the image off, it was Jed's turn to be puzzled.

"I'm sorry but I've got to ask, you said Ragea Atia ruled over the

Dark Lands and that black mist that was here when I sat down...is it your own type of magic?" he would have asked more but Telric raised an eyebrow and shook his head firmly Zeta, however, seemed happy to answer.

"We within the Forbidden Realms call the Northern Reaches, the Dark Lands...have you never noticed that all darkness and evil in this world seems to either be drawn to go up there or comes down from there? And yes the black mist is my own type of magic, we Stalkers are mages within our own right and the best hunters around, the unicorns are healers and hiders" he answered.

"Hiders?" This time the question came from Telric, Zeta gave him an odd look.

"Yes, Hiders...you know...their magic can be used to hide important things from anyone but themselves, they hide their foals that way so no enemies can kill the young ones when their parents go up to the grazing grounds. A very worthwhile trick if you ask me, I wish I had it three years ago" he said, his head hung low. Jed pulled his chair closer so he could get every reaction and hear everything.

"Why, what happened three years ago?" he asked quietly, the Stalker's nose scrunched up in a silent sniffle and he lifted amber-gold eyes to gaze at Jed.

"My mate had a cub, one solstice eve I went to hunt for her and when I came back she and my son were both dead, a rival Stalker who wanted my home for himself had come across them whilst he was seeking battle with me and killed them out of spite. You see when they have a cub by their sides, our females cannot use their magic...and they can only ever have one cub every three years. If I had the magic of a Hider my son at least would have lived on." His head sunk to the ground and Jed gave him a sympathetic stroke, his fingers found that Zetas fur was like smooth velvet.

Telric had remained quiet throughout the Stalker's small story but now he spoke, "I'm sorry for your hurt, I know what loss feels like; so you have my sympathy and understanding...but would you please give us the message from the Azale runner? Time is of the essence here."

The great cat nodded solemnly and lifted his head to its usual position, "Forgive me, it's one weakness of my kind to feel compassion and express our feelings and hurts with others, I hope I haven't lowered myself in your eyes."

Sitting back on his haunches, Zeta raised his forepaws and waved them in a strange manner, then his very long tail flicked forward over each shoulder and finally he spoke in a language that Jed did not know. The black mist came back and a roll of parchment dropped out of its depths and onto Telric's desk. The assassin picked it up and broke the wax seal on its side, a pointed ear next to a shining eye that threw off sparks of magic. He quickly scanned the page with his bleak eyes and smiled sadly before passing it to Jed.

The wizard read the message with more care:

Questors
~Friends we greet you with joy, we have been told of your noble journey and wish you to know that your names will be written in our history and years from now you will be well known heroes. We write this message to help you in the only way we can, our spies were able to give us this small slice of information before they were sadly collared.

Ragea Atia now commands the evil beasts in the Northern Reaches, they number by the hundreds, his own army of dark Eternal and men number close to fifty thousand and he has a fist of seers, one is known as 'Mysticism' and has the true sight, be careful of your moves and plans for she will surely see some of them.

Make haste.

~Your faithful servants
The High Azale of the Northern Reaches

Jed turned to regard Telric and saw the grey worry on his face that reflected his own and heard him sigh, "This is useless, my guild members number to five-hundred all in all and I can only spare half of them...where are we going to raise an army to match his within a week? And how much time does Karma have left?"

Jed shook his head, it did seem hopeless...then his staff perked up and butted into the conversation.

I remember you reading a book on battle tactics for war mages once...it said something about 'winning by making the main piece of the domino chain fall'...but that's all I can remember, can you think of anything to add?

It seemed that Telric and Zeta had heard the exchange as well, the cat shook his head but the assassin lifted a finger.

"Wait, I know what that means...have you ever made a domino chain?"

"Yes, of course I have"

"Well then, what happens when you tap the first piece to start the chain off?"

"Simple, the others fall from the weight of the piece and in the end, if your chain has been set up right, all the pieces are down"

Telric clapped his hands together and spread his arms, "Exactly, don't you see? Ragea is the first piece, if he falls then the rest should fall too, without a leader the army will be in confusion and we can use that to our advantage! All it will take is a stab in the back in the dark, perfect for my skills wouldn't you say?" He gave a grin, a dagger whipped out from a sleeve, whirled around his fingers and then slipped back into its hidden sheath within a trice. Zeta gave a low purr that Jed realised was the big cat's way of laughing and he himself smiled, it was true…but there was a catch.

"What about Karma?"

Telric's face fell for an instant and then it brightened, "I can get that information out of him with truth serum whilst I hold a knife to his neck…simple enough I'm sure," he nodded, as though assuring himself.

Jed agreed, as did Zeta, man and Stalker looked at each other with a smile, then the tablet Jay had given him to ward off sleep wore off, Jed's eyelids drooped and he yawned, standing he gave each of his friends a small nod.

"Forgive me, I am tired…I think that now we've sorted this out, I'll be a-bed" he turned to go, staff following along behind, when he opened the door he turned back, "when are we leaving?"

Telric grinned "We'll be setting off the day after the morrow, that should give you time to rest, me time to finish a bit more work and Zeta the time to prepare the cloaking spell he uses to travel about in light. Goodnight wizard," he said roughly. Jed gave a laugh and then left to go and sink into silk sheets, goose-feather stuffed pillows and the land of nod where he kept dreaming that a pair of violet eyes watched him and a high-pitched laugh followed him as he ran through corridors of an unknown place amongst the clouds.

*

The following day Jed woke at noon to find that his robe from the day before had been taken away and replaced with a red and black robe of simple if effective design and his saddlebags. Changing, he went over his things to find that his books needed to be re-spelled against dirt and water and that his usual, old, fraying cotton robe needed to be cleaned. Sighing he re-sung the spell over his books and picked up the dirty robe to go and clean it, when he felt something heavy and slim wrapped inside. After unravelling the cloth he found the silver flute with the red-ruby dragon pattern inside, smiling as he remembered the day he had received it. The flute glinted slightly as he moved it closer to the lamplight. He was about to put it to his lips and see how it sounded when his staff gave a start and said, *'Stop messing about, that robe won't get washed on its own you know...and I'm sure this guild will have a tailor somewhere in its depths, you need more than one robe...in fact you could use some travelling clothes. Do you know how many staffs snigger behind my back because of the fraying things you wear?'*

Jed sighed, the blasted thing was right. He placed the flute back into his pack, shoving it between a leather-bound volume of 'A hundred different spells of protection and single-handed sorcery' and a skin roll of writing tools. After washing his robe in the tub of water that he had bathed in the day before, he left it still dripping over a handrail and went to sit on his bed, cross-legged.

"What are you doing now?"

"I'm going to take some information from one of the assassins in the guild, I need to know how to get around this place if I have to get travelling clothes," he answered the now floating wood that had asked the question. His staff muttered and then came to hover at his side.

Jed gripped it in one hand and then went inside his head, finding the chest there he unlocked it with his key and let magic spill out onto his hands. The magic filled his view for a second or so and then the glow dimmed and he saw a path leading up to a blue-stone well, glaring at the path he put his hands to his hips and disappeared, he appeared a moment later next to the well and pulled a bucket up from the depths there. Taking a sip of the refreshing stuff he cupped some in his hands and watched as it sunk into his skin, then he grasped a thread of spirit and a handful of raw power and wound them together. Sending his mind out he found an assassin a few corridors away from his room, diving into his mind Jed grasped the power and sent it around the man's brain until it zipped back into his hands with what looked like a map. Using the thread of spirit he made a copy, sent the original map back into the man's head and then placed the copy into his own memory.

Returning to his body Jed shut the chest and opened his eyes. The first thing he saw was Zeta, the huge Stalker sat before him, gazing on with interest, Jed got up hurriedly and remembered something the great cat had said the night before.

"Good day Zeta...err...last night, I asked about your magic and you said you were a mage?"

Zeta yawned and nodded "Yes you did and I am...I know it seems rude to intrude but I have waited all morning and when I did check you were awake. I wondered if you would like to swap a few spells? I'm extremely curious about human spells and how they would work with my type of magic"

Jed grinned, here was a creature after his own heart, as the very same thought had popped into his mind "Of course you can! I'd be delighted to swap with you, in fact could we talk whilst I go to the tailors? My staff seems to think I need travelling clothes"

"That is fine, but really I don't see what it is with humans and clothes, I manage fine without them and I seem to have turned out all right," he answered whilst they both went out the door, Jed chuckling at the remark and his staff putting in a sour comment.

CHAPTER FOURTEEN
Freedom and Fur

The day with Zeta passed quickly, Jed found that the Stalker-mage had the same curiosity with everything as he did and they both enjoyed learning more spells, reading about the history of magic and how certain spells were used in certain ways at times of certain doom. They both swapped spells till the evening meal and practiced each spell as they learnt it, creating pleasing effects for passers-by to watch. In the end Jed's staff had to half-drag him towards the tailors (which he had forgotten to go to whilst getting caught up in the whiz of magic). Soon they had no more spells to swap...at least, no spells that they were 'allowed' to swap with anyone outside their own magic group, Jed came away from the tailors with an armful of breeches, black leather belts, cream coloured shirts and fur lined grass-green jackets for extra warmth. He even had a pair of knee-length boots hanging around his neck. When both he and his companion were back in Jed's room he was about to drop the heavy pile on his bed when his beard got in the way of a foot, tripped him and sent Jed flying forwards scattering the neat pile of folded clothes everywhere. He cursed and then glared at the beard and sighed heavily; clicking his fingers and shaking a hand he muttered a word and the clothes flew back into their neat piles and onto his bed. Zeta gave a purr-chuckle and jumped up alongside the bed, half of his body hung over the side and the mattress groaned and sagged underneath the creature's bulk. Stretching he rolled over onto his back in a rather kittenish way and said, "Why don't you cut your beard and hair? It must be a nuisance to have them that long"

Jed nodded, "Hot in summer, long, heavy and dragging when wet, useless to comb, forever getting tangled, tripping me up, getting caught on and in things, whipping around my head when its windy, it's a nasty burden and I wouldn't think to wish it on even my most cursed enemy"

"Then why not cut it?" Zeta persisted.

"Well...I don't know...frankly I can't see how anyone else in my guild keeps theirs in order...and personally I don't care, I guess I keep it for tradition..."

The Stalker rolled back onto his front and kneaded the bed with huge silver claws that made cuts and nicks on the sheets, oblivious to his destruction he replied, "Cut it anyway, start a new fashion or something…it doesn't all have to go, just cut it so its manageable"

Jed thought about it and then nodded; all the other advice from Zeta thus far had been good why should this be any different?

He was moving towards the bath chamber, which had a mirror, comb and scissors when his friend rolled off the bed with a thud and moved towards the door, calling over his shoulder he said, "I have to go and get my cloaking spell ready now, please excuse me, I'll see your new fur on the morrow when I bid your group goodbye" Jed nodded and watched as Zeta opened the door with a magic word and pulled it shut behind him by wrapping his tail around the door handle.

Once in the bath chamber he saw that fresh water had been placed in the tub yet again, after a moments thought he put up an index finger and said a word in Old Lore, the language of old, the finger heated up slowly, changing from red to orange to yellow to bright-white, when it was white-hot he thrust it into the water, the finger hissed and steam was driven up into Jed's face, when he took the finger out it was a normal pink shade and the water was steaming hot. Grinning he shed his garments quickly and hopped in. When his hair had been washed and was wet enough to handle easily he picked up a comb, positioned the mirror and took up the scissors, then he started to snip.

*

Dawn spun across the sky in twirls and swooping dives; she laughed lightly as the early morning wind caught her hair and trailed through it like long, smooth fingers. She flicked her hands, palm out, in all directions, throwing light forward to eat the night-time shadows and bring light forth to Mog. A faint flicker of…something crept into her memory and she scanned the earth below, she knew this place…it was the only one that all Gods and Goddesses, no matter how big or small, were interested in. Torath'Danar, the place held a tiny golden spark of high-power amongst the small dull blue slashes that represented humans to her eyes. She hovered in the air for a moment, indecisive but curious. In the end curiosity won and she brought her hands down in a sweeping gesture, veiling her body from sight.

When she touched the ground, light shone for a second before fading with each of her footsteps, the Goddess frowned. Something would have to be done about that, catching her flawless form in a rippling pool that lay next to her she frowned again; even dull witted mortals would notice her against their own pale, grim complexions. Dawn touched the water, letting its memory of faces flow into her head; she picked a feature from each face, a different limb from each body and quickly pieced them together. She ended up as an extremely ugly old woman who had gnarled hands and a stooped back, shrugging at her luck the minor Goddess slipped into the body and opened her human eyes...Everything seemed so different through mortal eyes, so bright and fresh, everything was exciting and every new day brought forth new wonders. She looked into the pool again...the next thing she would need was some clothes, simple enough. She yanked a grass blade and a purple flower from their homes in the earth and concentrated, the flower and grass blade grew and intertwined with each other, their natural material changed to rough wool and soon she wore a dull purple dress that fitted badly with a green face veil and hat. She smiled with smug satisfaction as she pulled them on and made her way towards the golden spark, still fixed in her mind.

*

An old woman wandered the corridors of the assassin's guild, how she had got in no one could say...it was as though she had just appeared. She had sheets hung over an arm and a kindly expression on her face. Everyone assumed she was just an old maid who had lost her way, though her legs moved with the speed and strength of youth and she walked down every corridor with the air of someone who knew precisely what she was doing.

Dawn watched as a man all in black came out of a door and went past her, his dark blue eyes unemotional and his handsome face half-hidden by the shadow that lay across his face from a wide brimmed hat that he wore. For a moment the Goddess watched him as he passed with interest...he was the same dull blue sash of most mortals, but he had flecks of red and black on his ...not normal, not normal at all...and with the roguish smile that he had fixed on his face, Dawn would have gladly investigated further. However, she could see the Gold-spark in a room two doors down from the door the handsome stranger had come from and she had already made up her mind. Moving to the door she placed an old hand on the handle and pushed down, entering she saw a large bedchamber with a huge four-poster bed in its centre. On the bed was a wiry looking man who gave off a brilliant shine of Godly power from his skin, though no human eyes could see it, she gasped as her memory stirred...

With a smile of delight at finally finding the child she went down to him and floated atop the water as she looked inside the crate at him. He had hazel eyes and soft eiderdown tufts of brown hair, as Dawn peered at his face he gurgled and smiled, waving a chubby arm in the air. The Goddess smiled and reached out with a finger, smoothing his head and kissing his nose...as she leaned back her eyes caught movement in his. A gold rim had appeared around his pupils and the hazel seemed lighter, Dawn caught the bottom of a delicate lip in a gasp as she saw a gold kiss-mark on the child's nose sink into his skin and add to the intenseness of the gold around his pupils.

Dawn stepped forward and carefully placed a hand on his head, seeing him as the child he had been, smiling softly at the remembrance of his gurgling laugh. She watched as his brow creased and he twitched violently in his sleep, words were muttered from his mouth and she felt concern as he flung out a hand and battled with a nightmare. Biting her bottom lip she reached out with her second hand and placed it at his temple. Dawn almost fell backwards with shock as years of information flooded her brain. She saw Jed as a schoolboy being beaten, saw him receive his staff. She jumped forward in his memories, and saw a beautiful raven-haired Eternal with the most amazing eyes and laughing nature...she saw the same Eternal cry out and fade as silver metal bonds that glowed appeared around her hands and neck. She saw a dagger in a clutched hand as the half-hidden man she had seen in the hallway whipped round and threw it, she also saw a little boy with a shining grin and eyes that reflected all the joy and spirit and wonder of a child as he ran with arms outstretched. She listened as she heard words whispered in her ear of a quest and she came to a decision. Literally ripping her hands from the mage in front of her she smiled softly as he now slept peacefully then leant over and flicked a wisp of hair from his face. Then she left Jed's chambers and trotted to the Azale maiden's room, it was at the heart of the mountain and inside everything was decorated in Azale style. Someone had obviously spent quite a lot to make the room seem perfect and she was willing to bet half her Godly-powers that it was the assassin guild leader she had seen in Jed's memories. The way that the mage portrayed both he and the Eternal when they were together was enough to give her a suspicion that they loved one another and this room assured it. A young maid who had been sat in a chair whilst watching over her sleeping charge stood when Dawn entered the room, unsure.

"Don't worry my dear, Master Zeal told me to come and take over for a while as I can't sleep, let you have a bit of rest. I hear that the cooks kept a good bowl o'food for ye and a decent swig of some strong drink...to keep the chills out of ye on such a cold night." She made up the excuse on the spot and ushered the young woman out of the room, "go on now child, 'afore it goes stone cold and the poor woman's effort wasted. Mistress Lanoelin will still be here when you get back," she said with a warm smile as she pushed the maid out the door calmly but firmly and shut it behind her. The Goddess sat down in the now unoccupied chair next to the Eternals sleeping form on her silk-laden bed. She reached out and touched the metal bands that surrounded her throat and hands, and as she suspected, ...they glowed amazingly brightly and made a whirring noise, she let go and glared at them. They had been made to specifically absorb Azale power to gain power for themselves...but her Godly, higher powers where too much for it...if she kept a hold of it long enough then it would burst...and that she suspected may be a side effect of the nasty little device.

The Goddess shred the body she had made for herself and showed the bands who she really was; then listened with pleasure as they hummed nervously, Karma stirred beside her and Dawn touched her forehead, sending her back to the land of dreams, there at least she could be free of trouble. She rubbed the tips of her fingers together till they gave off a light and then she attached them to the bands; one hand went around Karma's hand bands and the other around her neckband.

They glowed brightly and started to change colour, hue by hue they went from bright white light, to silver, to ice blue, to royal blue to deepest midnight blue and then to black...with each change came a dull echoing thud, then they started to shake and hiss and bubble and burn her hands. Dawn grit her teeth and held on, forcing more and more of her power into the bands...soon the blasted things began to smoke and little by little an opening appeared on each of the bands and the metal started to dissolve into vapour and fly up into the sky where it simmered quietly in a black cloud. Soon the opening was large enough so that Dawn could slip Karmas hands and neck through the wretched bands and throw them to the ground. She hissed like an angered cat and let her power flow onto her hands to heal the red burns there. As soon as she had thrown the metal bands to the side, the black cloud above her head had streaked towards them and joined back to the metal, once more forming it into a perfect circle, never to be opened once closed. The Goddess then muttered violently and grabbed the metal, searching and probing it with her mind as she wondered how the person who made the things got them to open...and what she found made an amber-coloured tear run down her cheek. Whoever had made the bands had made them well...and he had made them dirtily, the reason it had been so hard to get them off Karma, and the reason that they sucked up an Eternals power...was that they had been sealed with a human soul. In their making a Seer-spell had been cast, the soul was damned to keep the bounds locked and secure until they had sucked up all of the Eternals power, the more power they sucked up...the less time they would be damned in such a painful cycle and the sooner they could rejoin their loved ones in heaven. But there was a devious trick in the spell...for the soul could never suck up enough power to set itself free. After time caught up with the Azale it held captive and that Eternal had died, they would try to break free...only to find that they could not and would be clamped onto the next Eternal neck to be forced to do the same thing over and over again for eternity.

No one, not even Bironneann, king of the Gods, had the power to sentence a soul to eternal damnation! For that to happen the crime must be serious enough to be called before the court of Gods and even then there would be solemn discussions on the punishment of the mortal who would commit such a crime. Yet here, a mere Azale had been able to decree such a thing...a mere immortal being.

Dawn had been so caught up in searching the bands that she had not realised that Karma had woken behind her, then she heard the girl's gasp. Turning she saw the Azale's look of wonder and hope and joy and watched with a faint smile as her Eternal eyes returned to their normal wholesome shade of green, leaving no trace of pupils and spreading across the eye in one whole colour, she watched as Karma then held her magic to her heart and played it along her fingertips, then chuckled as Karma realised a Goddess stood in the room. The Eternal rolled out of her bed and dropped her head to the floor and smiled and waited politely to be addressed. Dawn did not keep her waiting long; she had things to do and the matter of the bands to discuss in the court of Gods.

"Karma this night I, Dawn Goddess of the morning sky, have

released you from the bands that bound you near to death. I cannot do this for all the Azale, the effort, even for me, would be too great. As I release you I decree that you and your companions will go forth and fight Ragea Atia...I will help when I can but it is Fate and Bironneann who play on the chessboard, I can only do so much without inflicting their rage on me. Also, I would ask you a favour...do this favour for me and I will grant you one miracle whenever you wish it...on whoever you wish it," she told her, raising Karma's chin up to see the girl's beautiful face as it flushed with joy.

"Yes Dawn, Goddess of the morning skies and keeper of Mog's daylight"

The Goddess nodded gravely; at least the child knew how to address her.

"I want you to look after Jed, I am the one who saved his life as a child and though he doesn't know it, I am also the one he stole power from as a baby boy in a wooden crate. He has God-like and High-power in him Karma, so far it has not surfaced as he would not be able to control it...yet soon it will be there. I do not know when so I cannot tell you and therefore wish you to keep it a secret from him till it does surface...but he will need help in controlling it and he will need someone there to catch any power that might escape. Mortal power is bad enough if it gets loose, Godly power is ten thousand times worse. I want you to be the one to catch that power if he drops it and use it as you see fit. He is like a child to me though he may seem to be a useless bumbler to you...*keep him alive for me my dear and you will have your miracle.*" The last words were whispered on the air as Dawn left, fleeing earth and returning back to her home in the Immortal Realms of the God's court...just before Fate checked the chessboard, which was just after the piece that was meant to be her got back before being noticed.

*

The morning came all too quickly for Jed, he woke up late to hear someone hammering on his door, the wizard gave a shout of "I'm up" and the person who had been hammering replied, "Good, now get your things together and meet the guild master and the others down in the main hall, hurry now!"

Muttering to himself he heard a snigger in the corner, turning he saw his staff bobbing up and down, as some people's shoulders do when their laughing, after glaring at it he rolled out of bed and pushed his glasses onto his face then grabbed a brush and a leather hair-tie.

When he finally reached the main entrance and entered via the top staircase, Jed looked completely and utterly transformed.

In place of the usual long, dragging, dull and shapeless robe, he had tan leather breeches that showed he had very lanky long legs, a cream coloured shirt that tied down one side with white leather buckles, a belt that had at least twenty different things hanging from it, a grass-green jacket that had been left open and had plain embroidery up the sleeves. His knee-length boots had proven to be very sweaty so he had discarded them for his old, battered, comfortable ankle-boots, tied around his neck with an odd knot was a short grey cape that gave him an air of mysteriousness (or at least that's what Jed thought). His hair had been cut to shoulder length and he had drawn it back into a tail, his beard was no longer there and in its place was a small goatee which he twirled around nervous fingers. In fact the only thing that had not changed was his hat, still the same pointy algae green cone. His staff flew down the stairs towards the others whilst its master lugged behind, dragging his saddlebags along over one shoulder. When Telric turned away from talking to Karma (who, Jed realised, he had not seen since he had entered the guild) the assassin raised an eyebrow and clamped his lips shut over a laugh. Lance turned to see what was so funny, he gave a grin and started to walk around, stroking an imaginary goatee on his chin whilst saying "Hmm, yes, yes that will do...hmm" then giggling for all he was worth. After seeing the child's antics Telric also joined in the laughter, Karma glared at them both and gave a soft smile to Jed. When he reached them she looked him up and down.

"You've certainly improved since we took you under our wing" she said, indicating to the others with a nod of her head. Telric smiled and clapped Jed on the shoulder (almost overbalancing him and making him fall).

"Too true, I can hardly remember the small, annoying, cowardly man who had no fashion sense to speak of," Telric told him.

"And you do, do you," the Eternal shot back with a sharp-eyed look, Jed butted in before the argument turned into a full-scale yelling match.

"Yes I have changed, so have you Karma. You seem a bit more...'aware' than you did the last time I saw you"

She smiled to him, and it was in that instant that he noticed her eyes...they were back to their normal green shining hue and he could see no pupils glittering from them, just two eye-shapes of pure colour. His mouth dropped in amazement as he quickly looked from her hands to her neck to see that the metal bands that had once bound her...had gone. She gave a laugh at his astonishment and grinned happily.

"Yes there gone...and you *won't believe* what happened" and then she launched into the most amazing tale Jed had heard for a very long time.

*

The group left the hall and snuck down the hidden passageway they had entered almost three whole days ago; when they were outside they found Autumn-wind, Winter-sky and Nightfall waiting for them. The beasts greeted their friends with shrill cries and as Jed looked around, the assassin questioned him.

"What are you doing? The horses are right in front of you"

"I'm looking for Zeta, he said he'd meet me here and I'd like to say goodbye...and where's Jester?"

"My spells must be getting better if they can fool your magic friend" came a low purring voice as Zeta appeared next to Jed in a swirl of black mist, Jed laughed and shook his head.

"No I'm just losing common sense, I didn't even use my magic to look for you, I checked with my eyes!"

The Stalker chuckled and sat on his haunches, sticking out a large paw delicately.

"Then we have both been fooled, I must depart as swiftly as possible Jed...but rest assured, when I have had a chance to debate it with my cousins and family in my realm, I will visit you at your guild. Farewell human mage, may our paths cross again on the road of friendship"

Jed shook the paw, cautious of the razor-sharp claws that were hidden under its velvety rug and replied in kind.

"And maybe, someday, I will be allowed to come and study and learn with the other creatures in the Forbidden Realms. Goodbye Stalker Mage and rest assured I will meet you on that road and will gladly join your company on the perilous highway that disappears amongst the hills"

With a nod to the others Zeta shook his head, gave a rumbling yowl...and then disappeared.

Jed felt sad, he would miss the one friend on this trip who could relate to him and his works...someone tapped him on the shoulder and he turned to see Telric pointing to Autumn-wind, Karma had already mounted and Jed felt a nagging question tickle the back of his brain.

"I know I'll probably get bawled at for this but...well...Karma doesn't have the bands on anymore, that means we have time to raise an army to go against Ragea...don't we," he said. The assassin nodded his head.

"Yes we do, dump your saddlebags on the floor, Lance will take them back...he's not allowed to go where we are about to go"

"And where would we be going?" Jed asked, his 'too sweet' voice masking sudden fear as Telric gave a crooked smile and showed sharp white, pointed teeth...his eyes caught a sparkle from the sun and shone for a moment before saying.

"We're going to meet King Saia and see what he's been up to whilst I was gone and then we're going to have a little 'meeting' with our friend the dwarf."

Jed gulped and mounted up as he felt a sudden and deep foreboding lay heavily across his mind...

*

Later on the trio were found trotting towards the palace, they crossed the training yards where men still practiced with their wooden swords and from time to time stopped to change partners or wipe down their sweating bodies. Jed eavesdropped as the drill sergeant taught some of the younger troops.

"You there boy, state your name and rank!"

"Erm, Graham Smythe, private"

"You tryin' ta be h'insolent lad? When you address a superior h'officer you finish every sentence with sah!" the man hollered with a smile, obviously enjoying himself.

"Sorry sir, I'm Graham Smythe sir, rank of private...sir" Graham Smythe said quickly, throwing of a sharp salute just to be sure.

The sergeant gave him a curious glare and pushed his fat red face into the smaller one.

"You tryin' ta be funny boy?"

"No sir, just following orders sir!"

"Good! And so ya should be lad Now you lot, this 'ere is a sword, 'ow to use it is relatively simple. You 'old the wooden end and the sharp end goes in yer enemy. 'Ow you use it well is by listenin' to me and your superior h'officers!"

Watching the display going on behind them Jed wondered how long and hard they practiced to keep in fighting fit order, after all there were no wars on. *'Yet,'* corrected his staff, and the last war that Mog had seen had been before most of these men were born. Jed speculated if they really knew the meaning of death and war, did they think it was some glorious game to be won and to cheer and drink about? Or did they know the harsh reality of death, would they realise that when they saw a best friend on the ground with a gaping hole in his side, that they couldn't bring that friend back to life. That every second they lost concentration of the enemy they were trying to kill, and thought about that friend, was the second when the enemy could pull out a trick and slice their throat? Seeing their harsh determination and focused eyes, the men worked to better themselves in the art of swordplay over hours of ruthless punishment on their bodies…Jed wondered what drove a man to become a soldier and kill countless people.

Finally, he wondered how that sudden knowledge of war had popped into his head, true he read a great deal…but war had never been his favoured subject…slowly he heard a slight, embarrassed cough in his mind, he turned to his staff and raised a curious yet serious eyebrow.

'Erm…sorry about that, you see…at night when you were asleep at the guild I liked to read and learn new things, and I liked to read about war and the types of magic that could be used. Manoeuvres! Tactics! Ambush! I loved it all and you never read any of it whatsoever…so I decided to read for myself at night, when I was bored, so that you wouldn't know,' it finished in a humiliated rush as Jed massaged his forehead with a hand and sighed. "Any other little secrets you'd like to tell me about?" He asked, staff turned as though to answer, and just then Telric called out from the front.

"We're here Jed hurry up!"

The mage realised he had dropped behind whilst getting lost in his 'wondering' and asked Autumn-wind if he would catch up. His friend obliged politely. *"Indeed I will Jed."*

He finished with a nod of his head and a flick of his mane.

Catching up to the others Jed dismounted so fast that he half-fell and half got off his friend. Giving Telric and Karma a forced grin, he nursed an arm he had scraped against the saddle while he followed on behind them. As they entered the palace by the huge gilded doors that Jed had spied on his way to the guild, he saw that inside everything was richly decorated with deep rose red, bright, eye-catching gold and rich, pearly cream colours. Ancient tapestries that were displayed through glass boxes hung on the walls, showing scenes of life from each King and Queen to have ruled in Torath'Danar…and how they had died. Jed tried hard but was still shocked to notice that they had all died by assassination, he caught Telric's eye and the man gave him what could only be called 'evil' grin, then the black look shrank back into his face and Telric walked forward with mild interest and one hand on a dagger hilt at all times. Metal statues and stone busts of past princes and princesses lined the corridors, along with the occasional piece of ancient armour or famed object from nearly every type of age imaginable. The carpet they walked on was a deep red with golden trimming and richly outlined tassels that small spoilt, rare cats with gem studded collars tore at viciously. It was the plain old working cats from the kitchen that tried to keep down the mice.

The ceiling had clouds made from mother of pearl and small golden children with sweeping feathery wings peeked out from behind them, seemingly throwing down precious jewels on golden ribbons that had been cleverly stuck into the ceiling by their hands. Jed didn't know how many corridors they passed, nor could he count all the tapestries and see how many monarchs had reined over the country. All he knew was that though it seemed rich and amazingly beautiful, it was definitely not as large as the assassin's guild. Watching the black-cloaked figure ahead of him he wondered if the palace had meant to be this small…or if the plans had fallen into the wrong hands and things had been changed. Perfumed oil lamps shone from grand, silver chandeliers and lurked at every corner, throwing light onto the people passing by, whether they wanted it or not. Important looking men with curved swords at their sides and uniformed hats tucked firmly under an arm strode past, each of them gave a knowing nod to Telric (who ignored them completely) and then went on their way, eyes front, hands on the hilt of swords and shoes squeaking annoyingly. After bowing deeply, serving men and women went about their tasks as though nothing unusual was going on…but Jed saw that they bowed a bit lower towards Telric than they did to the people with the hats and swords, and they were trying a bit too hard to get on with cleaning or running errands. He glanced at Telric and was shocked to find the man watching him with vague amusement and a cold smile. Jed replied with a hearty grin and then went back to looking around him in awe, the assassin watched him for a minute, head cocked to the side with a doglike curiosity and then his eyes snapped forward and he concentrated on three men at the end of the corridor where two large, gold doors stood. The doors had amethyst etchings of a crown and large throne in the centre, and two huge, ornate rubies were used for handles. One of the men was extremely fat and red in the face, he was obviously going bald but had made a pathetic attempt to comb the last strands of his hair over the top of his head to try and hide the fact. He could have been considered jolly, but his little eyes had a pig-like expression and he gazed at people by raising his chin high and looking down his nose at them. His chin and wrists seemed covered in deep, cream lace that hung from his golden cuffs and collar. His shirt and jacket were of the same velvet plum coloured material and was studded with semi-precious stones. In one hand he held a sharp looking silver cane with a golden handle that looked similar to that of the golden eagle (but Jed thought it looked more like a puffin), that he gripped with a podgy ring-encrusted hand. His other hand held a delicate looking handkerchief that had flowing initials sewn onto it and when he wafted it about a strong, peppery smell filled the air. His extremely baggy breeches almost hid a pair of cuirass slippers that curled at the tip. Another of the men reminded Jed of a stick; he was extraordinarily thin and wore ice blue silk from the neck down with a silver cloak that was attached via a golden sash. He had curled silver hair and a huge, oiled moustache, and on his head was a shiny black hat that had a buckle in the middle of it and a peacock feather on one side. His arms were folded in a very angry way and he pursed his lips with jealousy, around his silver painted and gold drizzled belt hung a shining silver sabre and a heavy looking purse that matched the rest of his outlandish and garish outfit.

The third man was much younger than the first two; he had large and intelligent red-gold eyes, which made Jed, think of the moon. His dark brown hair hung to his chin in a ragged style and made his pointed and foxy face quite handsome yet extremely mysterious and secretive. His long, black woollen cloak hung heavily around his neck and the rest of his outfit, which was dark grey and bark brown, screamed 'loner' a mile off. His long tapered fingers caressed the top of a simple looking dagger that seemed to be his only weapon and he wore long riding gloves on his hands but when he exchanged a grin and a handshake with Telric, Jed would have bet just about anything that on his left hand on the palm, was a red rose tattoo that dripped black blood.

"This is Kyder Moray, a very close friend of mine and my second in command when it comes to guild matters. Kyder this is Jed, the mage I was talking to you about earlier on…you might like to discuss your 'secret' with him later, I'm sure he'll find it fascinating and end up wanting to be bitten just to see what happens." Telric said as he clapped the man on the shoulder. Jed was about to ask what on earth the man was going on about when Kyder gave a quiet, humourless laugh and Jed saw very sharp, almost fanged teeth shining pearly white from his mouth. Instead, gulping down a sudden nausea that had reared up from his stomach, he swerved around his immediate curiosity and let his Staff investigate Kyder Moray whilst he nodded his head to the other two men, the ones who looked like lords dressed for a feast.

"And who are these two…gentlemen?"

"These two gentlemen, if gentlemen they can be called, are going. Now!" Telric told him in a tight-clipped tone, while carefully examining a fingernail. Jed watched with a sort of mad, half dazed expression, and half confused laugh as both men gave sweeping bows and walked off as fast as their legs could carry them (and in the case of fat-man it was not all that fast).

The mage turned back towards Telric to find that the assassin had already disappeared through the now open throne room doors and that Karma and his staff had followed, leaving him alone with Kyder Moray…somewhere that he did not want to be.

"Shall we follow?" the man asked, and each word seemed snapped and short, as if the man had a deep, dark secret.

The wizard nodded and quickly trotted through the doors and followed the other two through another set of doors, leaving him no time to gaze thoughtfully about him. The high domed ceiling and huge windows that had such long velvet curtains, that Jed could have stood on the top of two men and still not reached the zenith of one. They moved into a room to the left that led into a rather large study where an elderly man sat at a writing desk, quill in hand and parchment before him. His eyes glittered of old charm and finesse, his gait when he stood and walked over to the small group was graceful yet strong and admiring, his clothes could be considered simple to the ones that the two lords outside had worn but he made them seem elegant and grand beyond belief. He gave them a kind smile and bowed with poise over Karmas hand and welcomed Telric and Kyder with a short bow. When it was Jed's turn he gazed at the mage and even asked him a question.

"Good day, I do not believe I have had the pleasure of meeting you yet sir. Might I know your name? After all it would be considered quite rude by myself and others surrounding us, if I kept calling you sir all the time whilst everyone else was merely spoken to by their name," said King Saia of Torath'Danar with a noble smile. Jed had never met a king. In fact, he'd never met any sort of royal before in his whole life. He had only ever read about them in books, and what he had read was true. Certain members of the royal family had such a thing as a 'charm button' which they were able to switch on and off with apparent ease, whereas Jed had a 'clumsy/nervous button' which seemed to be stuck at 'on'.

"Err…I…I…I'm Jed sir, I mean…erm…King Saia sir…err, I'm a mage from the West Isles…your Majesty…sir…" he spluttered out whilst sticking out a hand to be shaken and at the same time trying to bow. The king cocked and eyebrow in amused surprise and turned to Telric.

"So he doesn't get tongue-twisted around the person who actually operates everything," he pointed to the assassin, "yet he falls over his feet if you place the word 'king' in front of someone's name," he observed politely. Telric chuckled and Karma shook her head in complete and utter disbelief that someone could actually be as blind as Jed when it came to certain things.

"Jed there's no need to bow, Saia here only helps Telric out on the political side of Torath'Danar and leaves the rest of the world thinking he actually controls things around here…geesh! I thought that Jay would have at least explained something to you about this place. Never trust first impressions for a start," the Eternal said.

Jed was about to answer back that he knew quite a lot of things *actually*, but never got the chance as he was plonked onto a chair next to Karma and Saia, as Telric and Kyder shuffled through pieces of paper and official documents whilst whispering in a secretive huddle and from time to time glancing at Saia with a hard look. The king took it all in with a graceful silence and twiddled his thumbs at the same time as appearing very interested in Jed's staff (who was currently talking to the King about wizards and its opinion of them...Jed wished it would shut up for a bit or at least say something nice about him and his fellow magic-makers). After an hour or so of what Jed thought was pure boredom, Telric grabbed a spare chair and hauled it forwards, sat on it, and with a respectable pile of paper clutched in one hand, he started to shout at the King.

"You have drawn up a document that allows people out of doors when the moon is full at night...what did I tell you about that? I made that law for a very specific and worthwhile reason man! If people go outdoors when the moon shines fully at its summit they will die, I can only protect the citizens of this country if you listen to me. It is the only night that they have to be inside for, any other time they can control it but not then...do you want to wake up one morning to find the streets scattered with dead women and children because you made a stupid mistake!" he said in a low, tense voice, his eyes fixed on the King's and his knuckles white from holding onto a chair arm tightly...presumably because if he didn't hold on, he was going to hit something, or someone.

"The people are talking Telric, they want to know *why* they can't go out at night when the moon is full. And y'know Telric, curiosity will drive the children out onto the streets anyway. It's bad enough if one of those *things* gets a street urchin that no one cares about, but if it got a family's child there'd be an underworld to pay. What we need is a reason for people to stay in at night. All the families in this town are intertwined, everyone knows everyone else and though they talk behind others backs and gossip and moan about one another, if by chance a family member was hurt then they would have their reason for staying inside ...we have to give a...a...demonstration...if you will." Saia told him quite calmly.

Jed pondered on what these 'things' might be and what 'it' was...then decided that he really, really didn't want to know. But catching Telric's eye he knew he would, and soon.

Then Kyder stretched, he did it with outward ease and boredom and Jed watched as his ears seemed to perk up sharply and he came and stood at Telrics side, disregarding the papers in his hand to let them fall to the floor. He leaned forward a bit and then twisted his head for a while, watching King Saia with apparent dislike.

"Wolves, King Saia, have a jaw that is four times stronger than a normal dogs...Werewolves have a jaw many times stronger than that and it is designed to be so quick, efficient and strong that they can rip out a man's jugular with astonishing speed and barely any effort. Werewolves are smart, because they have a human's intelligence, and they are an amazing species." He grinned widely and Jed watched in horror as two front teeth elongated to fangs and started to grow slightly longer and Kyder's eyes…'blurred' and were suddenly a different shape.

"You see there are many types of Werewolves, some that are permanently stuck in one shape, others that can only change when its full moon and there are a rare few that can change any part of their body at will. I am a Werewolf who is part of that rare 'breed'. We are not 'things' we despise being called 'it' and we are just as intelligent as humans, in some cases more so…but luckily Telric is smarter than all of us, otherwise, guess who'd be running this town? And guess who'd have to stay indoors every night instead of just at full moon, hmm?" he growled at Saia. And it was a true growl. The type of noise that you could imagine hearing at night in the forest, miles from any sort of civilisation, and made you very, very afraid.

The King, kept upright and didn't shrink backwards into his chair (as Jed was doing) but gave a rough smile.

"Forgive me, I spoke rashly…you can be assured that it won't happen again" he told the Werewolf. Kyder grinned happily and tore the document that Telric had been holding into tiny pieces. Then his eyes shape-shifted to those of normal humans, but they still reflected the moon. And his teeth shrunk to what could be considered (with effort) to be normal. Jed felt numb, and his brain went onto automatic. He raised a curious finger in the air.

"Aren't Werewolves meant to be extinct?" he remembered asking groggily.

"That's what most people believe, but here in Torath'Danar they thrive in the assassin's guild and make extraordinarily good and vigilant guards…Jed?…Jed?"

He heard the answer, but didn't know who was actually speaking, just before he fell off his chair sideways in a dead girlish faint.

CHAPTER FIFTEEN
Madness, Blood and Torture

Jed woke some time later, to find himself tied to the back of Autumn-wind.

"Oh good, you're awake…now untie yourself and sit up, my neck's killing me!" Snorted the stallion as he gave a whole body shake and blowed gruffly to the wind. The wizard complied and sat up stiffly, rubbing his eyes groggily and sheltering them from the afternoon sun. How long had he been out?

"About three hours, we were starting to worry", staff told him whilst it floated forwards and gently moved to lay in front of his master, Jed stroked it soothingly, like one would a cat, he started to feel calmer despite himself.

"I'm sorry…I guess the fact about…Kyder and his…kind…came as a bit of a shock," he admitted whilst cricking the back of his neck and forcing back a yawn.

"Hah, it surprised me too…but since you'd already blacked out I decided to try and play the strong card. Next time it's your turn to worry over me," it muttered, almost sleepily, Jed chuckled and pretty soon he got the feeling that Staff was asleep. He carried on smoothing the wood gently as he looked at his surroundings.

Up ahead Telric and Karma rode side by side, Jed gave a small cough and the Eternal turned her mount to come and ride beside her friend with a small smile.

"Back in the land of the waking then eh?" she chuckled.

"Yes, no thanks to you…any more surprises you might want to tell me about? The walking dead, vampires, that sort of thing…" he muttered at her grumpily.

"Oh we're pretty sure there are no walking dead about…but we've heard some rumours about vampires over on the dwarf lands. Telric says he's going over to check on them as soon as he gets the time" she said conversationally before going back to the assassin's side.

Jed gave a long groan and then tried to shake this new information from his mind, figuring that if he didn't think about it then nothing could happen.

Huge, old timber buildings creaked and groaned in a slight breeze. Rotten wood from black, half burnt buildings held cobwebs and swarmed with bugs. Rubble and chunks of stone and slate lay scattered about, debris lay in huge mounds, doors hung on one hinge or were broken in pieces, it seemed they had come to one of Torath'Danars less attractive areas. Karma and Telric rode just ahead of Jed and had their heads together, speaking quietly. Of Kyder there was no sign…but newly gained instinct made Jed look down at the thick, bog-like mud that the horses' hooves squelched along in, besides stones and scuffed shoe marks he saw a huge wolf print. It was at least twice as big as any normal timber wolf print that Jed had ever seen painted in the books he had read. He could make out small grooves where part of Kyder's claws hadn't been able to retract into the pad, presumably because they were so immense. Jed was now over the shocking truth about Werewolves, and (as Telric had predicted earlier) he was currently quite interested in them. Did they hunt in packs or alone? What exactly was it about the full moon that forced them to change? Did they have a similar hierarchy to wolves or were they all loners?

"Hey!"

Jed was woken from his wondering and jolted away from his questions, as Karma turned round to see he had recovered.

"Hurry up Jed, we're about to go and meet the dwarf. It'll only take a little time and then we can be off to finish this blasted quest" she called over her shoulder before spurring Winter-sky into a fast trot. Telric gave a glance over his shoulder to check on the mage, and seeing he was well threw him a quick smile before following Karma. The trio moved on through the burnt-down houses and on through the dust filled air till they reached what seemed like the end of the maze of buildings they had just come through. It wasn't the largest, in fact it wasn't in any way different to most of the ruins around them, but it was here that they dismounted and it was this building that they entered. Telric led the way and gently pushed the door aside, letting the others through before replacing it and taking great care to make it seem that the cobwebs around its frame had not been broken, merely stretched into a shapeless, limp form by the wind. He then led them through a small, pitch-black doorway that stood before them and down some damp, oily steps. Jed's clammy hands held onto his still sleeping Staff and clutched at the walls, his eyes soon adjusted to having so little light and he could soon see the faint outline of his friends in front of him and what appeared to be a pile of rubbish. Jed watched as Telric reached out with a glove-clad hand and pulled a piece off rag from the pile and then touched three more places on the heap in swift succession, when he had stepped back Jed raised his eyebrows in sharp shock at the opening that had silently appeared in place of the mound. Reaching behind their belts, assassin and Azale took out a torch and lit it with a spark of magical fire as Karmas eyes shone twice. The light revealed a set of winding steps that crawled downwards into darkness with only a faint glow from small stones that were mounted on the walls to see where you were going. As they descended, Jed felt a sad and deep fear start to settle around his shoulders like an unfamiliar cloak. At the bottom of the steps was a door, Telric unbolted it with shining eyes and when the door was opened Jed's nose and mind recoiled as one. The putrid, disgusting smell of blood and rotting meat that rolled from behind it hit him hard, Karma already had a cloth around her own nose and mouth, and with pitiful eyes, she passed him one and the wizard hastened to tie it around his own face and cut off the stench. But even with the thick cloth he could still feel the stink pouring into his mouth, clogging up his nose and crawling along his skin. Everything seemed to move in slow motion as Telric walked forward, his cloak flapped behind him like a pair of huge black wings and he grabbed a silver dagger from the wall. Kyder growled at him as he moved nearer, his huge black head pushed downwards, protecting his mangey throat. He snarled and showed large yellow-white fangs that dripped slightly, but when Telric moved nearer still and waved the silver in front of his face he stopped growling instantly and whimpered slightly. Backing away, his huge paws skittered on the floor and Telric frowned, then with awesome speed he caught the handle edge on the Werewolves nose. Kyder yelped in pain and then started to shake, his whole body moved from side to side, gaining speed and then an awful noise filled the air. Like the 'squelch' of a boot being sucked out of ankle-deep mud mixed with a loud sneeze. Suddenly long, shaggy brown and grey fur sunk into skin and large paws shrunk into five human fingers, claws shrivelled back to long fingernails and after a moment or so Kyder stood before them. His nose was bright red and he touched it gingerly, scrunching his face in displeasure at his pain. He was very disgruntled and his lips rippled slightly, like they had when he had been in wolf form and he was snarling. He was also very naked. Telric threw him a long cloak that hung on a hook that was attached to the wall whilst Jed blushed and Karma casually looked up at the ceiling. Kyder wrapped it around himself and then gave the guild leader an accusing look.

"Was there any need for that?" he asked in an annoyed tone whilst pointing at his now throbbing red nose, Telric nodded.

"You shouldn't spend so much time in wolf form...your becoming more wild and wolf like, this time you actually snarled at me and lowered your head. Though I'm sure I have no right to lecture you on something I have no first hand experience at, what happens to a Werewolf if he stays in wolf shape for a long time...I do have an idea. You start to lose touch with your human side, the intelligence that sets Werewolves apart from the average wolf. Try and control yourself will you?" he berated whilst placing the silver dagger back on the wall. Kyder nodded, sulkily, like a dog that had just been severely told of by its master and then he caught a large cast-iron key from Telric and opened the door next to him. It was solid oak and very heavy by the looks of it, Jed already knew that it was to keep the screams of the people being tortured behind it, in that room alone. The Werewolf trotted through the open door happily, Telric went to follow and then turned back.

"Karma I already know you won't come in here...but perhaps Jed would like to see this. It's quite an experience..." he suggested with glinting eyes.

Jed firmly crossed his arms and sat on the cold floor. He had made up his mind the moment he had smelt the stench of blood and felt the fear in the air.

"No thank you" he said coldly, he would not go to see some human being heartlessly harmed for information...he knew it was Telric's job, it was what he had been born for and it was what one God had given him as his lot in life...but it was not for Jed.

"Suit yourself" the assassin answered and then swept into the other room, shutting the door behind him.

*

Telric gazed at the chamber before him, in its centre was one huge slab of stone on which had leather and metal locks and bounds on it, to hold the 'prisoner' in place. At the far side of the long black tinted room was a wall with locked cupboards and these, he knew, were filled with sharp, menacing objects that shone in the torchlight and inflicted fear into a person's heart as surely as Kyder did in wolf form. The Werewolf in question was trailing his powerful, long hands over the cages at one side of the room. There were six in all, two had already crippled forms in them that had crusted, black-brown blood covering their amazingly thin, stick-like bodies and burn marks along their foreheads and spines. One figure's hands were nothing more than a lump of useless, infected flesh, which oozed slightly. The figure's eyes gazed into madness and they didn't move as their breathing came ragged and slow…Telric knew Kyder had been busy whilst he'd been away, but did the man always have to rush a torture? One of the cages to his right held a short figure that eyed him up and down with annoying insolence, the dwarf's weapons and armour had been taken from him and he had a gash on the side of his head. He'd have to tell the prisoner handlers not to be so rough to people, how were his victims supposed to last long enough for him to experiment different poison techniques on them when a rough guard had kicked them senseless?

Telric took off his hat and cloak and placed them onto hooks that stuck out from the wall. He rolled up his black shirtsleeves and un-attached four small daggers from leather straps that were bound around each of his arms. He positioned these next to his hat and cloak then went to the cupboards, placing small and large items alike onto a steel tray which he placed on a stand that stood next to the stone slab. Then he pulled up a chair and sat on it and watched as Kyder secured his long cloak and then unlocked the bars that held the angry dwarf. With one hefty hand the Werewolf grabbed its beard and tugged hard, dragging the dwarf (kicking and cursing) from his cell with ease and strapping him onto cold stone. The dwarf had lost his angry face and now he looked worried, his eyes even showed fear. Telric leaned forward, hand on chin, psychological effect was just as important as pain in this game.

"Hello, now I'd like to know your name please?" He asked, quite politely.

"I ain't tellin' ye nuthin'!" came the reply, but behind the fierce words Telric gave a delighted smile at seeing his victim gulp uneasily.

"Why not? It's a simple request, and anyway I'm on a solemn vow to not hurt any man who tells me their name. I'm Telric by the way, pleasure to meet you" for me at least, he added in his head.

"I'm…Yuric Deep-digger…" came the hesitant answer.

Telric put out a hand and Kyder placed a shiny scalpel into it with a grin.

Yuric looked worried.

"'Ere! You said that if I told yer me name…"

"Correction Yuric, I said that I would hurt no *man* who told me his name…sadly, you are a dwarf. Now I won't say that this isn't going to hurt. Because it really really is, the trick is to tell me everything you know about Ragea Atia and the high Azale before the pain knocks you out, and at the end you get a prize"

"Wot sort 'a prize?" Yuric Deep-digger asked in a small voice.

Telric leaned forward and grinned.

"If you can still run then...tonight?" he turned to Kyder for a moment, the Werewolf nodded eagerly.

"Yes, tonight I set you free in the city. If you can get out of the gates then you win the game and I will never come after you again and you can live in peace," he smiled, happily.

Yuric may have been stupid, but he was not a complete idiot, "Wot's the catch?" he said gruffly.

A warped noise was heard to the left and two huge paws pushed up on the stone slab as Kyder drooled with anticipation, he stood over the dwarf for a mere second before being pushed off and back down to the floor, but Yuric was now frozen with fright. Telric moved down to his ear and whispered.

*"The catch is that **they** will be hunting you...I wonder, how fast can you run? And how smart are you Yuric? Because I'd bet a good bit of money that in the end, you won't reach the gates alive. No one has yet, but just think...what if you do reach the gates? Are they silver? Can they still follow you if they want...or will you win the game?"*

He stopped his whispering torment and told Kyder to heat up some hot coals from the small furnace that was next to the cupboards; his friend did so reluctantly and eyed the fires with fear. Then he came back to watch, with a grin, as Telric leant forward, scalpel in hand...he had never had the pleasure of torturing a dwarf, so his 'technique' was not at its best. But there was a first time for everything and pretty soon he had wool stuffed into his ears to muffle the agonized yells, and he worked away with a faint smile as the blood drizzled to the floor to flow down the drains.

His deep, unemotional eyes were, for once, happy...content, almost blissful.

And he was humming a tune under his breath.

> *"Walk down a dark and lonely street,*
> *Who do you greet there and whom do you meet?*
> *If you're a noble count to four,*
> *Hear the assassin at your door.*
> *If you're an innocent turn your head,*
> *If you don't then you'll be dead"*

His quick fingers worked away, and soon he saw no more need for the scalpel, and reverted to a small steel instrument, made up of tiny bolts and screws, Telric hooked two of them over Yuric's thumbs and started to tighten them, slowly, thoughtfully, adjusting them here and there so that the screws drove through the exact centre of the dwarfs nails. Breaking them from the inside, and as he got further down...breaking the skin. Blood and pulped flesh was pulled away so that he could see what he was doing and concentrate. He didn't really care for information about Ragea...he had all the information he needed. And anyway, he was having too much fun to stop now, not for some simple questions to be answered. He nodded to himself and removed the torturing instruments slowly, so that each jolt of the metal painfully tugged up a bit more flesh with each twist. He stood and stretched; his back ached from leaning over in his glee. How long he'd been working on Yuric was of no interest here, Telric just knew he was going to carry on. He had hardly relaxed enough from that small session to stop yet. Moving to the burning coals he wrapped a thick cloth around his hand and grabbed a pair of pinchers that were glowing white hot in the fire then moved back to his seat beside his new 'friend'. By now Yuric was in so much pain that he could only sob and bit his lip till blood streamed from it. Kyder held the dwarfs hands firmly as Telric used the pincers to pull the mess that had been Yuric's thumbs up into black stumps. Then he amused his inner darkness by discarding the pincers and using his hands to unlock the metal manacles that held Yuric down and pull him to the floor. Once there he casually kicked him in the chest, hard, and backhanded his face, flinging him against a stone wall. Kyder gave a barking laugh as the pathetic, short figure tried to regain his feet and ended falling on his face, causing him to break his own nose. Telric found great joy in this, the fact that his prisoner was hurting himself...maybe; in the near future...he could try to find a way to get them to do that more. He turned his mind back to the current task at hand and pulled Yuric to his feet by his hair. Then flung him towards his right hand man.

Kyder leapt forward and caught the dwarf in mid-air, holding him easily in one hand whilst his other hand rippled slightly and grew larger, the nails becoming sharp claws. He slashed the smaller man down the chest, then changed his hand back to a normal mans. He let Yuric fall to his knees and then grabbed his left arm and twisted, viciously.

The dwarf gasped and choked with the pain of a broken arm and almost passed out as the Werewolf proceeded to snap each joint in his fingers and then bend them backwards and forwards, like a cat playing with a helpless baby bird, then Kyder passed him back to Telric, who nodded, impressed, and smiled as his master threw him into a metal cage that had been fixed halfway up the wall. Underneath, in a metal basket, sat bone-dry wood. The Guildmaster then took a flickering torch from the wall and looked up at his captive.

"Can you dance Yuric?"

The answer he got was a splutter of mumbles; his lips were unable to make real words as they were frozen in shock of the pain that wracked his body.

Laughter echoed around the chamber as Telric set the dry wood alight, the metal floor of the cage started to heat up and glow a dull red. Yuric jumped to his feet and hopped from one foot to another, the soles of his feet burning red raw painfully.

The bottom got hotter and hotter and hotter.

And Yuric danced whilst the laughter and pain washed over him.

CHAPTER SIXTEEN
The Hunt Is On

The sun was starting to set by the time Telric and Kyder came out from the torture room and into the hall. Jed was starving and half-asleep, his head resting on the wall he had slid down to sit on the floor. Karma was in no way tired. She was angry. Very very angry.

Being left to sit in a cold, dark corridor with no real entertainment apart from Jed, no food and no natural daylight had quietly worked away at the back of her skull until she was seething with pent up rage. Kyder leapt forward as soon as the door opened and ran past them on all fours, fur flying backwards as he sped along. Telric departed from the torture chamber with a bit more style and a lot less 'dog-like' elegance. Jed rose from the floor groggily, hand raised half-way to his mouth to cover a yawn.

"He seemed in a bit of a hurry" Jed observed, Telric nodded.

"He was, Kyder's gone to fetch some pals...we're going to play a little game with our friend the dwarf"

Karma strode forward; lips pursed angrily, hands on hips and chin tilted upwards. It has been said that no man can stand against his women, as Jed thought of this saying he saw that Telric (powerful as he is) was no exception to it.

The assassin winced when he saw the Eternal and shuffled his feet, trying to avoid her gaze.

"Do you know how long we've been waiting out here?" she asked, coldly.

"Four hours," came the muttered reply.

"Four hours! That's four hours that could have been spent organizing your guild into this so-called army you've been speaking about. That's four hours that you didn't once think to come out here and tell us what was going on and how long you'd be! I know you Telric, when you get caught up in that...that...that room you forget about everything else!" she paced the few steps from one wall to another, hands flying around in exclamation as she ranted over Telric's 'foolish' and 'mule-headed' ways.

By the time she had just about finished, Karma was breathing heavily and glaring at her friend ferociously. She drew a deep breath but before Karma could start off again Telric jumped forward, grabbed her hands and whispered something in her pointed ear. The Eternal lost her impatience and anger and looked at him curiously, a smile starting to spread on her lips.

"Really?"

Telric sighed, "Gods alone know why I'm doing this...but yes. Really" he replied gruffly.

Karma chuckled delightedly and turned her back on them. Before she disappeared from sight up the winding steps that led to the surface she called.

"The Gods may not know why Telric, but the Goddesses do".

The door shut behind her slight figure and the assassin turned to Jed, as all men will turn to another when a woman has left them clueless.

"Tell me Jed, have you ever fallen in love?" he asked.

Jed laughed loudly at such a suggestion.

"Love? Telric I may have a lot to learn about the world outside my guild but you have a lot to learn about mages!"

Patting his companion on the shoulder sympathetically, they walked away from the torture chamber and back up the winding staircase to Torath'Danar.

"Wizards scare the living daylights out of most women on the Western Isles, when you mess around with magic and stay hidden in a musty old guild all your life...well...people start to invent stories. Most of which are completely wrong. But the funny thing is that most women scare the living daylights out of wizards!" he chuckled whilst using Staff to walk with. Telric laughed along with him; for once he seemed relaxed and not so guarded.

"And what most people don't realise is that women are the stronger sex."

"Really? How do you know that?" Jed asked, innocently.

"Ok...next time Karma argues about something YOU stand up to her, she can wear a body away with a single glare and she can leave you weary beyond belief with that temper of hers. Just watching her argue is terrifying" Telric smirked.

Jed put up his hands in submission, "Point taken," he said.

*

Outside both men saw that Karma had already left. Mounting up, the two made their way back to the guild, speaking with Nightfall and Autumn-Wind as they went.

Outside the entrance of the assassin's guild they met Jay, who had a young woman on each arm and a happy grin on his face. Giving them a small wave he was about to head of towards the palace when a shadow bore down on him.

"Where's Lance?" Telric asked, whilst playing with a dagger in a very nonchalant way.

"Ah-ha...ha, yes, Lance. Karma's got him old chum and I must say she was in a very, hmm...'mixed' mood. And if you two are going to have a row I want to be well away from it. The last time I tried to intervene I got a nasty gash down my back. Goodnight to you," he told them and then strode off, joking with his female friends.

Together Jed and the assassin clambered off their horses and crept into the guild without a word. A man was waiting by a large copper gong next to the staircase. As soon as he saw Telric he threw off a casual salute and then asked, "Master Kyder, sir, said that tonight..." he trailed off when Telric nodded his head impatiently.

"Yes yes, it's all settled, now hurry up will you?"

The man saluted again and then hit the large gong four times. Telric stepped up his pace from a walk to a fast trot. Jed followed on behind him hastily as they made their way upwards through the guild. They jogged up what seemed like hundreds of small side-staircases and practically sprinted across landings till they stood outside a small room with a single metal door. Telric opened a small hatch that had been carved into the stone wall and pulled out what seemed to be a long metal tube with a funnel at the end. This he proceeded to talk into.

"Open up Dav, I need to get to the plateau. The moon will be up soon and I've found some entertainment for us all tonight"

The tube seemed to speak back, but all Jed could hear was, "Babada baba, bigely beep?"

"Yes, tell everyone to get up here and tell the werewolves to be ready. We have someone who's going to play a 'game' tonight", Telric replied and then replaced the tube and shut the hatch.

Jed looked at him curiously, "What was all that about...and what were you doing with that tube?"

The assassin grinned proudly, "Modern engineering Jed. You can't beat it for speed...and as far as the 'game' goes, you'll see soon enough"

Suddenly the metal door in front of them started to move, Jed took a step back and then gaped...the door was sliding open sideways. When it had finished its squeaky process Jed could see a very small metal room behind it. Telric stepped into the room carefully, it shuddered...then stood still. Jed let staff fly in before him and then slipped in after it, grabbing hold of the floating wood as he felt the room give a slight shudder. Telric had opened another hatch and was speaking down the tube he had pulled from it. He replaced it and the door closed...Jed whimpered as the room started to move. It climbed steadily upwards and the wizard heard a 'click, click, clunk, click, click, clunk'. Forgetting his fear in the surge of interest that pushed up inside of him, Jed studied the chamber with scholar's eyes. The metal that covered the room had been welded together and a grille was placed overhead to let air in so that they could breathe. Two glow-stones lit up the room easily and showed that the door they had come through was built into some grooves and had little wheels on the bottom of it. He could now hear a new noise added to the 'click, click, clunk', a whirring that came through the grille overhead.

"I'm guessing that this works by weights and pulleys?" he asked, Telric nodded.

"And people. In their spare time the apprentices take it in turns to pull the ropes and work the weights, it builds their muscles up after a while and they learn to judge how the weight of an object should be handled...for example, say they were out on an assassination job and they had to get past someone bigger than them. They'll know how to handle their own weight and the other man,s weight because they worked on the 'Move-room' weights. Good eh?"

Soon the room shuddered to a halt and the doors slid open with ease. Stepping out of it Jed looked around in confusion.

"Where are we?" he asked, looking around the flat landscape.

"On top of the mountain" the assassin smiled back, "Now follow me and we should see some fun..."

He walked over to a clump of trees that hid the mountains plateau from view. Jed followed and when they got through the foliage he saw that wooden chairs were placed around the edge of the plateau. And a solid timber fence was the only thing that stopped them from falling off.

As Jed held onto the fence he smiled and sighed in awe at the scene below him. The sun had just set, women and children went into their houses and men came home from work where they were greeted with smiles and laughter. A sort of calm had settled over the town of Hidden Heights. And suddenly dark shapes emerged from the foliage and stood around them, hidden in shadows.

"Master?"

"Get everyone up here, and then blow the warning horns. Tonight we're going to have some fun," Telric told the shadows, his face impassive and light mood gone in front of his guild members.

The shadows bowed and then sunk backwards into the trees.

"Telric, what fun? What's going on?" Jed asked, nervous after the shadows.

"Be patient and you'll find out" came the reply.

Jed was about to give the angry reply that, no he would not wait thank you very much! When Staff floated up to him and tapped its gem-head on his arm.

"Don't push your luck with this guy, just wait and be patient for once"

Suddenly the plaza was filling with black-garbed people, who were pushing forward to grab the seats around the edge of the Plateau. Karma appeared from the crowd and dragged Jed into a seat next to Telric. When everyone was seated a loud noise echoed in the night. It filled Jed's head and as he looked down into the streets below he saw people look up in fear. Men, women and children ran towards their homes, if a child fell it was picked up by any passer by and shoved into the nearest open door. There were a million tiny 'clicks' as people locked and bolted their homes and slid wooden shutters over windows. All the lights in every home gradually went out and left Hidden Heights in complete darkness. Telric leaned over and patted Karma's hand then stood up. The Eternal nodded and her eyes lit up brightly as she connected herself to a stream of Azale magic. The muttered conversations and whispers stopped as each guild member noticed their Guild Master standing silently in front of them.

Karma twitched a finger and sudden light, bright and blinding reflected Telric against the blue night sky, he put his hands out dramatically.

"Friends, tonight is full moon and I have some entertainment for us all. On my way here from Gin'ne four dwarves attacked my companions and me. All but one were killed and the last was brought here, to await our pleasure," he started pacing before the chairs. The light followed him and so did Karma's head.

"You all know I like to play 'games' and tonight our short friend will play with us".

A cold chuckle rippled through the onlookers as Telric sat down and patted Karma's hand again.

The Azale looked upwards and the clouds in the sky cleared, with amazing speed, revealing a full moon that had a faint red ring around its surface. Like blood.

Jed froze; anyone who used magic knew that symbol. Blood on the moon meant that someone was going to die…and Jed had a good idea of who that person would be. The moon shone down on the town, Karma's eyes flashed and glow-stones that were stuck on the side of buildings and on poles in the air gave a burst of light and shone brightly. Jed could see down every alley, up every street, no shadow was left in the town below and there was nowhere to hide. He watched as the lights showed small groups of street urchins clambering onto the top of flat roofed houses and banging on locked doors. But no one let them in. Then other shapes appeared in the streets, at the base of the mountain. Two men pushed a short, tottering figure forward. The dwarf looked in bad shape, his head rolled around on his shoulders unsteadily and one arm hung lifelessly at his side. He limped badly on both feet and every time he moved a shudder went through his whole body. His thumbs were black and stumpy and a gash on his chest leaked through his thin clothes and oozed downwards.

Telric stood up again and cupped his hands over his mouth to shout down.

"YURIC! YOU HAVE TEN MINUTES IN WHICH TO GET OUT OF THE CITY. TEN MINUTES YURIC AND THEN THEY ARE SET LOOSE".

The dwarf looked up groggily and shook his good arm at them in a fist, he shouted up an angry dwarfish curse and then one of the men next to him pushed him towards the streets.

And all of a sudden dark shapes came out of the mountain. The two men who had 'escorted' the dwarf outside stepped forward with the other shapes, into the moonlight. A rippling noise drifted up from below and the Werewolves formed a silent circle.

There were thirty-eight of them altogether.

Jed watched as the dwarf took one, frightened look behind him and started to run.

*

Yuric Deep-digger was not having a good day. In fact he'd not been having a good week. So far his three brothers, Guric, Muric and Huric had been killed. A man in black with cold eyes and a Werewolf by his side had shown him four hours of pure pain and he was about to be chased down by a pack of beasts that he had thought were extinct.

His short legs pumped away painfully beneath him as his heavy head swung from side to side, trying to think and keep an eye out for main streets. There was no silver anywhere, no fire either. His left arm hung uselessly at his side and the thumb on his right hand throbbed as he tried to stem the flow of blood coming from a deep scratch gash on his chest.

He had ten minutes, more than long enough for a healthy man to reach the gates. But he was shorter than any man and his legs were already shaking and shuddering treacherously. Yuric staggered down unknown streets, always moving forwards. He saw street children peeking over the top of flat roofed houses as he rushed past.

Behind him a howl started up.

The hunt was on.

In fright the dwarf sought a way up to the roofs, off the streets; he'd be able to see where he was going and where *they* were if he could just get up.

His quick eyes saw a pile of logs against a wall and jumped forward, grimacing as his burnt feet thudded against the wood and then groaned as his aching leg muscles pushed upwards as he leapt and grabbed a ledge above him with his good hand. What dwarves lacked in height they made up in upper body strength. Strong muscles strained and Yuric started to pull himself up slowly.

Small, rag-bound feet pattered towards him from the next roof and two children grabbed his hand.

Looking up Yuric saw two small boys with an arrow earring through their right ears and dark, large eyes.

He smiled at them, relief flooding his brain.

"Thank'ye lads...I thought I was dun fer a minute there," he stopped speaking as both boys looked at each other silently, then nodded and, grabbing his hand, pushed him off.

*

Telric smiled happily as he watched Yuric's progression through a spy-scope. He waved a hand and a woman came to stand next to him.

"Yes Master?"

"Those gang-boys down there, they belong to the 'Shadow-

Archers' gang...don't they?" he asked, passing the spy-scope to her. The woman glanced through it, and then nodded.

"Ah I thought so. In the morning send someone down with new clothes and daggers for each member in their little group, and get them some food...tell them that they've pleased me with their 'help' tonight" the Guildmaster told her.

The woman bowed and then trotted off to do his bidding. Telric offered the spy-scope to Karma, who shook her head, and then to Jed.

Jed took the long brass tube cautiously; afraid of what he might see through it's concentrated lens. He watched as the dwarf pushed himself up from the floor slowly and started to jog off down a street, his breath coming in pants. The Werewolves spread out, moving in groups of three or more, noses to the air, moving slowly...almost lazily. Jed thought he understood why.

Where was the fun in chasing something down if it was easy? Better to give the prey hope that it will live, and then take away that hope at the last moment.

He watched the assassins around him as they jeered and betted on the pathetically outnumbered figure below.

He watched in horror as Telric eagerly leaned forward, eyes glinting suddenly as his four-legged friends below stepped up the pace. Before, in the palace, as he watched Kyder in shock he wondered why the Werewolf hadn't bitten Telric, so that his kind could rule the country. Staring at the Guild leader he knew why.

If Telric could control the Werewolves now without being all that strong physically, just stupefyingly fast and extremely intelligent, what would he have been like with the added threat of being a Werewolf? The thought made him shudder, and though the man was his friend -of sorts- he thought that perhaps he was a bit mad...

Staff floated up, *"More than 'a bit' I think. And you would be too if you had his upbringing. Anyway, can't you tell he's different from the assassins around you? They only kill for a fee, he'll kill for the simple pleasure he gets from killing. He's not a 'refined' killer, like assassins are portrayed as...he's a murderer"*

Jed glared at Staff, "How do you know what type of upbringing he's had?"

Staff tutted.

"For a start I've had a look in his head, secondly I've been to look at the 'schoolrooms' they have here, for apprentices. You wouldn't believe the

classes they have...look! Dwarfies slowing down...the Werewolves are catching up!" said Staff, in a stunning effort to change the subject. Jed looked and bit his bottom lip, the dwarf was slowing down with each step and sometimes he was stopping, leaning against buildings and trying to catch his breath. The Werewolves were only three streets away and they were starting to build up to a run.

This was wrong. Looking at the laughing faces around him and the eager smiles, Jed knew that this had to be stopped. Karma was still sat in her chair, her face unsmiling and her body slumped...she wasn't about to intervene anytime soon. He felt something rise up inside him; it attached itself to the anger that burned in his head and spread through his body like a forest fire and glowed ferociously, it made his fingers tingle and his skin prickle.

Someone should do something!

And before he knew what he was doing Jed stepped forward and jumped off the mountaintop.

CHAPTER SEVENTEEN
Consequences

The thing that had risen up inside Jed was his magic, but it was like nothing he had ever used before- it was different somehow. The well of magic inside him had turned into a sea, and it was golden...but that was of little importance right now. Jed ran across the sky, his feet throwing off sparks every time his magic refused to acknowledge gravity. Yuric the dwarf was staggering, the Werewolves were at the bottom of the street he had just come to the end of...and they started to gallop. Jed leant forward and put his head down, streamlining his body and forcing a faster speed into his spell.

He hit the first Werewolf head on in the chest, just as the thing soared forward, jaws wide open. Both he and it rolled forward on the ground and as soon as Jed felt solid land under his feet he jumped up and flung out his hand.

"Flaming ball,
Fire of all,
I singe your fur and burn your soul!"

The hand was moved outwards and up. A wall of fire, hotter than any furnace, sprung up from the ground and blocked off the mage and dwarf from the Werewolves in front of them, but there were five running in from behind.

Yuric whimpered and scrabbled at the floor in a desperate attempt to get to his feet. Jed helped him up and shot out a hand, Staff was slammed into it within seconds and he gave it to the dwarf so that he could support himself, then turned to the oncoming rush of fur and fangs. He had no silver, not even any steel, no weapon whatsoever apart from his magic. By now it should have been drained considerably...but as he checked it momentarily he saw that the golden sea was still there...and he had barely scratched the surface of his new-found capabilities.

The first Werewolf to get within range got a ball of fire thrown at its head, setting it alight like a great mad beacon. The second and third advanced carefully and tried to circle around him whilst the third and fourth distracted him. Jed refused to let them and he wriggled his fingers, three red light-rays sprung from them and wrapped themselves around three of the Werewolves before squeezing them out of their wolf forms and into their human ones. Two men and one girl writhed on the floor in anger as they tried to break free; Jed turned to the last two and lifted his hands high above his head, both Werewolves looked at one another, then turned tail and ran.

Turning back to Yuric the wizard reached out with the essence of spirit and water and light, he brushed them over the dwarf and healed the gash across his chest and his thumbs and bruises...he'd have to deal with the rest later because right now they had to get out of here. He could hear more howls drawing nearer and the firewall he had called up was starting to fade, dark shapes loomed behind it. He grabbed Staff roughly, no time for manners, placing it sideways in the air he pulled Yuric up with difficulty and pushed him onto it, then clambered onto the back and held on with his knees.

"Fly, fly fly! Now Staff!" he yelled.

"Alright alright! Hold on!" it answered back.

And then they were zooming upwards so fast that Jed had to hold down his hat with one hand.

Up in the air, safe, he looked down in time to see the rest of the Werewolf pack snarling their rage as their intended prey escaped. Staff flew over to the mountain plateau and set them down amongst hundreds of grimfaced, angry assassins.

But before anyone could move Jed had already pushed Yuric into Karma's waiting arms with a, "Look after him till I get back". And then he had grabbed Telric's arm, oblivious to the hundreds of daggers that were drawn instantly and unaware of his friend's angry glare. Then grabbing the brim of his hat, threw it up into the air and clapped his hands together.

The hat floated down, slowly getting bigger and bigger...until it reached the ground, covering Jed and Telric in darkness.

Inside the hat Jed flicked a finger and an armchair moved behind him, he sat down on it without even looking, knowing it would be there. Then he glared at the inside of his hat until light lit it up and revealed what looked like a cone shaped room. It had hundreds of tiny shelves and drawers, all attached to the inside of the hat, a small bed stood in one corner and a table with a black cauldron bubbling on it in another. And above them, sitting on a little ledge was a small creature, no bigger than his fist. It had two grubby grey wings, a slightly forked tail and two feet that looked like a pair of clown's shoes. The funny thing wore a red waistcoat and a brown loincloth with a thick green belt that held it around its potbelly; it turned its hooked nose towards Jed and opened its mouth to speak. "Not now Horace you confounded hat-minx! I'll speak with you later but right now you're likely to get your head seared with a fireball, now stay still and shut up!" The wizard glowered up at the thing, crossing his arms and pouting. Horace the Hat-Minx gave a chuckle and then flew off to one of the shelves and dove into an open draw. Jed made an aggravated noise through clenched teeth and then mumbled, "I can't see the point of those beasts, forever tearing price-less spells, making a mess of the potion drawers-" he stopped his muttering with a sigh.

Telric was too stunned to remember his anger and even sat down on the bed when he was told.

But after gazing around for a few bewildered moments his eyes focused back on Jed (who had found time to dip a cup into the green mess inside the cauldron and was drinking it quite happily). Suddenly Telric was on his feet, fists clasped so tightly that they shook, his face was a pit of rage. "What on Mog do you think you are doing? Why in the underworld did you help Yuric? And what in the God's name are you going to do next?" he hissed. Jed was about to answer when he was grabbed by the lapels and held off the floor.

"Now tell me, tell me straight wizard...why spoil my fun?"

"You call torturing someone fun? You call hunting a dwarf down to be ripped to pieces fun?

Funny...I don't," he answered back, still angry that no one had tried to intervene but him.

"Yes it's fun. When all you had has been stripped away from you by death it's fun to give death to others, and spread it around...like some sort of disease. It's fun to feel powerful and to watch as people beg for their lives, you may know magic wizard, but I know true power" came the smug reply. Just then Jed muttered two words and Telric was thrown off his feet and slammed against a wall, he slid down it slowly and looked at Jed with disbelief as the mage sat on his chair again and flicked a finger. His cup, which had fallen to the floor, floated neatly into his hand and the mess the green liquid had left on the floor, vanished. The mage floated the cup onto the table and rested his chin on a hand.

"No, you know what power over people feels like. I do not know true power, that is Godly, but I do know that my power is far beyond your reach. Now, what were you asking me?"

Telric's jaw dropped, he couldn't believe that someone hadn't lis-tened to him, and he was sure he was crazy when the man who had so casually ignored him was Jed. Getting to his feet he stalked over to the bed and sat down, slowly and purposefully. If he had been a cat his tail would have been lashing from side to side.

"I said...why, did you save Yuric?" his reply was cold and distant.

Jed folded his arms, "Because no-one else would," he answered simply.

"Of course they wouldn't! You useless, lump of-...Jed, of course they wouldn't save him...he was entertainment" Telric said, angry at first but now speaking slowly, as though he was explaining something to a halfwit child.

Jed would never know how he had the courage to do what he did next.

"Why Lance Telric?" he asked quietly, whilst refilling his cup from the cauldron.

"What?" the assassin shot back swiftly, too swiftly...Jed had a lead.

"Why did you save *him*?" he sipped the green potion calmly and felt it healing his nerves.

"What are you babbling on about?"

"Karma told me that you saved him because he was alone in the gutter, but I don't believe that. You are a heartless man. You play 'games' that mean innocent people die for your pleasure, so why should Lance have been any different?"

Telric licked his lips nervously and his eyes darted around the hat, but there was no exit on any wall...not until Jed wanted one to be there anyway.

"Yuric was no innocent, have you forgotten that he and his friends tried to kill us?"

Jed shook his head, "No I hadn't forgotten. But he'd already suffered for that in the torture chamber. Now answer the question please, why Lance?"

"Lance was...special. He had no gang", came he reply, but his eyes darted around nervously.

Jed's eyes turned to narrow slits, there was some secret here.

"I don't think that he had any gang...because you told all the gangs to let him fend for himself,

I think that it was another of your games. But this time you didn't win-"

"That's not true!" Telric interrupted loudly, Jed raised his left eyebrow and swept his free hand across the room. Telric's mouth snapped shut and he was forced to be quiet.

"You will not interrupt me again. You will listen, clear?" Jed asked.

Telric clawed at his lips, trying to open them…but in the end he nodded sulkily.

"I think that Lance proved he was strong enough to survive on the streets, none of the

Werewolves got him…none of the gangs were able to catch him and he interested you. He was young, new to the town…someone whose origin you couldn't trace. I've read your Guild's rulebook in my spare time. It states clearly that every Guildleader must have his own personal apprentice, and when the time comes that apprentice must kill his master in order to take over the guild. Lance was good; you thought he stood a chance against you. You'd found your apprentice."

Jed stood and walked over to the table, placing his empty mug on it. Then he turned to his shelves and started to go through the drawers, taking pinches of certain things and throwing them into his cauldron. Telric watched, fascinated, as Jed picked up a wooden spoon and tried some of it, then nodded and muttered a word over the mixture (which had now turned grey). It gave off a bang and a puff of smoke and then glowed. Jed now got a metal spoon out and dipped the end of the handle in, so hardly any mixture got onto it. Then he turned back to Telric. "This is a truth potion, not powerful enough to last long but strong enough to get the truth about one subject out of you. Don't make me use it, please. Now tell me…why do you get so much fun out of killing folk? To see them writhe? To see them beg and plead for the lives of their family as they watch their children slaughtered in front of them? Because I'm sure, that at one time or another…you've done something like that. So tell me," he said, and lifted the silencing spell from Telric.

The assassin slowly rubbed his jaw and then scrubbed his fingers through his hair.

"When I was a boy…my parents were killed in front of me…they were all I had, all I knew and all I wanted. I was eleven at the time" he halted, and coughed…he'd probably never told anyone this before.

Jed gave him an encouraging smile; you could always catch more flies with honey than with vinegar.

"We were quite religious…my mother had lots of symbols hung around the house, protecting Gods and so forth. I'd hidden from the people who'd killed my family, and when I came out the first thing I saw, after my dead parents, were the symbols. The bandits had thrown them to the floor, laughing. The Gods had never protected my family. It was just an illusion. All the offerings, all the prayers, all the signs and holidays, it was one big lie as far as I was concerned," he spurted out angrily.

Jed put the spoon he had been holding threateningly down on the table, and shook his head.

"That's not true Telric, the Gods are always there, they're always watching and they know what they are doing. Sometimes they play games on a giant chessboard that lasts for centuries-

"What's that got to do with-"

Jed put up a warning finger.

"Listen. The game lasts for centuries and the chessboard is the world, each piece is a person and every move that is made has a knock on effect for the final round. Bironneann and Fate are the main players, but other Gods and Goddesses can join in behind the scenes…as long as no one else finds out. What happened to you was probably part of the knock on effect; something had to happen in your life for it to affect other lives that were vital to the game and how it would end. So don't blame the Gods, never blame them. Because if they are angered enough they will break off, even the vital game, to make your live a living underworld," he told the man severely.

"You don't understand, you never lost your parents!" the answer that was said in anger made the hat dim and made Jed seem pale and ghostlike.

"What do you know about me? I know that I never even got the chance to know my parents…I was found by the Archmage of the wizard guild on the west beaches on the Western Isles. I was in a wooden box filled with straw and it was amazing that I was alive at all. I grew up as an orphan in a cold magical world, where I wrapped myself in my studies and my work. I was not rich; I had nothing of my own…everything I've ever owned was given to me by my Archmage. I had no friends; I only had my magic…to create illusions of what my friends would be like if I had any.

You think you've had it bad? You've had it worse than some, but I'm one of the few who can relate to your problem. So don't say that I don't know what its like to lose my parents, because I've never known what it was like to have any. All I ever found out is that a man and a woman were washed up onto the shore with the remains of a small fishing boat a few days after I was found. They were both dead and they are both gone and I won't linger on them," he answered.

The light in the hat brightened soothingly and Jed got out of his chair, pacing the small room back and forth, tapping the head of his staff in the palm of his hand. His eyes flickered about and he stopped suddenly, and turned to Telric.

"I bet I know what you were like when you were a child Telric...after you'd lost your parents, would you like me to guess?"

Telric gave no outright answer but Jed thought he heard, on the edge of his hearing, the muttered words "Why not? You've done everything else so far"

Jed sat down again and crossed his legs, let Staff float away and made a bridge out of his fingers. "I bet that you ran from the home that held your dead parents, you ran and ran. And really, in your head, you're still running, you came to a big city and saw how everything worked, you saw the gangs on the streets fighting with one another and picking on the weaker children. You decided there and then that you would never be the one that got beaten, so you snuck in with the best gang around. You won some fights and enjoyed the feeling of control you got over a dominated opponent; you won more and more battles and gained more and more respect. Pretty soon the gang leader was asking you to be part of his 'inner circle' and you accepted. You 'played' at being friends until one day; you killed the gang leader and took his place. Soon you had all the gangs under control and everyone was scared of you. At first you'd been fun, you'd been new and interesting. But now children kept out of your way and walked with their eyes down.

Children enjoy playing and fighting and talking and relaxing with children like themselves, but you had stepped over that mark, you were now someone they were scared of. You were a murderer. Anyone who was shy, or small or different or who challenged your command met with accidents. You grew to be a young man with a reputation and with very high and very dangerous intelligence. You took over the country you had skulked in for so long, after all, how many people did you have under your control in each city? Hundreds? Thousands? Street urchins that had been shunned for generations rose up and took power. Some became too used to the power and forgot who gave them it; you had those few hunted down by the 'special' friends you had found among your gang - The Werewolf children. And then you put a sign on each of their hands, reminding them that really…they weren't powerful. You were powerful and they were just something that could be thrown away easily, and you were always watching, you had them marked. After you tattooed their left hands you took the mountain as your main threshold." Jed took a deep breath, calmed his shaking hands and checked his magic…the sea refused to budge, then delved once more into Telric's memories.

"Soon you became bored with the little paradise you had created for yourself and looked to other countries. You learnt of an assassin's guild far off, you left someone in charge, went to the assassins and took over, added the refined killers to your gang 'collection' and taught them all to kill efficiently. You had come back with more skills and knowledge than when you had left…and if any harboured thoughts of killing you…well, they melted like snow in the full summer sun." he stopped and licked his dry lips. Telric was stunned and very white.

"How…how did you know all that?"

"It doesn't take a lot of skill to read someone's memories, but it is very impressive."

"Then why didn't you do it before, so you didn't have to ask me the questions? It would have been easier…"

"Yes, but the thing about magic is when not to use it…and anyway, that would have been prying into affairs that aren't mine, you told me of your own free will," the mage answered.

"Then what are you doing now if not reading my mind and prying into my affairs?" spluttered the assassin.

Jed thought it was time to change the subject.

"Guess what sort of boy I was when I was a child" he said firmly.

"You were the one that got beaten" he answered, slowly. Jed nodded.

"You have to remember sometimes that, deep down inside of you is a good person Telric. I saw him when he was a child in your memories but then something else took over, some kind of beast. I've never had a beast inside me, I have knowledge and magic instead. You've also got to remember that the boys who are beaten are often the boys who will come back and beat you, after a lot of thought and careful planning. I don't need that. I have my own type of power. But I keep it in check, I keep it in line and in return I get to keep that power. The Goddess Majickia chooses mages, even if Birroneann were to create a life he would have to ask her if it was worthy to be a mage. You need to keep your own type of power in line; a welcoming hand is always accepted in better cheer than a punch to the face."

Telric looked confused.

"What's this got to do with me having fu- I mean, playing the 'game'?" he asked. Jed pulled his chair forward so he was within arm reach of the assassin, then he reached out and touched his temple. "That was just to calm you down and relax your guard. I'm going to do a spell now, it won't last long but it will seem to last for years. I'm going to put you in my shoes and then in Yuric's, but in turn I have to see what life was like through your eyes. Get ready," he told his friend quickly and before Telric had time to so much as blink he stopped time and saw the world through different eyes…

…Jed opened his own eyes minutes later, and even though he knew the spell did not, in reality, last long, he was still shocked. Telric had opened his eyes at the same time and then jerked away from the wizard's still outstretched hands. Jed felt across his face and neck for scars that should have been there, but they weren't…however they were on Telric's face and the mage had to shake the feeling that he should have bigger muscles than he had at the moment. And he was worried when his hands kept reaching for hidden daggers that were meant to be up his sleeves and strapped to his back. Sighing he sat back and watched as Telric blinked again and froze, experiencing what Yuric had felt like for the few hours he had been in the assassin's 'care'. When Telric came out of the spell he sat, shocked as Jed had been, then his fingers moved over his face and for some reason…he kept twiddling his thumbs.

"Well…"

"Yes, well" Jed replied, slightly amused at the fact that for the few seconds before re-living Yuric's torture, the assassin had an expression on his face that could only remind Jed of himself. The wizard stood and clapped his hands together, his chair sunk into the hat's wall and the light started to fade, Telric put a restraining hand on Jed's arm before he could do anymore.

"You do know that my guild members could loose faith in me entirely, because of your little episode?"

"Yes I do, and as soon as we get out of the hat, the spell I have prepared will be released into every single person outside, apart from Karma and Yuric. Your members will think that Yuric was killed horribly and you and I went into the hat to discuss future plans for Ragea Atia. All cleaned up, see?"

Telric nodded, relieved but then put out his hand again, "But if they see Yuric outside...won't they know he's still alive?"

Jed cocked his head to the side and sent his magic through the guild; he soon heard the dwarf and Karma talking to each other.

"Don't worry; he and Karma are in her room. She's just finished healing him and the dwarfs after your blood. When we get out of here you have two options" he said pleasantly whilst waving his hands and throwing powders from the pouches around his belt into the air.

"They are?"

"Apologise to Yuric before he sees you or have me whisk him off to his home in the country of Deepest Dunville, where he will arrive very confused and sorrowful for his dead brothers", Jed carried on throwing the powders and started to mutter an incantation under his breath.

"I think that option two is more suitable, I hate apologising to people I've just tortured" came the reply in a conversational tone.

Jed nodded and started on the last part of his spell.

"...up and out and fly about,
Listen as I chant and shout,
Though I decreed this hat a room,
Turn back to natural form, I say, or suffer a terrible doom!"

And before the room started whirling inwards on itself Telric had time to ask, "How can a hat have a terrible doom?"

"I don't know", came the reply, "I suppose it'd get unpicked with a pin, stitch by stitch...anyway, I don't make up these spells you know. They're regulation."

A thundering noise filled the air.

"Meaning what exactly?" Telric shouted over the roar of noise.

"If we aren't taught them our teachers get the sack, now steady your legs or you'll fall flat on your face when we get out of here!" came the loud reply.

There was a flash inside the hat that looked suspiciously like lightning, and when the flash disappeared...Telric and Jed were nowhere to be seen, and the hat-room started to shrink.

*

When Jed's eyes had cleared of the blinding light, he saw that he was outside his hat, as was Telric, and his spell had been released. Assassins laughed and joked with one another about how horrible

170

Yuric's death had been. Those who had placed bets cheered or grumbled, depending on who they'd betted on, and soon maids in black and grey and silver uniforms were bringing drink up to the plateau.

Jed reached towards the floor and picked up his hat, dusted it off, and plonked it on his head.

Telric watched his guild members guardedly and then, seeing that Jed's spell had worked, smiled with relief. Outside the hat, amongst his own kind, Telric once more took charge. And after grabbing a wine bottle from a passing maid he nodded to the metal-room and moved towards it, swigging with satisfaction as he went. Jed followed nervously, holding onto staff, and checked his magic supply. He shouldn't have been able to hold so much magic...it wasn't physically possible...looking inside his head he found that the sea inside of him was slowly draining away, becoming smaller and smaller. Jed's face fell and he called for it, standing on the shrinking shoreline as he did so, but it was going...and in the end Jed let it.

It wasn't his magic. It couldn't be. Someone had let him borrow it, for a short while...and the price for borrowing it was that he had to give it back.

Making his way to the metal-room, he looked up at the stars, noting the constellations instinctively and staring till his eyes were sore. Who had loaned him the magic?

He was positive that no mage in the whole of Mog possessed so much, and Eternal could only share their magic amongst their own kind...had a God or Goddess given him a smidgeon of it?

That thought was instantly disregarded; mages couldn't hold Godly power within them unless they'd had it from the first year of their life. Sighing he muttered curses of frustration and stamped into the room, it shook as he did so but he was too deep in thought to register it. The room shuddered and they started to move down and soon the door was opening and they were on the move again.

By now Telric had finished the bottle of wine (he had said it was to 'calm his nerves' when Jed asked him if he was trying to kill off his kidney) and was playing with a very small dagger and a rose. "Drinking and sharp objects don't mix well Telric" Jed told him pertly whilst they moved towards the centre of the guild.

His friend laughed, "It'll take more than one bottle to make me drunk, and when you have a friend like Jay, drinking soon becomes a fulltime job."

Jed rolled his eyes and started to trot faster, keeping up with

Telric's long strides. Soon he saw Karma's room ahead and was shocked to find it wasn't painted black, like all the other doors they had passed so far. Instead it had an Azale scene on it and a metallic green border. The handles were gold and had been carved into miniature trees. Knocking on the door both men waited until Karma stuck her head out. She frowned at Telric and gave a warm smile to Jed.

"Come in...both of you" she told them.

"Ah, I think I'll just stay here Karma, Jed's going to send Yuric back to his home" Telric told the Eternal whilst trying to smile innocently. Karma's hand shot out and two sharp fingernails grabbed the assassin by the ear, "Oh no you don't! You're saying sorry to this poor dwarf, now come in," she said, pulling the protesting guild leader behind her. Jed chuckled as he stepped into her room and smiled to Yuric who was sitting on a padded chair. The dwarf smiled back, gratefully, and then glowered at Telric whilst twiddling his thumbs, as the assassin had done back in the hat.

Telric rolled his eyes and gave a pleading look to Karma, she raised an eyebrow and shook her head. Sighing sulkily Telric folded his arms. "Sorry about...what's happened...Yuric. But considering your attack it seemed suitable at the time" he offered.

"Aye, well. I will nae be fergettin' what ye dun Master Zeal, nor will I let ma children. If ye set foot on Dunville ye'll be in fer a nasty time, I guarantee it" the dwarf answered back, his strong accent becoming gruffer by the minute. There was a moment of heated glaring between assassin and dwarf, and then Yuric turned to Jed with a smile."Well now, ye'll be the wizard who saved me, aye?"

"Aye, I mean...yes I am" Jed said, sitting down on a chair that was near him...the sea of magic had drizzled down to a lake now... "I'm sorry that you can't stay longer Yuric. But my magic is starting to drain; I'm going to send you home. Now, under which mountain do you live in Dunville?"

"Aye it do be sore news that I cannae talk some more with ma saviour, but I'm sure we'll be meeting agin friend. I live under the mountain called 'Bigger than wee digger mountain but smaller than medium sized digger mountain, digger mountain'" he smiled at them. Jed repeated the words slowly, he was slightly confused.

"Did you say 'Bigger than wee digger mountain but smaller than medium sized digger mountain?" he asked. Yuric shook his head, "Nae, I said 'Bigger than wee digger mountain but smaller than medium sized digger mountain digger mountain', ye ken?"

"Erm...I think so. Right...err...just...just sit still will you? You'll be home on...your mountain soon" he said slowly, wondering who Ken was.

He closed his eyes and started to grasp the magic that was slowly draining away into a handful, throwing it around Yuric's form and stitching it about him like a huge scarf. His fingers groped into the bags hung on his belt and he tied certain herbs and powders into the scarf's fibres.

He pulled at a strand of spirit, that was sticking out from the scarf and as he pulled he unravelled the scarf and started to mutter and flick his fingers about. Yuric span round and round making a "whoah...whoah...whoah!" noise as he spun. Purple and electric blue sparks started to shoot out from his beard and hair and fingers.

He laughed, shouting "Aye this be great fun wizard! Just ye wait till I tell the boys up in Mega-mineshaft Mountain that I were mixed up in magic afore I got 'ome! Hey, it'll be a grand un fer the story makers!" And then he vanished.

Jed watched in dismay as the last of the lake of magic drained and reverted back to his usual, little well.

Sighing he rubbed his eyelids and moaned to himself silently.

Karma patted him on the back, "Well done. You look tired Jed, why don't you go and sleep...it's almost midnight and we have to get up early on the morn."

"Ohhhhh! Do we have to?" he asked; his moment of wise wizardly appearance instantly dissolving with his childish outbreak.

Karma chuckled and nodded, "Yes we do, we've already wasted one day here. We need to be on our way, goodnight Jed" she smiled to him and opened the door. The wizard went through it and turned back suddenly.

"Aren't you coming Telric?"

The assassin looked as though he was about to say 'Yes' when Karma covered his mouth with a hand. "No he's not, not yet anyway. He promised that we'd...talk about certain things, and if he breaks this promise I may have to lose my temper with him," she smiled. Jed rolled his eyes and moved away, as Karma removed her hand from the assassin's mouth he thought he heard the words - "Right that's twice you've humiliated me today! Come here!"- and Karma's laughter before he shut the door.

*

Jed retired to his chambers groggily, the after effect of using all the magic he had done today hounding him into sleep. Yet his thoughts were a blur as he pulled the black silk covers over his body. So many new questions arose in his mind as he tried to turn into sleeps outstretched arms. Having watched so many scenes of agony from behind Telric's eyes Jed now thought he had an insight as to what went on in that sinister mind. Yet as his eyes started to become heavier and heavier, he also knew that the assassin teetered on the edge of both insanity and darkness. Telric had been walking a fine line since he had first flung death upon his fellow human being, and now, as he sought to try and balance his wrongdoings with this quest; he was slipping more and more towards the evil in the world.

Shuddering as he finally clawed his way into what he thought was a dream, Jed found he was trapped in a nightmare full of dark shadows, laughing faces and pain.

Fate held his breath as one of Birronneans main playing pieces started to turn aside. The sound of stone upon stone grated loudly in the players ears as the piece started to darken and grow. Fate smiled, showing more teeth than a shark and more malice than any monster ever created. Bironneann, usually cool and in control of his temper, roared loudly and slammed his fists beside the chess board.

The light that surrounded him burned brighter and he turned from the game to let loose a storm across the sky. Turning back he flung an accusing finger at his opponent.

"CHEATER! LIAR! BENDER OF RULES!" he bellowed, ignoring even the light-handed touch of his Lady to face down his enemy. Fate frowned in confusion and shrugged for all to see, lying back in his seat casually and taking a drink from his wife's hand. "Sire, you accuse me of such deception? Lord I tell you true I have not once cheated in this game from the beginning of time, why should I start now?" he asked, for all the world seeming polite and confused as to his brothers anger.

"You stole my piece, watch as it completely turns against me! See how it takes your colours!"

Birronnean shot back, heat radiating from him as he sought justice.

Their other siblings watched and frowned as the piece did as the king of the Gods said, queried over its strange behaviour and looked for an answer. It was then that Seria stepped forward, bowed deeply and offered an explanation.

"Good brother, be not so alarmed. Was it not your choice that every playing piece should have a will of its own? Not I, nor my lord nor even you can completely control its actions. Fate did not cheat; none here saw him do such a thing. It is the playing piece's choice. It has turned away from you sire, this is all" she said, smiling sympathetically before stepping back beside her husband. Fate rose and gave a forgiving nod to Birronnean.

"Come, let us forget this misfortune and return to the game. I have already forgotten the accusation and it is already forgiven, sit brother. Mayhap one of my pieces may turn as well?"

Birronneann frowned and sat heavily, crossing his arms as he watched those about him.

"Aye, it may yet happen. My outburst was disgraceful; I should have known not to accuse you of such a thing Fate. My thanks for your forgiveness" he nodded and turned back to the board.

Fate contained his excitement as he watched his opponent throw the dice. With this piece, with this one playing piece alone he could do many wonderful things…yet more important than those was that he could **win**.